Maple Street could be any town, but this fictional small town in New York is the story of Americana: Italian immigrants who passed by our Statue of Liberty seeking a better and new life for their families, who learned about their new home, developed skills, and worked to make America a better place. In *The House on Maple Street*, Marian Rizzo weaves a tale of exciting intrigue, proving that you really can "come back home" after you leave to find a big city career.

~Paul Ferguson
Reporter, Editor, Author, Printer—Retired

Marian Rizzo's *The Leper* is far more than just a simple, uncomplicated Bible story you've come to expect from Sunday School; all fluff and flannel graph with no soul, no danger, no depth. Instead, Rizzo imagines a first-century world where real human beings interact with real human motivations: greed, lust, distain, ambition.

She crafts a main character with flaws—major flaws—making readers waffle between feeling sorry for Eleazar and truly disliking him. She paints the backdrop between the cosmopolitan melting-pot of Alexandria and first-century Jerusalem with a broad brush, bringing the City of David to life and populating it with the poor and rich; with pompous religious leaders and disdainful Romans; and with those who follow a popular new teacher reported to have miraculous powers. Ultimately, *The Leper* is a timeless tale of sin and consequences, of damaged people finding faith and redemption.

~Paula K. Parker
Author of the *Sisters of Lazarus* trilogy

Marian Rizzo gives her readers a realistic look at the life of a young minister and his family in this exciting novel. [*Presence in the Pew*] is gripping, convincing, and gives a true-life account of a packed narrative. "Perceptive, vivid, and engaging" fits into this novel. A truly astonishing survival tale of ministry and marriage will keep you from putting this book down.

~Pastor Wayne King
48 years of pastoral ministry and church planting

If you are looking for a spine-tingling novel that touches on the reality of spiritual warfare in the church today pick this up! Great warnings of dabbling in the darkness are arrayed against the faithful preaching of the gospel. Don't miss [*Presence in the Pew*].

~Art Ayris
Kingstone Studios

[*In Search of Felicity*] gives voice to those of us who find inspiration and insight into our own lives through great works of literature. Rizzo's work will resonate with Rawlings fans and even those who will take up her books for the first time.

~Florence M. Turcotte, literary manuscripts archivist
George A. Smathers Libraries
University of Florida, Gainesville

Truth be told, I am not a novel guy. But I have to admit, Marian Rizzo's *In Search of the Beloved* drew me in from the first page. I love how she weaved her characters in and out of the search for the Apostle John. Great read.

~Dr. Woodrow Kroll
Creator of *The HELIOS Project*
Radio host, *Back to the Bible*

Plague is historic fiction at its most timely! Marian Rizzo's narrative style is perfectly suited for this clinical yet intimate perspective on how the invisible threats among us tear at family and society. This family drama is wonderfully told from the perspective of a nurse and mother married to the town physician as they witness their community besieged by the deadliest flu in American history.

~Aaron Shaver
PR guide
Author of Furious and other works.

Marian Rizzo is a gifted storyteller, whether it be for news reporting or fiction. She has a keen eye and ear for the intricacies of a story, which translates into very powerful narratives. Marian can turn the mundane into the magnificent through the masterful weaving of character, context, and scene-setting.

~Susan Smiley-Height
Journalist and editor

Plague thoughtfully presents the emotional trauma and feelings of helplessness healthcare workers experience while caring for the sick and dying. Its poignancy and vivid exposition highlights how little has changed over the last 100 years of responding to pandemics.

~David Kuhn, M.D.

Faith yields courage is what strikes me most about *Plague*. Marian Rizzo skillfully takes us back a century to remind us we are not the first to pray for God's protection of America's brave doctors and nurses, or who had such a desperate need of their aid.

~Gerry Harlan Brown
author of White Squirrels and Other Monsters

THE HOUSE ON MAPLE STREET

Also by Marian Rizzo

Angela's Treasures
Muldovah
In Search of the Beloved
In Search of Felicity
Presence in the Pew
Plague
O Holy Night: A Christmas Gift Book
The Legacy of Mrs. Cunningham
In the Boat with Jesus
Silver Springs (with Dr. Robert Knight)

The House on Maple Street

a novel

MARIAN RIZZO

WordCrafts Press

The House on Maple Street
Copyright © 2023
Marian Rizzo

ISBN: 978-1-957344-08-9

Cover design by Mike Parker.

Author photo by Doug Engle Photography. Used by permission, all rights reserved.

Published by WordCrafts Press
Cody, Wyoming 82414
www.wordcrafts.net

*This book is dedicated to the village I grew up in,
East Rochester, New York, also known as "Little Italy,"
and the backdrop for The House on Maple Street.*

*Also dedicated to the Class of 1960, and to classmates
who have passed away, with special memories of
Joyce Rumpf and Nancy Colegrove Kuhner.*

I was at my desk at the newspaper office, racing to make deadline, when my cell phone vibrated. I looked at the screen and felt my heart squeeze. I knew before I answered. Gram had died.

In an instant, one phone call carried me back to the house on Maple Street and Gram's kitchen. I pictured her sweet, round face, her mass of white curls, and the sky-blue eyes that always sparkled at the sight of me.

I shared her name—Francine Maria Capellini. I even looked like she did in her younger years—long brown hair, round face, petite frame.

"She went peacefully in her sleep," Mom sobbed on the other end of the line. "We will miss her."

"So will I." Tears flooded into my eyes.

"Can you make it to the service? It's Saturday at two."

I brushed the tears from my cheeks and ventured a glance at the cubicle on the other side of the aisle. I didn't want my friend Valerie to see my grief. She would leap from her chair and get the entire newsroom staring at me and wondering what was wrong.

"Of course, I'll be there," I promised my mother. "The *New York Dispatch* can do without its star reporter for a couple of days. I'll fly to Rochester on Saturday morning. No need to pick me up. I'll take an Uber."

Mom mumbled something indistinct, then said a tearful goodbye and hung up.

During the next two hours, I managed to wrap up the piece I'd been working on and sent it sailing through cyberspace to

Jane Dawson, my editor and the current overseer of my life. I checked my watch—almost noon. I grabbed my purse, my cell phone, and a spiral notebook and started away from my desk. Valerie swiveled around and stared wide-eyed in her familiar need-to-know expression. I shook my head and swept past her.

"Lunch?" she called after me.

"Not today. Too much going on." Then, in response to her pronounced huff, "I'll call you later, Val. Gotta go."

I hurried out the door and hit the street running.

Somehow, by late Friday, I'd completed two more stories and sent them flying to Jane, caught her nod of approval, and left the office for a Chinese dinner with my boyfriend, Brian. When I arrived, I found he'd already placed my order of sweet-and-sour chicken and had chosen braised duck for himself.

While we dined, I filled Brian in on what had happened to Gram and my plan to go home for her funeral. I studied his face, a blend of handsome ruggedness and gentle compassion. A flicker of concern filled his chocolate-brown eyes, and the deep wrinkle on his brow told me he was really listening.

He placed his hand on mine and gently squeezed. "She was pretty special to you, wasn't she?"

I nodded. "If I could make time stand still, I would. I'd keep her around forever."

"She was well into her 90s, wasn't she?"

I frowned at him. "She was as alert and active as you or I, almost to the end."

While we ate, I rambled on about the wonderful times I'd had with Gram. How every day after school let out, instead of going home I'd make a side trip to Gram's house and, while enjoying her freshly baked cookies—still warm from the oven—and a glass of milk, I listened to Gram's wild and wonderful stories. Brian listened with the patience of a preschool teacher, just smiled and nodded his head at appropriate times.

After dinner he guided me outside, his hand protectively bracing my arm. Knowing I had to catch an early morning flight, he kissed me good night at the door of my apartment and left me to my packing. Was that sort of consideration typical of young lawyers? Did listening to people's problems all day gift him with a rare compassion known only to counselors and medical people? I could see myself spending the rest of my life with that man. He'd asked me often enough. Now the question was, could he wait long enough for me to say yes?

As planned, I caught an early flight to Rochester, then took a 45-minute Uber ride to my former hometown—Cittadina, the Italian word for *Little Village*.

When I arrived at my folks' Victorian house, it was already teeming with relatives I hadn't seen in years. The place had come alive with aunts and female cousins carrying platters of cold cuts and cheese to a table already laden with casseroles, salads, and side dishes. Everything smelled like Italy, from the sliced sausages and roasted peppers to the piles of spaghetti and meatballs and the chicken cacciatore.

I sought out Mom in the kitchen and let her know I'd arrived. She dried her hands and gave me a welcoming hug. Then I made my way to the parlor where I found Dad and the uncles sitting in a cloud of smoke. Dad set aside his cigar, and we held each other for several long minutes. The last time I saw such pain in his eyes was ten years before when his father died. Now he'd lost his mother.

I spent several minutes interacting with relatives I hardly recognized. Then, I made my way to the table and put together a plate of food. I carried my lunch to a vacant seat at the kitchen table and watched my mom and my aunts bustle about like servers in a busy restaurant. Though stuffed, I poured myself a cup of coffee and sampled the homemade almond cookies, fig bars, and coconut macaroons.

Gram's service was set for 2 PM. At one o'clock, a wave of black-attired strangers flooded from every crevice of the house, surged out the front door to waiting cars, and headed for the church in one long cavalcade of mourners.

An otherworld aura bathed the sanctuary in a solemn glow of candles and brought back a time when I sat in that church and suffered through incense-laden rituals that left me gasping for air.

I still remembered the guilt-rendering sermons voiced by Father Piccoletti, an aging priest who pounded the pulpit and breathed fiery threats of damnation on us. But Father Piccoletti wasn't there that afternoon. A far younger priest conducted Gram's service, which included two hours of public testimonies. Then, everyone flooded back to my folks' house, where the women got to work in the kitchen, and the men returned to their cloud of smoke in the living room, where they argued politics in voices so loud the neighbors would have locked their doors if they hadn't already joined the crowd in my parents' house.

I had forgotten how noisy suppertime could get when all the relatives got together and everyone talked at once. My cousin Clara chose the seat next to me and kept pumping me for stories about life in the big city. Her ebony eyes sparkled with a mix of admiration and envy.

After supper, the women swarmed into the kitchen to help with the cleanup, and the men retreated once again to the living room, each of them with a tobacco-filled pacifier in one hand and a snifter of brandy in the other. The noisy chatter continued throughout the day.

That night, I escaped to my former bedroom, surprised to find it looking the same way it did fourteen years ago when I left home. The familiar pink-and-white quilt still covered my bed. Matching curtains hung at the window. My stuffed animals had taken residence on the closet floor. But my track trophies and framed academic awards covered the top of the bookcase, while novels and fashion magazines dominated the shelves. It was as if I'd never left.

As soon as my head hit the pillow, I was seventeen years old again. Without warning, throaty sobs erupted from my throat, and tears spilled from my eyes. I had drifted back into my past and was reliving the night I learned my boyfriend, Jeff Petrino, was seeing another girl.

For a teenage girl in love for the first time in her life, it was the end of a safe and happy world. After graduating, I fled to college and immersed myself in the study of journalism. I wanted to forget the pain of a broken first love. I didn't want to return to Cittadina but planned to head straight for New York City and a fresh start.

Back home again, I had unexpectedly come face-to-face with the old me. My life in New York City had faded. The truth was, I hadn't run away from my past at all. I'd taken it with me, buried it for a time, and now it had surfaced amidst my grief of losing Gram.

On Sunday morning, I passed on the breakfast Mom offered and settled for a cup of coffee and a slice of cinnamon toast. Then I packed my bag and told Mom I was going home.

"So soon?" she moaned. She flipped a pancake on the griddle. "I suppose it *is* a little crowded with all the relatives here. Why don't you come back next weekend? They're going to read Gram's will."

I offered a sympathetic smile and shook my head.

"Sorry, Mom. My work is piling up."

She kept flipping pancakes, layered them on a platter, and poured more batter on the hot griddle. Then, she set down the spatula and wrapped her arms around me. I tucked my forehead against her fluff of hair and inhaled the recent application of henna dye. I shut my eyes and allowed myself to be five years old for the moment. It wasn't for me, but for her. Then, as quickly, I let it all go and backed away from her.

"You can always come to the big city and visit *me*," I offered. "We can eat out, shop at Bonwit Teller, go to the Museum of Modern Art."

She tilted her head, her eyes questioning my sanity. Eat out?

She preferred to cook in her own kitchen. Shop? She bought a new dress maybe once or twice a year, usually for a wedding or a funeral, then she left it hanging in her closet until the next time someone got married or died. As for modern art, she preferred to root around in thrift stores.

She patted my arm. "My little girl has grown up. I guess I'll simply have to love her from afar."

"I love you too, Mom."

I left the kitchen and went looking for Dad, found him sitting on the front porch, the morning newspaper spread open in his hands. I leaned close to kiss his balding dome.

He looked me in the eye. "You're not staying for church?"

"My flight leaves in two hours."

Disappointment crept across his brow. I realized with a sense of despair, my parents had aged. Mom was a little shorter when we hugged. And I'd caught signs of gray the stylist had missed. Dad's hairline wasn't the only part of him that had receded. So had his chin, and his once muscular arms. With all my grandparents gone, my parents had moved up to the top. It wouldn't be long before they were gone too, and that troubled me. Perhaps I should come home more often, at least for holidays.

"You know," Dad said, waving the *Gazette* in front of me. "This isn't a bad newspaper. You could work here if you wanted to."

I shook my head and smiled. "I already have a job, Dad, with a major publication. Why would I take a cut in pay to work for the *Gazette*?"

"Well, you can save money by not paying rent on your high-priced apartment. And you won't have to eat out anymore. Not with your mom cooking up your favorite foods."

The poor man didn't put up such a fuss when my brother moved out. Tom had done what sons do. They grow up, go to college, and find a career, sometimes in another town. Daughters are a whole other breed to Italians. They also grow up, but they remain at home until they marry. They have to stay in the same town, hopefully live on the same street, and raise children their grandparents can lavish with attention. I must have disappointed my parents when I did what they assumed only boys do. I chose college and a career in the big city.

Choosing not to continue our debate about the rest of my life, I planted another kiss on Dad's forehead and left him sitting there with the newspaper crumpled in his hands.

It was time to leave. As I headed off to the airport, I momentarily relived my last visit with Gram two years ago when I went home for Christmas. Like she had often done while I was growing up, Gram invited me up to the attic amidst her collection of antiques and thrift store treasures.

"This place is off-limits for now, Frannie," she told me with a wink. "But someday, after I'm gone, I want you to come up here and root around to your heart's content."

Her words stunned me. After she was gone? I thought she'd be around forever.

Then she pointed toward a trunk in the far corner. "You're gonna have fun with that. But you'll have to wait. Promise me you'll wait."

I squashed a sudden inkling of interest and decided it would be an easy promise to keep, because I didn't plan on coming home again any time soon. I told myself to forget about that beat-up old chest and the rest of the castoffs in Gram's attic.

The farther away I got from Cittadina, the easier it was to leave behind the memories and promises. Mile after mile, I shed the brokenhearted young teenager and morphed back into the formidable career woman I'd become.

By the time I settled into a seat on the plane bound for LaGuardia, I was already looking ahead to tackling a busy workload and spending my free time with friends. For the moment, it was like nothing had changed. I gazed out the window through passing clouds and, as we drew closer to the city, I searched for the familiar skyscrapers for assurance that I'd come home.

onday morning came quickly. A slew of press releases and assignments sat on my desk. I plunged into my work. Things were back to normal. Or so I thought.

On Tuesday, Val and I had lunch out. On Wednesday, Brian took me to dinner and a show. Back in my old routine, I breathed easier.

Then, on Friday, Mom called again and hit me with news that would change my life.

"The lawyer read Gram's will today," she informed me. "You're not going to believe this, Frannie. Gram named you in her will. I kind of expected she would. Of all the cousins, you were always her favorite. You knew that, didn't you?"

"I guess," I said, remembering clearly how Gram pulled me away from the cousins to spend one-on-one time with me.

I searched my brain. Whatever could she have left me? Her cameo pin? Her gold wedding band? The diamond-studded wristwatch she kept wearing even though it had stopped working years ago? I kept shaking my head. Other than her collection of Hummel figurines and a set of Italian dinnerware, I couldn't recall anything of value in the old house.

"Sorry, Mom. I can't imagine her leaving me anything."

"Well, I hope you're sitting down. Your Gram left you her most prized possession, Frannie. She left you the house on Maple Street and pretty much everything in it."

I caught my breath. "I don't want the house, Mom. I live in New York City now."

She chuckled. "You have no choice, dear. Gram insisted."

"Why don't you offer it to Tom? Or to one of the cousins?"

"I can't, Frannie. Gram was specific."

"Then, put it up for sale."

"Can't do that either. It needs a little work. Mostly cosmetic. Your dad and I have been mowing the lawn and dusting the inside. Daddy had an inspection done."

Mom must have had her phone on speaker, because my dad's voice came over, loud and clear.

"The plumbing, electricity, all of it's up to code, darlin'," he said. "There are no termites, no mold, just a few minor repairs needed. I found a decent handyman who can help with the renovations. And your mom and I will do as much as we can."

I released a sigh of frustration. "Can't you oversee the work and sell it?"

"No, honey." Dad's voice was firm. "I have a full load at my accounting office. Plus, I'm head of the lodge meetings, and your mother has too much on her plate. You know, clubs and volunteer work. We don't have the time to fix up this old house. You're gonna have to do it yourself."

Do it myself? I sensed a hint of victory in his tone. Those two had been conniving to get me back there for years. A wave of heat rushed to my cheeks.

Dad was still talking. "You know, Fran, if you spend some time and money on the house, you can make a tidy little profit. That is, if you don't fall in love with the old place and want to live there yourself."

I wanted to scream. My dear, sweet Gram had chosen to hang this albatross around my neck. Knowing how she felt about me, I had to believe she'd done it for my good, not to hurt me.

"I need to think about this," I said at last. "I'll call you in a few days and let you know my decision."

If my Mom got her way, I'd be back in Cittadina with a paint brush and a hammer in my hands. But such an image had me cringing. That wasn't me.

Of course, I ran everything past Val and Brian. Val was ecstatic. "What an opportunity, girl. It'll be like those TV home improvement programs where someone transforms an old, rundown house into a showplace. You'll have to take before-and-after pictures, maybe keep a journal and write an article about it when you're done. You could submit it to a magazine."

The blonde-haired, blue-eyed former beauty queen, saw only fame and fortune behind the project. Somehow, she hadn't considered the back-breaking work and claustrophobic existence I envisioned.

Brian was less enthusiastic. "I'm gonna miss you something awful, honey. How long do you think the renovations will take?"

"I don't know. A month or two."

I fretted and fumed over the next few days. I pictured the dollar bills floating out of my savings account. My dream of promotion faded. All the while, Gram's face kept interrupting my thoughts, her cheeks cheerfully pink, her blue eyes sparkling with anticipation. If I didn't know better, she was already standing in the kitchen holding a plate of cookies and waiting for me to come through the door.

Somehow the old girl knew I couldn't turn down her gift. My brain had stored up far too many memories for me to ignore them now. Gram guiding my little hands on a rolling pin. Gram running a comb through my long hair. Gram walking with me through her garden while we gathered tomatoes for the sauce and lettuce for the salad. Gram filling my head with tales about an imaginary, free-spirited girl who sought out one adventure after another.

For some reason, Gram had chosen me over my brother and thirteen cousins to take possession of her precious house. In typical Italian style, she'd given me an offer I couldn't refuse—but without the threat of violence. Gram's weapon was love, the kind that pierced the heart and incited loyalty.

Reluctantly, I applied for a leave of absence at work, sublet my furnished New York apartment to an art student, and—hardest of all—I said goodbye to Brian. I couldn't expect him to wait until I finished getting Gram's house ready for sale. It could take several weeks. Or months. Nor could I ask him to leave his job at the prestigious Phineas T. Judd Law Firm and go with me, not even for a little while.

The good news was, Brian had his own workload. My boyfriend had been taking extra classes in hopes of transitioning from real estate law to corporate litigations where the big money was. Maybe the time would fly by, and he'd hardly know I was gone.

Both Val and Brian promised to come out some weekend and help me with renovations. And they assured me of regular phone calls. But I know how flimsy such promises can get when people are distracted by other activities.

Val had her boyfriend, Glen, a curator she'd met at a local museum while working on a story there. A twenty-minute interview had turned into three years of dating and a ring on Val's finger.

With a lump in my throat, I thought about how much I'd miss the city. The aroma of ethnic foods floating on the air outside my apartment. The sound of the traffic, steady and buzzing with life. The symphony, the art museum, the nightclubs. A familiar adage—paraphrased by me—kept running through my head. *You can take the girl out of the city, but you can't take the city out of the girl.* For my own sanity, I had to keep focusing on coming back. For only a little while I'd live among Cittadina's 5,000-plus residents, most of them Italian immigrants or their descendants.

I remembered my home town with a touch of nausea. Rows of identical houses lining every street. Front stoops with wrought iron railings and fancy scrollwork, and every porch displaying two flags, America's red-white-and-blue and the red-white-and-green of Italy. So predictable. So boring.

From what I remembered, Cittadina's downtown area also lingered in the past, making such a move a difficult adjustment for this zealous New Yorker. Those mom-and-pop storefronts, diners, and barber shops couldn't compete with the glass-fronted department stores and fine dining restaurants I'd gotten accustomed to. An occasional visit to see Gram was one thing. But I couldn't imagine moving into that dilapidated, old house—not even for the required couple of months.

A plan began to evolve. If I wanted to sell the place and come away with a profit, I needed to squash my anxiety and settle into small-town life for only a little while. I had to make repairs, update the decor, then stage the rooms for a quick sale, like they do on HGTV, as Val would point out.

Not one of my cousins contested Gram's will. Cousin Clara got the cameo and the Hummel collection. Aunt Marta got Gram's jewelry. Tom and each of our cousins received $100 from her meager savings account.

Not only did I get a house I might not be able to unload, but I also stood to deplete my own bank account fixing it up. On top of everything else, I had to rent a car. I hadn't owned one since I moved to the city ten years ago. Like many New Yorkers, I rode buses, subways, Ubers and cabs, or I walked wherever I safely could. When I needed to go somewhere outside the city, I rented a car.

Cittadina didn't have a bus, except the one that took its school's athletes to away games. The town had one cab driver, but certainly no Ubers. Everybody walked everywhere from one end of the one-mile-square village to the other. While growing up, I walked to school, to church, to the library, to the lone movie theater, and to the five-and-dime. Now I would need a car.

Thankfully, I'd kept my driver's license current. So, before I left New York for the trip home, I leased a white Honda Civic with the idea it would only be for two months. Then, I loaded it with three suitcases filled with my clothes and basic essentials. The rest of my personal belongings I stowed in Val's spare bedroom, with her blessing. That delusional woman thought my inheritance was the best thing ever, and she wanted to hear the details of each step of the renovations.

Even as I balked at the thought of tearing down wallpaper and installing new appliances, one spark of curiosity kept troubling my mind—Gram's old trunk, stashed in a far corner of the attic. It sat there like a relic from the past, and it was beckoning me to open its lid.

I left New York early on a Monday, grabbed a coffee and Danish at a cafe near my apartment, and started out on a five-hour drive to one of the most remote little villages in Upstate New York. I moaned. I was traveling from fast-paced living into a life of obscurity.

From the moment I left the city, I ceased to be Francine Maria Capellini, independent professional woman. As the miles ticked off, I gradually turned into Frannie Capellini—shy, unassuming teenager, returning to a life she'd been trying to forget.

As I drove north, I left behind the early morning lights of the city, and the world around me began to change from plate glass and steel to tree-lined highways, green fields, and small towns popping up along the way. I'd been caught up in the rat race for so long, I'd forgotten how peaceful the unadulterated environs of small town America can be. This was the part of New York State where farmhouses, fields, and silos dominated the landscape, where cows grazed and horses romped, where clouds filled the sky with interesting shapes during the day, and the moon and stars broke through the darkness at night. Such scenes had all but disappeared amongst the artificial, man-made, and mechanical environs of city life. I rolled down my window and breathed in the crisp country air, a refreshing change from the metallic taste put out by the buses and cars that filled the city's streets.

I'd been on the road less than an hour when my cell phone rang, and Valerie's photo came up. Blonde, blue-eyed, and beautiful, she never took a bad picture. With her tall, slim physique, she could have taken a job as a high-priced fashion model. She was one of the most photogenic people I'd ever met. But she'd turned her back on a life of glamour and had chosen to labor daily as an investigative reporter at the *Dispatch*. While other beauties posed for the cover of *Vogue*, she preferred to get her hands dirty in political scandals and corporate crimes.

I might have been jealous if I didn't like her so much.

"What happened? Did you fall out of bed?" I quipped.

Val yawned. "I couldn't let you get too far away without buggin' you."

"I'm already missing you, Val."

"And I'll be counting the days until you return."

"You can always come to Cittadina and visit me."

"I said I would. I'd like to help, if I can."

"Make sure you wear your work clothes then. And bring plenty of Bengay."

Then, my heart sinking, I asked about work. She filled me in on her latest breaking news story, which stirred a fresh surge of envy inside me. I longed to be back at my own desk, rifling through a pile of assignments, instead of on my way to dullsville. By the time we hung up, my eyes stung, and I had to blow my nose.

Outside of Albany I picked up Interstate 90 and headed west. Cittadina was located halfway between Syracuse and Rochester. Things had not changed much since I left home. A few more businesses had moved to town; a few new homes had been built; some new shops downtown, so maybe the nightlife had improved.

As I breezed through the agricultural part of New York State, my thoughts were interrupted by the aromas drifting off the landscape. A recent spread of manure, mashed corn for feeding the cows, and the sweet smell of clover and alfalfa wafting off bales of hay reminded me I had returned to a different part of New York State far from the big city and the place I'd been calling home for more than a decade.

Instead of blaring horns, wailing sirens, and screeching tires of hurried traffic, the countryside hummed with the rumble of tractors and the grinding of gears as farmers prepared their land for autumn crops. Then there was the bleat of sheep in a pasture and the lowing of cows in the field. Birds soared overhead, and none of them were pigeons.

The taste of homegrown vegetables came to mind. Tomatoes fresh off the vine, rich in flavor. Green beans that snapped when you bit into them. Apples plucked from a tree, crisp on the outside and juicy sweet on the inside. An unexpected nostalgia swept over me.

About the time the morning sun reached a point directly overhead, I caught sight of a mileage sign pointing toward Cittadina. I turned right onto a street that brought me directly into the center of town. Somehow, I'd missed this view during my ride from the airport a couple of weeks ago. What had I been doing in the back of the car as we rambled through the village? Checking cell phone messages? Scrolling through emails? Not once had I looked out the window.

Now I *had* to look, because I was driving, and to be honest, I was mesmerized.

"Why, this place hasn't changed much at all," I said aloud. "It's like the whole town has sat here, frozen in time, like Rip Van Winkle, waiting for my return."

Of course, I knew better. Things *had* changed. While the village was still one mile square with a wide Main Street running down the center, the spindly foliage I'd walked past as a kid had grown into large, expansive shade trees. Main Street had become a mix of the very old and the very new. Several glass-fronted monstrosities had set up shop between the hundred-year-old, frame-and-brick storefronts.

However, one thing had stayed the same. The intricately planned network of roads made it easy for even a stranger to maneuver around town. The large avenues running east and west were named after our nation's presidents—Lincoln Highway, Washington Boulevard, Grant Avenue. The cross streets bore the names of different trees—Elm Street, Pecan Loop, Rosewood

Drive, Cherry Lane, and so on. Each street was lined with the trees that matched their given names. I navigated the well-planned grid as though I had never left, convinced I could find every house I had visited as a youth.

My folks still lived on Almond Lane, two blocks away from Gram and Poppa Capellini's home on Maple Street. My father ran an accounting business in town, though he often preferred to work in his home office. Except for the historic section that boasted Victorian and Tudor homes, I recalled that the rest of Cittadina was dominated by single family homes with similar front porches and clerestory windows, small patches of green lawns with flower beds, bird feeders, and shrubbery. Long ribbons of cement sidewalks were chalked with hopscotch markings and linked the homes together like parts of a picture puzzle. Of course, this was before Nintendo and Xbox drew the kids indoors for a different kind of entertainment.

Now, as I maneuvered around corners and up and down the tree-lined streets, I began to appreciate Cittadina for its humble origin. Like many small towns in Upstate New York, the village grew out of a steady influx of immigrants from across the ocean, most of them from Italy.

The first to settle there came at the end of the nineteenth century. At that time, the peninsula of Italy was struggling with social discord and violence, particularly in the south and on the isle of Sicily. Widespread poverty prevailed. The promise of a better life in America motivated many young men to buy passage on ships traveling across the Atlantic.

Among the more than 300,000 who emigrated at that time was my great-great-grandfather, Salvatore Capellini, who came to New York harbor in 1887. Three years later, he moved to Upstate New York and built the house I had just inherited. Thanks to Salvatore, I'd now been strapped with a 130-year-old albatross.

Of course, when I was a kid, I never thought of Gram's house as a wreck. Back then it was a place of refuge, a warm and friendly escape from the pressures of school and household chores. While I nibbled on freshly baked almond cookies and milk, Gram filled my head with homespun fairy tales.

By the time I hit my teens, the population had diversified with the arrival of Poles, Germans, and Irish immigrants. Still, the Italians made up about 80 percent of Cittadina's population. Italian families owned most of the businesses in town. The bakery, the barber shop, the pizza parlor, plus several specialty shops. Italian men held public offices and controlled pretty much every decision having to do with home ownership, local taxes, and public works issues. They organized parades, festivals, and civic events, all centered around their Italian heritage. Everyone else— no matter what their nationality—jumped in with both feet, not wanting to miss out on the grilled sausages, homemade pastas, pizza, pastries, and beer, as well as the raucous but exhilarating concerts created by trombones, mandolins, and bass drums.

I hadn't planned to come back to such an antiquated way of life. My chosen future held more college classes, a master's degree, and, eventually, a desk with a placard that said, *Francine Capellini, Editor-in-Chief.*

But my dream faded the day I became the sole owner of a 1,300-square-foot antique of a house. I was 32 years old, and I had no experience fixing anything. I only had to pick up the phone and call the super. Now here I was, a pampered city girl, taking on a massive renovation project with no idea where to begin.

CHAPTER THREE

It was past one o'clock when I wrapped up my drive around town. I pulled up in front of Gram's house and took in the scene. The front lawn looked smaller than I remembered. Like I'd noticed during my last visit, the yard had little color. One maple tree stood at the far left corner of the property, and a flagless flagpole commanded the center of the lot inside a barren circular flower bed.

I got out of the car and walked around to the back. At the far end I spotted what appeared to be a dead vegetable garden inside a chicken wire enclosure. With unmasked disgust, I continued to survey the backyard. A brick patio contained a dirty wicker table and three chairs, plus a rusted charcoal grill. Off to the right stood a wooden park bench beneath a dilapidated trellis. Dying wisteria vines clung to its sides.

There were four trees—two maples like the one out front, and two pine trees, one in each far corner, like lonely soldiers on guard duty.

I eyed the house. Someone had whitewashed the vertical clapboard siding, leaving one less job for me to tackle. The roof looked new and might not need any patching. I wasn't about to climb up there, so I would have to hire a handyman to check it out and maybe do some other odd jobs. In addition to sprucing up the brick patio and the furnishings, I could handle a lot of the outdoor enhancements myself—maybe a few flowers, shrubs, and a couple of bird feeders to create some curb appeal.

Concerned with what I might find inside the house, I went

back around to the front and mounted the porch steps. The boards squeaked slightly under my tread. At the top I found a vase of cut flowers and a card, probably from Mom. The note confirmed my suspicion.

"Dear Frannie,

Daddy and I came out this morning to air out the house for you. We did a little cleaning, nothing special, just vacuumed the carpets, dusted the furniture, and washed the bathrooms. There's a baked ziti casserole in the fridge, and some soda pop.

Like Dad told you on the phone, we already had the place inspected. Enclosed is a check to help you with cosmetic enhancements. Daddy insisted, so please don't offend him by giving it back. We know how proud and independent you can be. We're so happy you're home, dear. Call when you get in.

Love, Mom."

I unfolded the check and gasped. $1,000! Tears sprang to my eyes. Suddenly, my insurmountable mountain didn't seem quite as daunting. My parents had opened their hearts and their wallets to me. And why not? Their baby girl had come home.

Home? I shook my head. This place hadn't been home in fourteen years. When I thought of the word, *home*, New York City came to mind. Not Cittadina.

I lifted the vase of flowers, straightened, and started across the porch. The floor seemed solid, no ugly cracks in the weathered boards, no groans when I walked across them. Two white rattan rockers sat side-by-side at one end, as though expecting Gram to come out of the house with lemonade and cookies. At the other end was a matching porch swing with a big floral cushion. Gram and I used to sit together on that swing. She'd kick it in motion, and we'd sway back and forth while she told me another fantastic story or filled my head with Italian sayings.

But there was no Gram, no lemonade, and no cookies. No idle chatter and no stories. A stark silence greeted me on that lonely front porch. Though I had survived losing Poppa, who seemed more like a fixture in the living room, smoking his pipe and reading the newspaper, I hadn't yet accepted the fact that Gram was gone.

I fumbled with Mom's envelope and found a set of house keys inside. Two looked like they fit the front door lock, and a different one might open the back. They were attached to a key chain with a tiny silver fish and the initials INRI. I had seen it before, hanging from the steering column of Mom's car. I smiled at the memory.

Keys in hand, I unlocked the front door and stepped inside. A blast of cool air struck me. Mom had turned on the central air system, one of the modern additions Poppa had installed about twenty years ago. I located the thermostat in the hall near the kitchen. It read 73 degrees. I reset it to 78.

In the doorway of Gram's kitchen, I closed my eyes for a moment and inhaled the undeniable aroma of roasted garlic and olive oil. Did I really want to paint away the vestiges of Gram's cooking? Couldn't I just fix up the place and sell it before I got attached?

My taste buds started tingling, and for a brief moment, the swish of slippered feet against the tiled floor, the distinct rattle of cutlery, and the sizzle of sausages frying in an iron skillet had me thinking Gram had returned to fix my supper. My mind's eye pictured her wearing a white chef's apron over one of her flowered housedresses.

I opened my eyes to an empty kitchen, no pans on the stove, no dishes in the sink. No sign of anyone having been there in recent months. The one sound came from Gram's red-and-yellow rooster clock, hanging on the wall by the back door, ticking away the minutes. The emptiness sucked the life out of my heart.

Whether I wanted them or not, memories abounded. This was where my family gathered on most Sundays after church. Like clockwork, we entered Gram's house to aromas reminiscent of Italy. She'd be in the kitchen, pressing her knuckles in a mound of bread dough, her pink cheeks dusted with flour as if she'd used it as makeup. A few loose strands escaped from her cloud of white hair and were pasted to the sides of her flushed face. Her pale blue eyes sparked to life at the sight of loved ones coming through the door.

She'd stop her humming long enough to call out a quick, "*Buona giornata, miei cari*," and after planting a welcoming kiss on my cheek, she'd return to her kneading and her humming, her frying and her stirring, her tasting and her nods of satisfaction. With amazing agility she flitted about the kitchen from stove to sink to table.

With those images lingering on my mind, I strolled through the rooms and soaked up the atmosphere. More memories surfaced; the dining room table laden with Gram's traditional Sunday feast—chicken parmesan, homemade pasta, meatballs the size of tennis balls, and Gram's famous *brasciole* immersed in roasted peppers and marinara sauce.

Everyone gathered around the table. Gram insisted on carrying the large platter of spaghetti herself, her slight frame bent beneath the weight of the huge dish. She'd set it in the center of the table, and then she'd step back and wave her hands at us. "*Mangia, mangia*," she'd sing out. "Eat, before it gets cold."

After supper, Gram often took my hand and stole me away to the front porch, or we squeezed together on her rocker by the fireplace. I leaned close to her. She'd shed the cooking aromas and now smelled like Cameo soap.

We didn't just sit there rocking. Gram told the most outlandish stories about an adventurous girl who'd climbed the Italian Alps, rode a camel up Mount Sinai, and went rafting on the Snake River in Nevada. Her stories stirred in me a desire to go traveling. Perhaps that was where my spirit of adventure had begun. The place where I'd shed any fears I might have had of venturing out into the world on my own.

"Let's call her Francine," Gram said about her make-believe character. "You can pretend it's you having all those amazing adventures."

Gram told those stories with such detail, she had me laughing out loud, cringing in fear, and chewing my fingernails. And she always left me wanting more.

"You should write novels," I told her once. "They could make movies out of your stories."

She snickered and shook her head as though my suggestion was less believable than her wild fabrications. In a day when I could still be molded by someone older and wiser, Gram also managed to insert little slices of wisdom in her stories.

"*La vita e un sogno.* Life is a dream," she once said. "Never allow anything to keep you from your dream."

Another time she said, "When something looks impossible, that's when you need to tackle it."

The truth was, Gram not only encouraged me to dream, she also incited me to act on those dreams. She supported my decision to go to college. And she was the one member of my family who didn't question my move to New York City.

I returned to the kitchen. "I did it, Gram," I whispered into the air. "I went to college. I have a great job. I followed my dream."

Then I thought about Gram's dream of sharing everything she had with me. More than once she'd taken me up to the attic where we rooted around the piles of junk. She dressed me in vintage clothing, looked for old toys we could repair and give to the needy, leafed through obsolete magazines and newspapers, and reminisced over the changes that had happened over the years.

Then, there was the old trunk in the corner. It must have held some private treasures only Gram and I would understand, things she wanted to share with me at the right time.

As though being led by an unseen force, I headed for the stairwell, went to the second floor, and approached the door leading to the attic.

Gram's attic.

Off limits for years, and now I could enter at will. I opened the door. A narrow stairway disappeared upward into the darkness. I hit the wall switch and a solitary bulb bathed the stairs in a soft yellow glow. With one hand gripping the railing, I mounted each step. As I drew closer to the top, the air became close and dust-laden.

Sunlight streamed through one of the clerestory windows and illuminated the ever-present cloud of particles. I breathed in the smell of old magazines, rusted pots, and thrift store clothing. Nothing had changed in the dingy attic. All around stood boxes and bags that gave off the familiar stale smell of the very old and forgotten. Now that I had the freedom to root around up there, I could go through Gram's sewing bags, her boxes of kitchen tools, and piles of worthless items she never could bring herself to throw away. Best of all, I could open the mysterious trunk. I bypassed the piles of clothing and books, the jumble of lamps and furniture, and went straight to the far corner.

With only a glimmer of light pouring through the clerestory window, I knelt beside the tired old chest. There was no key and no need for one. The lock opened easily in my hand.

My heart fluttered a little as I lifted the lid and peered inside. There were no gold doubloons, no jewels, no treasures of any kind. Just a lot of what a nostalgic grandmother might accumulate. A photo album, a small jewelry box, journals, and other memorabilia.

On the top was an envelope that bore her recognizable script and my name clearly spelled out. I opened the envelope and withdrew the handwritten note.

My darling Francine,

If you're reading this then I have passed away. By now you know I have left you my most precious possession. The house on Maple Street. And now, this trunk. If the contents do what I'd intended, they will open your eyes to a history you never knew you had. You'll get to know your ancestors, including me, and, hopefully, you'll come away knowing yourself a little better too.

You were always special to me, I think you knew that. Which is why I selected you to go on this little adventure with me. Follow my instructions, and you'll understand the chronological history of this house. It's my prayer that you will learn many valuable lessons from the folks who lived here before you. Hopefully, you'll apply what you learn to your current life and to your future goals. May you be blessed beyond your wildest dreams.

All My Love, Gram

The second page contained a numbered list of instructions, notating which items to remove from the trunk first, beginning with my great-great-grandfather's daybook.

Daybooks had been around since the 1800s. They were used to record business transactions and financial records. People today call them ledgers or journals. But to my Gram, this was a daybook, and so, that was what it was to me.

Like a small child following her teacher's commands, I reached for the ragged leather-bound daybook with *SALVATORE CAPELLINI* scrawled in large letters across the top. Gram had attached a Post-It note with more instructions.

You'll need to spend a lot of time in this daybook. Don't skim over anything, even when the details seem boring. Your great-great-grand-father was a skilled carpenter and craftsman. Trust him to help you appreciate our home for its unique design and sturdy construction.

Clutching Salvatore's daybook to my breast, I resisted the desire to look deeper into the trunk. I lowered the lid. I carried the daybook downstairs and set it on the kitchen table.

With one eye on the daybook, I rooted around in the refrigerator. In addition to the pan of baked ziti, Mom had left an entire bin of cold cuts and cheese, plus all the condiments I might need. I made myself a ham-and-cheese sandwich, then I carried everything to the living room and settled in Gram's rocker with the daybook on my lap. I hadn't even unloaded my car yet. Instead, I'd followed after an impulse that took me up to the attic and into Gram's trunk.

And why not? I had already started out on the adventure Gram had set for me.

CHAPTER FOUR

I spent the rest of the afternoon immersed in my great-great-grandfather's daybook. From the moment I opened the ragged cover, I traveled back in time more than 130 years.

Salvatore's certificate of immigration and his naturalized citizenship papers lay inside the cover on top of the first page. I set them aside and fingered the frayed and yellowed pages of the book, fearing the fragile paper might break apart in my hands. The first page bore his name, *Salvatore Capellini,* and his age, *29.*

Twenty-nine?! So young when he built the house.

There was a date: *May 10, 1890.*

Young Sal started the text with a little bit of history, something I hadn't expected but now read with interest.

Three year ago, I come from my home in Albi, Italy, left behind mia madre, poppa, three brother, three sister. Come alone to America, to find my fortune. I take with me a small suitcase and 50 lire. The journey long and the sea rough. I think, do I make mistake? But when we come to New York Harbor I see Statue of Liberty, two year from France, greeting me, like she knew I come. Many strange feelings fill me. I feel rich, and free, and brave, like the song say. And I have hope. No mistake. This my new home. This my new country.

Like other men on ship, I show passport and papers at Castle Garden in Manhattan. In Italy I farmer, I come to America with no trade. But in New York I find job and learn to build. I make good money, send some home to Mama, save some. I go to night school. Learn English. Learn to read and write my new language. Then I apply to be citizen of America.

This transplant from Italy was already embracing his new land. Not that he ever shed his heritage, but why couldn't a person enjoy the best of two worlds? For that matter, why couldn't I? I had New York, but I also had Cittadina, at least for now.

I read on, eager to burrow deeper into the heart and soul of my great-great-grandfather.

I here short time when I meet Rosanna. She work in office, keep records, hand out pay to workers. First time I see her, I love her. I no can help myself. She beautiful. Long black hair and dark, smiling eyes. The men hang by her desk like flies on honey. They talk loud, make jokes, but I win her with flowers and soft words.

My mama teach me and my brothers respect women. Mama say, treat like fine china. She say, pull out chair, open door, take the hand when crossing a street. Never talk mean, and never, never strike a woman. And, most important, no rush to the marriage bed until the ring is on the finger and the priest say you are man and wife. And always stay faithful to your chosen one, no cut the grass in another man's yard. Me and my brothers, we knew what she mean.

I stopped reading and lowered the book to my lap. Was it possible such a man existed? Polite, considerate, respectful of women? And his mother had raised four of them?

Salvatore had followed a whole list of rules his mother had set down for him and his three brothers. He won the girl, built the house, and sired four sons of his own. And he must have passed on his mother's advice to his own kids. Advice that then passed on to the next generation and the next all the way down to my father. I had seen the way he treated my mother, with tenderness and compassion, the same way Salvatore had been taught.

As a teenager, I had been shocked to learn some men cheated. Some men, like my first boyfriend, Jeff, treated their wives and girlfriends like they didn't matter.

Now that I'd read Salvatore's account, I knew there might be more men out there who respected women and relationships. Men who didn't cheat or lash out at their women. Considerate men who knew how to love unconditionally.

I caught my breath, convicted by my own words. Perhaps there already was a type of Salvatore Capellini in my life. Perhaps he existed in Brian Kelly. I reflected on the many times my boyfriend had opened a door for me, had pulled out a chair, had taken my hand when crossing a street. Not only that, but Brian listened—really listened—when I talked. Not like a lawyer in a courtroom, but like a man who was in love. If I didn't know better, I'd say Brian had come straight out of that homespun kitchen in Albi, Italy, where my great-great-grandfather had been raised.

I breathed deeply of the realization. Maybe all this wasn't simply about an inheritance. Maybe Gram was right when she said I'd be learning something beyond the physical makeup of a house, something only my ancestors could tell me.

The next two pages covered the courting and marriage of my great-great-grandparents. Salvatore was quite liberal in his praises of the beautiful Rosanna.

Il mio amore move to New York from Palermo, Sicily, five year before I come here. She speak good English. We go out for nine month, then her papa say okay to marry.

Mr. Mancini, a friend of Rosanna's papa, he come to see me, selling deeds to lots up north. I take chance to go. I leave Rosanna with her mama and papa and I go to upper New York to build our house. It take six months.

At the young age of 29, Salvatore Capellini had set his claim to a half-acre lot, and he himself had laid the foundation for the house where I now sat reading his daybook. I looked around at the living room walls, the brick fireplace, and the hardwood floors, all of them there from the beginning. My great-great-grand-father had planed every board. He'd pounded every nail. And he'd mortared every brick.

I thought about how the house looked now, situated on a tree-lined street with neighbors on either side. I tried to imagine what the area was like before someone paved the roads and put in sidewalks, before utility poles, fences, and landscaping. Was it an open range where cattle roamed and chickens ran loose? Were there straggly trees and clumps of scrub grass? Such an image didn't compute with all the development that had gone on over the years. But someone had to settle the land in the beginning. Someone had to plant the gardens and sod the lawns and carve out roads. It didn't just happen.

While growing up, I'd mistakenly taken for granted that Gram's home had always been there, that the lawn had always been green, and the flowers had always bloomed. Now I knew better. Now, while reading Salvatore's daybook, I could picture Cittadina as a wasteland that needed developing.

Eager to read on, I saw that the next paragraphs revealed more about the hardworking man who'd toiled day and night to provide a home for his woman.

I take no more jobs until house built. Need to finish and bring Rosanna here. Need my love by my side. Neighbors come with shovels and picks, help clear my land. Offer help with footings and foundation. I no refuse. I no proud. I trust people who know. But the framing I do myself. I learn from job in New York to be good carpenter.

I couldn't help but smile at his innocence. Italian men were either Mr. Macho, dominating the household, or they were like Salvatore, a mild-mannered child in a man's body. My great-great-grandfather had dedicated his life and work to creating a home for his wife and family. He had no other powerful goals driving him. Just a home.

I pressed his daybook to my heart and pondered this for a few minutes. The house at 122 Maple Street was more than a collection of wood and bricks. It was a living, breathing part of my ancestry.

Salvatore next described, in detail, the kind of materials he needed.

...very old wood, stronger than fresh-cut, with many tight rings and no chance to rot. I measure, then go to lumber yard and buy 2-by-4 dried and milled boards. I want the best for Rosanna's house.

I borrow Mancini's horse and wagon, make many trips to the mill. Get wooden pegs to hold boards. I choose the new platform frame for my house, not the old balloon frame. Easy to install, much safer. I hope for big family, so I make four bedrooms. Downstairs, kitchen, dining room, and sitting room. This my masterpiece. This my house forever.

I broke away for a second. Platform? Balloon framing? Wooden pegs? I nervously surveyed the living room, curious that the walls were still standing after almost a century-and-a-half. Wasn't this termite fodder? Obviously not, according to Dad's inspection report. But how trustworthy were those wooden nails?

I went to my computer and searched the internet for house construction in the late 1800s. There it was, complete with diagrams. Balloon framing had 20-foot to 30-foot outer studs traveling vertically through two stories, from the foundation all the way to the rafters. Another diagram showed my great-great-grand-father's choice—platform framing, which was recommended. The boards were 10 or 12 feet long, which made them stronger and more sturdy, like Salvatore had said. They stopped at each floor where horizontal wooden supports tied them together. The accompanying text said the newer pattern was cheaper and easier to build, and it was far safer if there happened to be a fire. It was like building two separate houses, one on top of the other.

I thought about the kitchen situated directly under the bed-rooms and shivered at the thought of a fire racing up the longer boards to the second floor. Thank God, my great-great-granddad had the good sense to use the shorter boards, a technique he must have learned while working as a contractor in New York City.

"Thank you, Salvatore," I said aloud. "More than 130 years ago, you built a house that could stand the test of time. Because of you, I'm gonna feel safe sleeping here."

I went back to the daybook. Salvatore's notations continued on the next page.

August 5, 1890
House finished. Need well. Neighbors come with spades, we dig all day, dawn to dark. Next bring stones from river. Mr. Mancini help with mortar. Mr. Dorio install pump. Water fresh and clean. Rosanna will like.

I couldn't help but consider all the backbreaking work Salvatore had endured to provide a proper home for his bride. As a skilled carpenter, he completed the framing and woodwork in three months, almost completely by himself. They had no electricity back then, and no plumbing to speak of. So, where did he put the outhouse? I had a fleeting thought of my great-great-grand-mother and her boys traipsing out the back door in the middle of the night to use the potty. I went to the kitchen window that overlooked the backyard. There was no sign of such a structure. Torn down years ago, I assumed. The property appeared barren, except for a lawn that needed mowing and the remnants of a few gardens. But no outhouse. What a relief that one of my ancestors later installed indoor plumbing and electric lights.

Salvatore's next notations described the wood-burning stove, the brick fireplace, and the oil lamps strategically placed in every room. He built custom cupboards and furniture out of left-over lumber and, after bringing Rosanna to their home, he trusted her to fill the house with color.

God bless me with kind neighbors, he wrote. *They come, welcome Rosanna and me to our new home.*

I imagined people rushing out of their houses, kind of like an 1800s Italian Welcome Wagon, with women carrying loaves of bread and men bearing jugs of red wine. Salvatore finally had his wife by his side. My heart surged with joy for them.

Salvatore went on to describe how his bride added her own touch of creativity to their home.

November 20, 1890
Rosanna, she sew curtains and bed sheets, and blankets and quilts. She make kitchen smell like my mama house, baking and frying and roasting and stirring whatever she put in the pot. I in heaven. I think it can't get better than this.

Like magic, Rosanna turn our cold, wooden house to a warm and loving home. She seem happy here, always laugh, fly around kitchen cooking and baking. We ready now for Thanksgiving and Christmas.

There was a break in the text. Then, Salvatore added a few more notations.

I start business. I build houses for people who move here. Next door

and many more down the street, on other roads. We make a village. I make tables, chairs, bureaus. Sell or trade. Then come special orders. Custom make. People see what I have and want the same.

There were no more dates, just a few scribbled notes on the next page.

We have four sons. First come our twins, Franco and Giovanni. Next, Armando, and then, Enzo. I so happy I think maybe I shout from rooftop.

That was it, a brief mention of the boys. Perhaps Salvatore had lost his passion for writing. Perhaps he'd meant the daybook to be strictly about the house. Puzzled, I found myself wishing he had written more. So far, it had been like reading an old novel, filled with characters that meant more to me than mere names on a page.

Enzo, their youngest, was my great-grandfather. He died before I was born. I paused briefly to think about the photos Gram had shown me. Enzo, a little boy with dirty knees, Enzo, a smiling groom in a starched shirt and fitted suit. Enzo, an old man in a rocking chair.

Such fleeting images never gave me a true impression of who my great-grandfather was. I could only hope Gram's trunk would hold more information.

Now that I was picturing actual people living in the house, going to bed that night was going to feel a whole lot different from what I had expected. I wondered, which of the boys slept in the room where I would stay? Perhaps it was Enzo.

I had reached the end of Salvatore's notations. Except for one final paragraph, he'd left the rest of the pages blank.

I leave house and this writing to my children and to their generations after them. I want they look past the wood and bricks and find the love I put in. I pray the house Rosanna and Salvatore built will stay in our family forever. God bless the precious one who is reading my words now.

My heart nearly stopped beating. I'd been privy to what it took for Salvatore to build the house Gram left me. At that moment, I wasn't looking at a collection of boards and mortar and nails. Like my great-great-grandfather had wanted, I was able to look beyond the work and see the heart of the builder. I pressed Salvatore's daybook to my breast. I sat like that for many minutes, unable—or unwilling—to break away.

My mind sailed back over the pages to the beginning when Salvatore first traveled to America and made a life for himself. I thought about the work he'd put in, his love of Rosanna, his joy at completing the house for his family.

Inhaling a deep breath, I rose from the chair and carried the daybook into the dining room to Gram's hutch, where I carefully laid it on an empty shelf, the first of many treasures I expected to place there.

As I closed the door on my great-great-grandfather's daybook, a terrible guilt settled on my heart. Though Salvatore had built the house with the idea that it should stay in the family forever, he could not have predicted what might become of it after he was gone. True to their legacy, his sons and grandsons had kept the house in the family for decades. That was all well and good. But now that I had possession of the house on Maple Street, I couldn't help but wonder what my great-great-grandfather would say if he learned that one of his descendants was getting ready to fix it up—and sell it.

CHAPTER FIVE

I'd been so absorbed in Salvatore's daybook, I hadn't phoned Mom to let her know I'd arrived. I punched in her number. She answered on the second ring, her voice lilting with joy. Her little girl had come home. Now, I needed to help her understand it was temporary.

"I'm only here for a month, Mom. I'm going to fix up the house and get it ready to sell. That's all."

"I know, dear. I promise, your dad and I will stay out of your hair until you need us."

"Thanks, Mom. I'll let you know if there's anything you can do. For now, I kind of need to figure things out for myself."

I thanked her for the food she'd left. "And Daddy's generous check," I added. "It's going to help a lot. One thing though, I need the contact information for the handyman Dad found."

"I believe he left the guy's card on the counter."

I went over to check and found a dark blue business card with the name *Fred Amati, handyman,* and a phone number embossed in silver lettering.

"Found it," I said. "I'll give him a call tomorrow."

After a few pleasantries, we hung up. I opened the refrigerator door and found Mom's baked ziti on the shelf. While it warmed in the oven, I carried my bags up the stairs to the second floor. Several boards creaked beneath my footstep. I chuckled. No need to install a burglar alarm. I already had a built-in system right there in the stairwell.

I paused in the doorway of the smallest bedroom, found the

wall switch, and illuminated the close quarters. The four walls were covered in a bold, suffocating pattern of pink and red roses.

"That's coming down," I announced aloud. I planned to paint every wall with an off-white color. Wasn't that what real estate agents recommended? Stick with neutral colors?

The furniture was another story. With the right decorative touches, most of Gram's antiques could stay. I could sell the house furnished. Lots of folks love to own such treasures, like the four-poster bed, the heavy bureau, and the padded bench.

I took the time to unpack my things. Hung my sundresses and blouses in the closet, placed my underwear, shorts, and jeans in empty bureau drawers, and arranged my grooming essentials in the bathroom.

Though I'd heard Salvatore had designed the original house with four bedrooms, someone during the past few decades had turned one of the bedrooms into an upstairs bathroom with a large linen closet. There was a sink, a toilet, and a claw-foot tub, but no shower stall. I allowed the wheels of design to turn in my head. I could have the handyman install a walk-in shower in place of the closet. A luxurious bathroom suite would be sure to draw the right buyers. And I could picture myself enjoying the spa during my own stay in the house. I could turn the project into a mini vacation of sorts.

I returned to the kitchen, and with Mom's baked ziti and a glass of red wine before me, I began to figure out a plan. Though I'd enjoyed Salvatore's daybook and my journey into the past, I firmly reminded myself that I'd come here with a definite plan in mind. The house at 122 Maple Street needed to go through a transformation if I expected to get it sold. The wood-frame structure was as strong as it was in the summer of 1890 when Salvatore first wielded a hammer and nails. Except for the creaking of a few floorboards, it was solidly built. No groaning water pipes, no squealing hinges.

But there were a few signs of wear and tear. The cracked and yellowed ceilings bore telltale stains from all the pipes and cigars that had come to live there. The countertops in the kitchen had suffered the abuse of Gram's cutlery. And the gas range had seen the last of its better days. Thankfully, Poppa had updated the refrigerator, and he'd installed a dishwasher—a real blessing for an aging grandmother who still liked to put out a decent spread for a houseful of guests.

I sat at the kitchen table with a pen and pad and began to make notations. Before I purchased a single can of paint, I had to remove as much of my grandmother's belongings as possible, a very difficult task for my aching heart. I had to clear the walls, the bookshelves, and the cupboards of everything that reminded me of Gram.

Later, as I got ready for bed, I continued to deal with the dilemma. My heart was torn between preserving as much of my grandmother as possible and buckling down to the job that loomed before me.

I walked to the one window in the bedroom I'd chosen. It overlooked one of the maple trees in the backyard. A cloak of sadness had settled on the property. In my child's eye, I remembered the brilliant colors of Gram's garden, the flowers and plants that created a veritable Garden of Eden. I recalled the afternoons we spent picking tomatoes, beans, and cucumbers from the vegetable section toward the back. And I remembered how fresh and real everything tasted, not those watered-down flavors products get after sitting for days in a vegetable bin at the store. Tomatoes tasted like real tomatoes. Corn melted in my mouth. Sweet potatoes were really sweet, not like paper imitations.

I let my eyes wander over the places where colorful blooms once filled the backyard. As a child I had romped there, a wonderland of color where my imagination could soar. Now the property looked like a graveyard. Gone were the clusters of pansies and petunias. Gone were the azalea shrubs with their pink flowering blooms. Gone were the lacy trails of wisteria, the sprays of ivy, and the long borders of tulips and irises. Gone was the row of rose bushes that framed the back of the house.

Though my memory had revived Gram's garden for the moment, the reality struck me hard. Would I have time to restore some of the color before I left?

Sighing, I turned away from the window. I sat on the edge of the bed and phoned Brian.

He answered on the fifth ring, as I was about to hang up.

"I was in the shower," he apologized. "Couldn't get to the phone fast enough."

"Do you need a few minutes to dress?" I offered.

"Sure. Hold on. Don't go anywhere."

When he came back to the phone, he was panting.

"Are you okay?" I said, frowning.

"Yes, I'm fine. I didn't want to lose you."

"I'm at Gram's. I have nowhere else to go."

"Right. So, what do you think of the place?"

"Well, it's been a long time since I was here last. Except for the gardens, which have gone to pot, everything looks pretty much the same. Like my folks said, it needs some cosmetic changes, but nothing major."

"What's your first plan of attack?"

"Not sure yet. If I write out a list of projects and set financial limits, the work should move along easily. Dad said he'd help. He gave me the number of a handyman, but I want to do as much as I can by myself."

He chuckled. "Why am I not surprised?"

I smirked, though he couldn't see me. "Okay, Brian. You know me too well."

"Now that you've seen the place, can you afford the upgrades?" His question revived my own concerns.

"Well, my folks gave me $1,000. And I have a couple thousand in my savings account."

"I'll be glad to help, Fran."

"No," I responded a little too abruptly. "I don't want to borrow money from anyone, especially not from you. I don't want to take advantage of our friendship."

"Friendship? What we have is more than a friendship, don't you think?"

"Yes, but, well—you know what I mean."

We both went silent for a few seconds, then I broke in with, "Why don't you tell me about your work."

"Well, I settled a claim today, to my firm's advantage. And, I'm actually breezing through my classes. It's like I was meant for corporate law."

"I'm proud of you, Brian," I said with complete sincerity.

"And I'm proud of you," he countered. "You've taken on a tremendous task with that house."

"I have one purpose, to sell it and get out of here," I reminded him.

"Like I said, I'd be glad to help. In fact, I'd like to come up there in a couple of weeks and give you a hand."

"Sounds great, Brian. By then I may actually know what I'm doing."

We both laughed. Then we murmured our usual endearments, with Brian being the first to say, "I love you," and with me mumbling a similar reply.

I went to bed that night, assured that Brian hadn't given up on me. He had a full plate of his own to tackle. And I could tell from the tone of his voice that he missed me.

With confidence I could settle into the task before me. I had a job to do, and if I ever wanted to get back to the city, I had to get to work. I lay there for a while and mentally sorted through the various projects. Remove Gram's possessions. Pull down the claustrophobic wallpaper. Paint the walls. Polish the wood floors. Decorate to my heart's content. And if time allowed, restore Gram's garden.

Then the work, the wallpaper, the painting, and the gardens faded into the back of my mind. Something else had consumed me from the moment I'd revisited Gram's attic, and I thought again of the trunk in the corner. Salvatore's daybook had whet my curiosity for whatever else I might find in the old treasure trove. I knew that, despite the regimen of work I was about to create for myself, I had to work in another visit to the attic.

Early Tuesday morning, I shuffled downstairs in my pajamas and took stock of the fridge and pantry. Gram's cupboards were nearly full, thanks to Mom. Canned peaches and tomatoes, boxes of pasta and bags of rice, herbs and spices, and an assortment of condiments, including three kinds of olives and several bottles of olive oil.

I rooted around and found a bag of ground coffee and an old-fashioned coffee pot, the kind that bubbles inside a little glass ball on top. I recalled how Gram preferred it to the Mr. Coffee my folks bought her. I took the ancient pot to the sink, filled it the way I remembered she had, and started my first cup of coffee in the old kitchen.

There wouldn't be much for me to do as far as cleaning. Mom had disinfected every cupboard. Even the hardware glistened. A lidded glass jar, filled with homemade chocolate chip cookies, stood on the counter. I brought it to the table along with my coffee.

My mom had welcomed me the only way she knew how. I shook my head in amazement. Roberta Capellini still thought of me as her little girl. She couldn't help herself. This was the Italian way. Take care of your own. Protect, pamper—and please, never let the kids grow up.

I scribbled out a grocery list of my personal favorites—power bars, bananas for smoothies, and an assortment of veggies and dips, plus two or three microwave meals.

Next on the agenda, I had to figure out what supplies I needed to start the renovations. And of course I had to factor in the cost. Dad's gift would only go so far.

The resulting numbers had me swallowing hard. Paint, brushes, and rollers, plus Spackle, drop cloths, and masking tape came to just under $300, a painful chunk out of my budget. The good thing was, those supplies would cover most of the walls and ceilings downstairs.

I fixed myself some scrambled eggs, poured an orange juice, and ate my breakfast while savoring a few minutes of respite next to the window that overlooked Gram's withered garden. For someone who loved homegrown vegetables, she had to have been very sick to let her little plot go to ruin. I vowed that if I had the time and the funds, I'd bring that 6-by-12-foot remnant back to life. Not for me or anyone else. I'd do it for Gram.

For my first order of business, I needed to clear the down-stairs walls of all the pictures and curios. Someone—probably Dad—had broken down several packing boxes and had stacked them in a corner of the kitchen. I pieced one together and began filling it with items I pulled from the kitchen walls. I set aside the rooster clock to use in the final decor. Nothing like a ticking rooster clock to create a country kitchen feel.

Adjacent to the kitchen was a combination laundry/powder room, probably added by the same person who installed the upstairs bathroom. I decided to stack the boxes in there until I could figure out what to do with them. Perhaps the church thrift shop or a women's shelter might be able to use some of those items.

Realtors recommended removing personal items. Buyers had to think of a place as their own, not someone else's. That was the hard part for me. It broke my heart to relegate so much of Gram's precious collections to cardboard boxes. It was like putting little pieces of her away, never to be seen again.

I did the same in the dining room and living room, leaving none of my grandmother's personal effects on the walls, the tables, or the bookshelf. Photos went into one of the boxes to share later with my parents and any other relatives who might want them.

As I cleaned off the fireplace mantle, I came across a black-and-white photo taken at a family gathering when I was about three years old. All my aunts and uncles were there, including Uncle Paulo in his Army uniform. He later died in the conflict in Afghanistan. Some of my cousins were in the photo, squatting on the floor in front of the adults. And there I was, peaking out from behind my mother's skirt. Poppa stood front and center. His bearded face had a huge, proud grin. Beside him stood Gram, youthful, vibrant, smiling with joy at having her family around her. I clung to that photo for a few seconds, then set it aside. Though I'd never been much of a collector, I wouldn't be able to part with that one.

Sighing, I went back to work. Each item generated another lost memory. For the rest of the morning, I cleared the walls and tables until the rooms echoed.

In the end, I decided most of the furnishings would stay for the staging. Gram's rocking chair and sofa still had a lot of wear and tear. I tested Poppa's Victrola and found it still worked. The Formica table and padded chairs would remain in the kitchen. And Gram's solid oak table, hutch, and sideboard would give the dining room a homey feel. Except for a few classics and Gram's Agatha Christie novels, I removed all of her books from the shelf and boxed them up for the town library.

I broke around one o'clock for lunch, then headed out the door for town. First stop was the Cittadina Bank & Trust. The teller, an older woman and friend of my mother's, remembered me, which made it easy for me to cash Dad's check.

I passed up going to the town's little hardware store and opted instead for a Home Depot I'd passed on the highway on my way in. The prices in town had to be a lot higher than what I might spend at the megastore. With the help of a young man named Carl, I came home with a carful of painting supplies.

Back at the house, with the hours ticking away, I laid drop cloths everywhere and applied the blue masking tape around windows and doors. Starting in the kitchen, I tackled the ceiling with a long-handled roller. Thankfully, I'd remembered to purchase a painter's cap and had tucked my hair inside.

One coat of eggshell paint covered all the cigarette and cigar stains, while also diffusing the cooking aromas that had lingered there for years. Once again, I sensed I was painting away a huge part of my grandmother.

It was after five when my cell phone rang. I peeked at the screen. Brian. I wiped my paint-stained fingers on a rag and answered his call.

"I've got some news," Brian said, intensity in his voice. He had my full attention.

"What is it?" I pressed. "Something good?"

"Not only good, it's great!"

"Did something happen at the office? Have you been promoted?"

"Sort of. The management wants me to go to UCLA for a two-week negotiations workshop."

"And that means?"

"It means they've targeted me for some kind of advancement. The skills I'll learn at that workshop will set me up for the transition I've been wanting. No more sitting behind a desk dealing with real estate transactions. No more juggling numbers. I'll be out there. In the courtroom. In the *news* even."

If Brian could see the look of apprehension on my face, he might have lost his passion. I didn't want to spoil his joy, but I had to ask the question that was pressing on my heart.

"Does that mean you might have to move?"

He let a few seconds pass then answered with less enthusiasm. "Possibly," he replied. "Not to California, of course. I'm going there for the workshop. But the group *has* opened auxiliary offices in a few cities. There's no telling where this will take me."

An instant of panic squeezed my heart. I had feared my absence from New York might cause Brian to lose interest in me. I'd been gone only a couple of days, and already he had carved out a new path for his career.

"You don't have to worry, honey," he soothed, as though reading my mind. "I won't make any decisions without talking to you first. Have I ever given you any reason to think I might exclude you in my decisions?"

"No," I said, hesitantly. "It's just that, well, I wasn't prepared for this." I took a breath.

"But really, Brian, it sounds like a wonderful opportunity for you. When do you leave?"

"Not sure. Soon. The bosses will make the arrangements."

"I see."

"Remember, I'm planning to come up there. I want to see you before I leave."

"Yes, of course."

"I'll let you know as soon as I have more information about my trip."

While we continued to talk, I put my phone on speaker so I could wash my hands and open a can of chicken noodle soup. I stood by the stove, stirring the pot, and we chatted about other things. I complained about the crick in my neck from painting ceilings, laughed about the splatters of paint on my T-shirt, and shared my relief that I'd had enough sense to wear a painter's cap.

"At least my hair is splatter-free," I giggled.

Then, seated at the dining room table with my bowl of soup and a plate of crackers, I brought Brian up to date with what I had accomplished thus far.

"I filled a dozen boxes with Gram's possessions, mostly knick-knacks. I'm telling you, Brian, sound bounces off the walls now."

"Sounds like you jumped in with both feet. Maybe you can wrap things up sooner than you expected."

"Maybe. There's still a lot of work, though. I haven't tackled the upstairs yet. And there's the front porch, the back patio, Gram's gardens, and—"

"C'mon, Fran. You're not gonna *live* there. Do the basics and come home."

I set down my spoon. "Brian, I need to turn this old house into a showplace. Not for me. And not for the buyer. For Gram. When I first arrived, I thought, like you, that I'd merely get the place fixed up for the sale. Just the bare minimums, that's all. Then, I don't know what happened, but lots of memories surfaced.

Nice ones about my Gram and the good times I had coming over here. I want to do the best job ever. Plus, you know what a perfectionist I am. Once I start something, I have to do it right. You're like that, too, so you must understand."

"Sure. I guess that's why we get along so well. We understand each other."

He ended the call saying he needed to get something to eat. "I'll go to our favorite Chinese restaurant and think of you."

I smiled. "And I'll think of you while I finish painting the kitchen. Tomorrow, I'll tear down the floral wallpaper in the dining room and paint those walls."

We ended the call, and in the sudden silence, my shoulders sagged as I looked around the kitchen at the yet unfinished walls. At that moment, I felt very much alone.

Only a few days ago, my life had been completely different. Sitting behind a desk typing on a computer for the past ten years hadn't prepared me for the most backbreaking work I'd ever done. All the aerobics classes and jogs in Central Park hadn't trained my body for standing in an awkward position, with one arm extended upward and my head tilted back.

Releasing a sigh, I forced myself to get back to work. I was able to cover the kitchen walls much faster than the ceiling. I even removed the boxes from the powder room and laundry and painted in there, too. I was like a crazed artist, painting everything in sight.

Sleep came easy that night. I lay exhausted in the big four-poster bed and gazed around the room at all the antique furnishings. It was easy to envision myself living in another era, decades past, when Salvatore's four sons played on the floor in that very bedroom. I had to smile at myself. I'd fallen inside a time warp of sorts, part of me living in the present, and a huge piece of me grasping onto the past.

It was Gram's fault. Gram and that mysterious trunk of hers.

CHAPTER SIX

I awakened the next morning, eager to get back to work. After a quick breakfast of scrambled eggs and toast, I continued the frenzy I'd begun the night before, this time in the dining room. The flowered wall paper came down easier than I'd expected.

I took a minute to call Fred Amati and left a message on his voicemail. Then, with paint roller in my hand, I worked in rhythm to the sounds of "La Traviata" spinning on Poppa's old record player. I had to stand on a step stool to paint the ceiling, applied big swirls with the roller, then tied them all together with broad sweeps of the brush. For the moment, I felt like a real artist with a modified version of the Sistine Chapel. I joined Pavarotti in song, my voice echoing against the bare walls. I didn't feel the least bit foolish. Val wasn't there to laugh at me.

Over the next few days, I followed the same routine in the living room and hallway. I even took time for the backbreaking, knee-scuffing chore of touching up all the baseboards. By Friday afternoon, I was able to stand back and admire my handiwork. The rooms literally glowed, and the entire downstairs smelled like an artist's studio.

With most of the downstairs painting done, it was time for some self-pampering. I settled into Gram's claw-foot tub, added a generous splash of her bath beads, and, with a glass of white wine and an Agatha Christie novel in hand, I spent the next half-hour getting pruney.

Afterward, refreshed and eager for another visit with Gram's trunk, I dressed in my pajamas, ventured upstairs to the attic, and retrieved her next note.

Welcome back, Frannie dear,

You'll find your next journey into the past inside a thick bundle of envelopes bound with a red ribbon. They're very old, so handle them with care. I've arranged the letters in chronological order by date. Keep them that way. They'll make more sense as you read through them. Beneath the letters you'll find a small jewelry box. Don't open it until you finish reading the correspondence between your great-grandparents, Enzo and Catherine. They lived a true love story if there ever was one.

Love story? My great-grandparents? Until that moment, I hadn't pictured any of my ancestors as lovers. Gram had kept a framed black-and-white photo of Enzo and Catherine on her dresser. The faded images showed a white-haired, wrinkle-faced couple in the winter of their lives. Two old people, a pair of senior citizens I had never known. It was hard for me to think of them as romantically involved.

But Gram's mention of a love story got me thinking about my parents, two people who depicted what romance in marriage was all about. I couldn't remember one time when they'd had a fight. They discussed things, sure, but they rarely argued. In fact, one of them—not always the same one—inevitably acquiesced to the other's wishes at one time or another.

My parents appeared to enjoy doing everything together. They had a date night once a week—without my brother Tom and me tagging along. When we were old enough to stay home overnight by ourselves, they went on cruises and took overseas vacations.

My parents had the ideal marriage, the kind I wanted, the kind of dream Jeff had all but destroyed with his infidelity and arrogance. My parents' home life was busy, if not hectic. They volunteered with charitable organizations, always together, like they'd been cut from the same mold. Now it appeared my great-grandparents had enjoyed a similar marital bond.

With newfound eagerness, I located the bundle of letters, carried it down to the living room, and placed it on the table next to Gram's rocker. I grabbed a soda pop from the fridge and put together a plate of potato chips and pretzels. I arranged everything on the little table, creating a cozy corner where I could immerse myself in more of Gram's memorabilia while snacking on my favorite foods.

My heart fluttered as I slid the first envelope from the stack. The postmark was dated *May 30, 1917*. With great care, I removed the note paper. As Gram had warned, the fragile letter's light blue tint had faded some and the edges had frayed over the years, but the ink was still legible. The note bore Catherine's signature.

My dearest Enzo,

I'm still reeling from your decision to join the Army. Everything happened so fast. One day, our world seemed fine. We wanted to start a family. We got a baby's room ready. The next day, a dark cloud descended on our home. You told me you wanted to join the war effort, and my whole world came crashing down.

Do you remember those first days of spring before you decided to leave? As soon as the snow melted away, you tilled the ground for our flower beds. On April 1, we planted six rose bushes out back and a row of azaleas in front of the house. At the edge of the property, you made room for holly bushes. You said they'd look great during the Christmas season.

The next day, President Wilson declared war on Germany, and I sensed you wouldn't be here to enjoy those beautiful holly bushes this winter.

At that moment, the conflict that was being waged on the other side of the world had entered our living room. You pored over the newspaper articles, clenching your jaw and closing your fingers into a fist. I watched you change from a mild mannered bank teller into a fearless soldier, ready for battle. The transformation frightened me. Like a whirlwind, you signed up and left Cittadina along many other young men and went off to war.

Of course, I couldn't stop you—wouldn't stop you—because I knew your heart. From the time we moved into the house, you'd been raising the American flag out front, like your papa had done since he arrived in this country. With your mama gone, he remained with us. Every evening after supper, he sat in the rocker on the front porch and read his Bible. And he always wanted the flag out there, so he could praise God for his new homeland.

Salvatore was a naturalized citizen. He didn't always live in such comfort. He often talked to us about the poor village where he grew up in Italy. Ever since you left for boot camp, I've been listening to his stories over dinner every night, how he struggled to find work in the old country, how he saved every penny he earned so he could come to the land of opportunity. He's repeated those stories so many times I could recite them from memory. The point is, your father is a true patriot, Enzo. And now he has passed that passion to you and to your brothers.

If you recall, your brother Franco was the first to sign up. His twin brother, Giovanni, followed the next day, then Armando. All three left wives and children behind. I shouldn't have been surprised when you followed after them. The day you left on the bus, I gathered with the other wives at Franco's home, and we wept and prayed together. Even with the children running in and out of the house, making all kinds of noise, we managed to keep our thoughts on you men.

I ask only one promise of you, Enzo. That you come home to me. I'll be waiting with open arms.

Love always,
Your Catherine

I paused to absorb my great-grandmother's words. Through that first letter, I began to get a picture of ancestors I'd never met.

First, I'd been introduced to Salvatore, a true patriot and lover of his new country. Rosanna, a doting wife and mother of four sons. Enzo, a humble man who'd responded with fervor to the call to battle. And Catherine, while troubled by her husband's decision to go to war, remained strong and committed to wait for his return. Did these qualities exist in my own genes? Did I care about my country? The people in my life? The turmoil that was happening on the other side of the world? Iraq? Afghanistan? Ukraine? Could I wait for Brian if he went? Most importantly, had I become so self-absorbed that I'd lost sight of everyone else?

I had to admit, the issues that held first place in my own mind involved my career, my lifestyle in New York, and protecting my heart from more pain. Unlike my great-grandparents, I couldn't see myself risking any of it.

I set aside Catherine's letter and sipped my soda for a few minutes. Then I reached for the next envelope in the stack. The date, *June 10, 1917*. This one from *Enzo*.

My dearest Catherine,

I received your letter today. By the time you get my answer, I'll be finished with training. I lost count of the number of pushups I have to do every morning after they rouse me from bed at an ungodly hour. We go on long marches into the brush, even in the rain, just slosh through the muck for ten miles or more. We have regular weapons drills, and we practice combat moves with each other, taking care not to hurt one another. Don't worry, darling. I'm fast on my feet.

We have inspections every morning and drills before bedtime. None of us guys had any military training before coming to camp. The men in my unit were fishermen, factory workers, farmers, and a few, like me, people who worked in offices and banks. I lost track of my brothers. They placed us in different companies. But I keep an eye out for them. Perhaps we'll find each other one of these days.

The Army has issued me a khaki uniform in an ugly shade of green—not my best color—also a helmet, and size 10 trench boots.

Each of us received a Springfield .30 caliber rifle with bayonet and an ammo belt, a canteen, a wool blanket, two pairs of socks, and a bag of grooming essentials, all of which we will take with us when we board the ship for France in two weeks.

Yes, my love, I've received my orders. I'll be part of the U.S. infantry's wave of troops to reach foreign soil. Pray for our safety, and please don't worry. I promise. I will come home to you. Nothing can keep me from it.

All my love,
Enzo

I stared at my great-grandfather's script, stunned that someone in my bloodline possessed such courage and determination. Beyond my intense fear of spiders and snakes, I couldn't imagine going to war against strangers carrying guns and hand grenades. Yet my great-granddad hadn't thought twice about it. He saw the need, and he went. So did a lot of other men, and women too. Even today, women take part in the U.S. missions abroad. They accept the same duties and receive the same battle scars as their male counterparts. Some come home injured. Some never come home. They perish on foreign soil. My selfish heart had rarely thought much about them before reading my great-grandparents' letters. Like everyone else in my circle of friends, I mutter lame regrets, pass over the news reports, and return to my prime rib and glass of wine, back to my popcorn and TV movies, back to my life of freedom that our men and women in uniform purchased for me.

Though I longed for peace in the world, I didn't do much to bring it about. I was consumed by my own business and pretty much forgot about what was happening on the other side of the world, until the next casualty happened. Then it got about five minutes of my time before more pressing needs took over, like a shopping trip to Nordstrom's with Val, or a walk in Central Park with Brian. I existed in my own comfortable little world, rarely giving a thought about those men and women who were risking their lives overseas.

Now my great-grandfather, Enzo, had put a face on the soldiers who'd responded to the call. In a sense, he'd introduced me to another time and another set of circumstances, not very much unlike the world I lived in. Here I was, back in the place where I was born and raised, and I'd entered another school of life, this time with my great-grandparents as my teachers.

I read a few more letters, which said pretty much the same thing. Catherine, pining for her lost love but encouraged by the gardens that were coming to life at the touch of her hand. Enzo, exuding the spirit and courage of a soldier on his way to war, while allowing his own heart to grieve for the one he'd left behind. Such a mix of emotions. Two people, deeply in love but accepting the path where their decisions had taken them.

Brian came to mind. While we also were separated for the time being, I hadn't lost my feelings for him. In fact, my love had grown, partly because I truly missed him, but also because my ancestors had introduced me to a new dream and a new hope for the future.

It was late. I left the letters on the table by Gram's rocker and went upstairs. Still thinking about the words that had passed between Enzo and Catherine, I was getting ready for bed when Mom called me.

"Is something wrong, Mom?" I said.

"I just wanted to invite you to church on Sunday. Please say you'll come. Your father and I can bring lunch to your house afterward. We want to see what you accomplished this past week."

Like my folks had promised, they'd left me alone all week. Now they had asked one thing of me. To give them Sunday.

"Of course, I will," I told her.

That night, I made two phone calls—one to Val so I could catch up on the latest happenings at work—and the other to Brian, who'd become even more special to me since I'd been reading my great-grandparents' letters.

Brian admitted he'd been scrambling to complete the corporate taxes course at the university so he would be ready to leave for the workshop in California. At the same time, he also kept a tedious 9-to-5 schedule at the office. I didn't have to worry about him meeting someone else while I was gone. He didn't have the time or the energy. *What's more,* I kept reminding myself, *Brian is not Jeff.*

That night, I slept better than I had all week. I awoke to a sunny Saturday morning, a perfect day to take a drive to the city park. I donned shorts and a yellow top with spaghetti straps and slipped into a pair of comfy sandals. Then, I packed a basket lunch, and I grabbed the book I'd started reading. Feeling free for the first time in a week, I loaded up the car and took off for one of my favorite spots along the river.

As I settled on a blanket with my back propped against the trunk of an elm tree, I gazed upward at the feathery umbrella that was shading me from the bright summer sun. In the midst of deep repose, I looked out at the gently moving river and nearly choked on the memory that surfaced. Fifteen years ago, I'd caught sight of Jeff Petrino and bikini-clad Denise Conn, leaping into the water, laughing and shrieking. They had become a couple after I broke up with him. I had been sitting beneath this same tree, unable to pull my eyes away, helpless to ward off the daggers that pierced my heart.

In an effort to shake off the bitter memory, I reached inside my tote for the novel I'd brought, *And Then There Were None*, by Agatha Christie. Nothing like a good murder mystery to distract me from reality.

I was immersed in Chapter Three when the crunch of gravel drew my attention to the walk leading to the parking lot. In the glow of sunlight, a dark shadow approached. I could tell from the outline it was a big man. My heart caught in my throat.

He took a couple of steps toward me, not in an aggressive way, but hesitant, as if he wasn't sure he should disturb me.

"Frannie?"

The voice sounded familiar.

I nodded cautiously and shaded my eyes.

"It's me," he said. "Jeff Petrino."

I'm certain I gasped. I couldn't speak. I was aware of the hot flush rushing to my cheeks.

"I heard you'd come home." He stepped closer. When I didn't respond, he backed away. "A friend of mine works at Home Depot. He said he saw you there, shopping for paint."

I swallowed hard and glared at him. Like my mother, I had eyeballs that could plunge a knife in a person's heart. Neither one of us could disguise our true feelings, especially when we were angry. William Shakespeare once said, "The eyes are the window to your soul." I believed him, and Mom insisted it was true. If Jeff could read my eyes, he would have run for his life.

Thankfully, at that moment, I was hiding behind a pair of dark shades. He had no idea I was sending a slew of poison darts at him.

"Mind if I join you?" He began to lower himself on the grass beside me.

"Yes, I mind," I snapped, halting him in midair.

He hovered for a moment, not quite touching the ground and no longer standing upright. He looked so comical, I almost burst out laughing. I rose to my feet and clutched Agatha's book to my chest.

"What do you want, Jeff?"

He was on his feet again. "I–um–wanted to talk, maybe catch up." The confidence had left his voice. How wonderful to watch him grovel.

"No thanks," I grumbled.

I gathered up my picnic basket and tote and started for the car, didn't turn to see if he was following me. After I slid into the driver's seat, I ventured a glance at the elm tree. Jeff was gone. Like an unwelcome apparition, he'd vanished. Had he really been there, or was my mind playing tricks on me? It didn't matter. Jeff Petrino was the last person I wanted to connect with during my time in Cittadina.

I felt my cheek and brought back another hard memory. Jeff's hand, leaving a red imprint on my face. After we'd been dating for almost a year the thing that set him off was for me to question where he'd been the night before. I frowned and clenched my teeth. At seventeen years of age I'd made a vow never again to let a man get close enough to hurt me the way he had. So far, I had kept that vow. As a result, I'd left a trail of confused suitors in my wake. Brian was the only man who'd had a chance with me.

I was still scowling as I meandered my car along the town's thoroughfares back to Maple Street.

Please, God. Don't let Jeff come to Gram's house. There's no telling what I might do or say.

I ended up eating my picnic lunch while sitting on the bench swing on the front porch, my eyes warily scanning the street. If Jeff showed his ugly face on my block, I'd run inside and lock the door.

Of course, Jeff wasn't ugly. He was one of the best looking guys in the twelfth grade. Stark black hair, shining eyes that looked like lumps of coal, a broad jaw, and a whimsical smile. The school quarterback, he had a physique like the pros, and his innate charisma had the power to melt the frost off any girl's heart. Breaking up with him had been the hardest, but also the best, decision I'd ever made.

I was ten times stronger now, and after reading my great-grandparents' letters, I had an entirely fresh perspective about what makes a relationship work. I'd seen it fleshed out in my parents and my grandparents. Reading Salvatore's daybook had given me a window into the life of my great-great-grandfather. I saw how he could think of nothing else but to create a decent home for Rosanna. Now I'd begun to read the letters Enzo and Catherine had written, and I understood how true love could wait, not only for the right time, but across the miles.

I spent the rest of the afternoon reading more of their correspondence. Then I took a walk around the property and tried to envision the gardens the way they must have looked when

Catherine tended them. Her letters were filled with images, so detailed I could picture the gardens the way they looked a hundred years ago.

A spark of excitement stirred my heart, and I knew I wanted to restore some of those plants and flowers. No longer was I only concerned with the work that had to be done on the inside of the house. I wouldn't be able to leave Cittadina without bringing Catherine's gardens back to life, no matter how long it took or how much it cost.

CHAPTER SEVEN

Early Sunday morning, Mom called and reminded me about church. "Mass starts at 10 o'clock," she trilled.

Other than my grandparents' funerals, I hadn't stepped inside a church since I left home. Brian attended a non-denominational church. I didn't go with him, but I did acquiesce to a Wednesday night Bible study now and then. I found the fellowship refreshing, the food satisfying, and the instruction interesting, though a lot of the jargon went over my head. For the first time in my life, I was drawn to the word of God, and I began to read passages in a Bible Brian gave me for my birthday.

Still, I didn't know how to say a decent prayer. The truth was, I'd strayed so far from God, I didn't feel like I deserved His attention. It wasn't that I was a bad girl. I just didn't know how to be spiritual.

When I was younger, my parents took me and my brother to church every Sunday and on all the religious holidays. I still remembered the rituals of mass—the standing, kneeling, bowing, the recitations, and all the incense and holy water being spewed about. I could perform the entire service in my sleep, but the words and litany met nothing to me.

Brian kept telling me the rituals and recitations contributed only a small part of what it meant to worship God. A personal connection was much more important, he insisted.

"It's not about religion, it's about a relationship," he said.

I wanted to understand, tried to understand, but I'd been caught up for so long in my work and lifestyle, I hadn't made time to get to know God. It was something I'd put off for later.

One thing was certain, I already knew what to expect when I met my folks in front of Saint Agnes Church. As I stood on the sidewalk, I recalled how imposing the tallest structure in town had appeared to me as a child. The steeple rose high above all of the other buildings in the village. Now it didn't seem so daunting.

The brick-and-mortar sanctuary had been standing on the same rise of hill for almost a hundred years, with the same eleven cement steps leading up to the front door. Though the bricks had faded some over the years, and numerous cracks marred the front steps and sidewalk, the rows of stained glass windows gave the structure an ethereal quality that could not be denied.

In the past, Father Piccoletti would have been standing at the top of the stairs, greeting members of his flock. But instead of the aging priest with the bald head, bulging stomach, and cigar smoke on his breath, a much younger man stood there. He was handsome, had a full crop of brown hair and a closely trimmed stubble of beard. He hadn't chosen the cassock and collar, but stood slim and tall in black pants and matching vest over a white, short-sleeved shirt.

Mom must have caught me staring. "That's Brother Patrick Sullivan," she whispered. "Don't you remember him? He did your grandmother's funeral."

I shrugged, but truthfully, I hadn't been paying attention at the time. I'd spent most of the service wiping away tears that blurred my vision.

The guy is Irish? Interesting. So is Brian.

"He came here five years ago when Father Piccoletti retired," Mom went on. "He's changed everything. Wait till you see. The organ's gone. A group of young people play guitars and drums. He insists on being called *Brother Pat,* I guess to be closer to the teens. He gives a terrific sermon. Your dad actually stays awake."

She was almost giddy with delight. She grabbed my arm and ushered me up the steps, then introduced me to the smiling priest with the sparkle in his green eyes. He gripped my hand and smiled, like he was genuinely happy to meet me.

I walked with Mom and Dad to their chosen pew, squeezed in beside them, and noted the changes that had taken place in the church of my youth. Gone were all the life-size statues. Gone was the rack of votive candles at the front. A massive projection screen graced the wall beyond the pulpit. Images of nature flowed across the screen, accompanied by soft, ethereal music. Gone was the crucifix with an ailing figure of Jesus, a sight that had both transfixed and frightened me as a young child. Now a plain and simple cross hung from the ceiling. No body of Christ. No reason to mourn, for the crossbar bore the words, "He is Risen."

The image transported me to one of the Bible studies I'd gone to with Brian. The leader had made the same point over and over again. "Jesus has risen," he'd said. Then, he'd read something from the Gospel of John.

My interest piqued, I searched the pew rack and found a Bible amidst the hymn books. I flipped through the pages until I came to the Gospel of John, but for the life of me I couldn't find that passage.

At that moment, a group of young people mounted the stage and began to play guitars and drums. A young, blonde girl stepped forward with a mic in her hand. When she opened her mouth to sing I thought an angel had descended upon the church. I don't remember what song she performed, only that she sang it beautifully. It impressed me to see teenagers using their talents in such a way, and I regretted having missed such a blessing while growing up.

I followed the service, opened a hymn book, and sang along with the congregation. Then Brother Pat began to speak. He didn't pound the pulpit, didn't growl or shout at us, merely talked to us from his heart.

I listened to every word he said, but one thing stood out to me. After reading a lengthy passage of scripture, he used the text as a springboard to life. "Remember, he who builds his house on sand, when the rains come, it will wash away. But he who builds his house on a rock, it will last forever."

I thought about Gram's house, the firm foundation Salvatore had lain, the hard labor that had gone into the walls, the floors, the gardens.

"Now, you know Jesus wasn't simply talking about actual houses," Brother Pat went on. "He was talking about life. He was talking about hearing the word of God and doing it. He was talking about basing your faith on something solid. Not good works or prayer or attending church. Those things matter, but there's something even more necessary. God's gift of Jesus Christ should be the foundation of your faith. You must then build everything else upon that foundation."

It was as if those sharp, green eyes of his were staring right through me. His words penetrated my heart, and I began to understand what Brian had been trying to tell me all along. While I had been working hard at my craft and struggling to make a good life for myself, I'd missed out on the one thing that could give me the foundation I needed.

"Take this message to heart, people," Brother Pat concluded. "Apply it wherever you can. Examine yourselves and see if you're building your personal house on a rock or on sand."

I had to admit, I'd been building my life on sand. Such a foundation could wash away in a heartbeat. For the first time, I wanted what Brian had. I wanted to learn more about a foundation that would weather a storm.

As I left the church, Brother Pat again shook my hand. "I understand you've been living in New York City," he said. "And you're here fixing up your grandmother's house."

I glanced at Mom who responded with a sheepish nod of her head. She'd been talking about me again.

I could have told Brother Pat that if it had been my choice, I'd still be in the big city, planning to go out for dinner and dancing, instead of scrubbing floors and getting paint under my fingernails.

"The streets of New York are a lot noisier than Cittadina's," I said instead. "The most excitement I've had since arriving here was the shrieking of two tomcats fighting beneath my bedroom window the other night."

"Well, let's hope you can adjust to the peace and quiet of country living," he said with a sincere smile. "You might find you prefer it."

I caught Mom staring at me, a flicker of hope in her dark brown eyes. That woman spoke more with her eyes than with her mouth. Throughout my young life, I had no trouble decoding her messages. At that moment, she was thrilled that the priest had planted a seed of encouragement in my wandering heart.

Still, she never said a word about it, merely gave me a hug in the parking lot before we parted.

"We'll bring dinner over in a little while," she offered, her lips smiling but her brown eyes still flashing with anticipation.

I went home trying to think of ways I could return Mom's love without giving in to her demands. I didn't want to lose myself within someone else's dream for me. I had to hold onto my own plans for my life.

As I drove back to Gram's house, Brother Pat's sermon came tumbling back to me, and I couldn't help but connect his message to the entries I'd read in Salvatore's daybook. My great-great-grandfather had toiled with his bare hands to build that house. But he didn't simply hammer boards in place. He first trusted men who could help him build a foundation as strong as a rock. Then he built the rest of the house on that firm foundation.

The biblical analogy had given me food for thought. The whole idea of different kinds of foundations had taken me to another dimension, one less tangible than the actual building of a house. I determined to spend more time studying Brother Pat's passage of scripture, if I could find it again.

As she'd promised, Mom brought a casserole of macaroni and cheese and a box of cannolis to Gram's house. I set the table in the kitchen where the smell of paint had dissipated. Dad entered the house with his head swiveling left and right, his eyebrows raised in surprise. With a broad smile he conveyed his approval over what I'd already accomplished.

Surprisingly, my mother gave me little advice about the work I was doing. In fact, she was all praises as she looked at my newly painted walls. Then Daddy pointed out the good job I'd done on the baseboards and trim.

"So, what are your plans for the house?" Mom ventured to ask.

I didn't want to stir up an argument about whether I was going to stay or sell it, so I went through a partial list of my ideas for renovations.

Mom and Dad both listened intently, nodded their heads and uttered an occasional, "Mm-hmm."

"Do you need any help yet?" Mom asked, though she already knew the answer.

I shook my head. "No, I want to take my time and do it myself."

Dad took a long drink of water, then he leaned toward me. "Don't be proud, Princess. We want to help, if we can. There are a lot of things we old folks can do. I can wield a paintbrush as well as the next guy. And I've been known to pound a nail or two. So far, I've kept the lawn mowed. But we can help in other ways. Just say the word."

Mom nudged him with her elbow. "Leave her be, dear. The more Francine does by herself, the longer she'll stay in town. Who knows?" She shrugged. "Maybe she'll never leave."

Though Mom's remark made me feel wanted, it also sent a shiver down my spine. Never leave? As soon as the For Sale sign went up, I'd be out of here. With a Realtor handling the sale, I could sign the papers over the internet. Or the agent could mail them to me.

After lunch Mom and I did the dishes, and Dad went outside and took a stroll around the property. I figured he was checking out more work for me to do. From the kitchen window, we watched him walking and gesturing like he was making decisions. While Mom had her hands in the dishwater and I was drying, our conversation turned to more personal issues.

"How's that man of yours?" Mom said. "I believe his name is Brian."

I felt myself blushing. I hadn't talked much about Brian except for telling her his first name and that he was a nice guy.

"We're friends," I said, though we'd been together for more than a year, and she knew it.

She didn't mention engagement, though I suspected the possibility had been on her mind. For a few minutes there was the clink of silverware and the clatter of dishes. I started talking about my job and the classes I planned to take. Mom commented softly, but I detected a hint of disappointment in her voice. She was never going to give up her dream of having me back home, married, and pregnant. She wanted more grandchildren. With Tom living in Boston, she rarely enjoyed her little grandson. The sad truth was, her hope of grand-parenting now had fallen on me. And I wasn't even married yet.

CHAPTER EIGHT

On Monday morning I had to switch gears again. I put a temporary freeze on delving into the past and tried not to think about the trunk in the attic. Back to working on the house, I approached the old structure with fresh enthusiasm. Thanks to my great-great-grandfather, Salvatore, the house had withstood the ravages of time and weather.

I sat at the kitchen table and made a new list. Fortunately, Gram's insurance had replaced her roof about six years ago. Someone had whitewashed the exterior siding, so that was another thing I didn't have to worry about. I would have to wash the windows, polish the wood floors, and spruce up the front porch. As for the landscaping, it would have to wait until the end.

Since the day I learned I had inherited Gram's house, I'd been watching home improvement shows on TV to try to get some idea of what I needed to do to make the property more sellable.

At the top of my list I wrote, *New stove for the kitchen, plus a shower and double sinks for the upstairs bathroom.*

By removing the huge bathroom closet, there'd be enough room to add a nice, big, walk-in shower stall. I'd have to get Fred Amati to install everything, that is, if the handyman ever called me back.

I also wanted to put in a farmhouse sink with crookneck faucet and sprayer, the kind home buyers seemed drawn to. And, I would replace Gram's battered countertops with new butcher block.

As for the plumbing and electrical systems, everything seemed to work fine—the toilets in the main bath and downstairs powder room both flushed, all the drains worked, no drips, and all the light switches and electrical outlets had passed the inspection.

After breakfast I started out for Home Depot, the male-dominated store that had drawn my interest away from Dillard's and Saks—at least for the time being. Totally out of my element, I went up and down the aisles until I got to the appliance section, all the while, looking left and right and over my shoulder, in case the worker who'd ratted me out to Jeff might be there. Since he seemed to have known me, I assumed he was someone from our high school days, but I hadn't recognized him.

This time, an older gentleman helped me select my purchases, giving plenty of fatherly advice about options and tax incentives. He promised to have the kitchen items delivered by Wednesday, adding that the delivery guys could install the stove and take the old one off my hands. The countertop and upstairs bath items required major carpentry work, so I'd have to hire a handyman, who could take the measurements and order the right products. I checked out using Dad's remaining $700, and some of my own savings.

As I was leaving the store, Jeff popped up from out of nowhere. It seemed he had the habit of doing that. I turned away from him before he could speak, but that didn't stop him. He scooted around in front of me and held up a business card.

"I'm a contractor." His tone was as arrogant and boastful as ever. His face flushed red in stark contrast to his mop of ebony hair. He set piercing dark eyes on me. "I can install your purchases," he boasted. "And I'm cheap."

I had no doubt about that.

"Look," he said, thrusting his card at me. "If you can't find anyone else, give me a call. And, guess what? You won't find anyone else. I'm the best handyman/builder within fifty miles of this town."

Reluctantly, I accepted his card. My pulse had begun to speed up. Was it attraction? Fear? Anger? Perhaps all three. I'd gotten over him years ago, and I didn't want to fall into his trap again. As I walked away I was determined to find someone else to do the work, even if I had to call a handyman from Rochester.

I turned once and caught Jeff watching after me, a smug grin on his lips.

My face burned. I had sworn I'd never let that man near me again. Had I just considered hiring him? Where might things go from there? I still had lots of work ahead of me, and if I wanted to finish the house and get back to the city, I needed to hire *somebody*. I just I didn't want it to be Jeff.

On Tuesday, I went through Gram's kitchen cupboards. Mom had left all of the dishes and bowls, plus the pots and pans Gram had collected over the years. I boxed whatever I didn't need to survive for the next few weeks. I labeled the boxes for the thrift store, and added them to the ever-growing pile in the laundry room.

I was about to check my list, when someone banged on the front door.

"Please don't let it be Jeff," I growled under my breath.

With no peephole to look through, I had no choice but to open the door. I lunged backward in shock. Valerie was standing there, a big smile on her lips and a Dunkin' Donuts carry-out box in her hand. On the porch floor by her foot stood a cherry red suitcase with her initials engraved in gold on the top.

"Surprise!" she shouted, her blue eyes sparkling with mirth.

"Valerie? It's really you?"

"In the flesh," she said, grabbing the handle of her suitcase. She barged through the open door, nearly knocking me over.

I stepped aside and let her pass. My best friend had dropped everything to come and help me.

"Say something," Valerie challenged me. "I didn't come all this way for you to stand there gawking. By the way, where do I put these?" She raised the box of donuts. "Is that the kitchen?" Then she charged ahead with me following in her footsteps.

"It's Tuesday. Aren't you supposed to be at work?" was all I could think of to say.

She let out one of her familiar giggles that sounded like a cross between sleigh bells and a witch's cackle.

"Work?" she said, turning to face me. "Don't worry about it. I agreed to do the cops beat next weekend in exchange for two days off. Of course Dawson agreed. She has a hard time getting people to work weekends."

"You made quite a sacrifice," I said, knowing how tedious the cops beat could be. Whoever got stuck with it had to sort through all the petty thefts and misdemeanors in order to find the real story.

"But Val, I have to ask you, why?"

She set the donuts on the kitchen table, then swung around and faced me. "Why? Because my best friend is tackling a humongous job all by herself, and I couldn't let another day go by without giving her a hand, that's why. You see that suitcase?" She bobbed her head in the direction of the red bag. "It's full of work clothes."

I eyed her with amusement. There stood Valerie looking like she'd come straight from the hair and nail salon—her hair perfectly coiffed, her long nails painted a bright red, and her skin creamy smooth, like she'd had a facial and a full makeup job.

I also nodded toward her suitcase. "Only work clothes?" I couldn't imagine a fashion queen like Valerie owning anything made of denim, unless it was diamond-studded.

"Well," she said, coyly tilting her head. "I must admit, there might be one or two cocktail dresses in there." She shrugged. "In case we take a break and do the town."

A laugh burst from my throat. "Do the town? I'm afraid there isn't much of a town to do. You're gonna be disappointed, girl. This isn't the city."

She managed a sympathetic smile and rested her hand on my

shoulder. "Don't worry, honey. We'll find *something*. But believe me, it's *not* gonna be all work and no play." She put her hands on her hips. "Now," she said with an air of authority. "Where do we start?"

I reached for the box of donuts. "We start with these," I said. "I'll make some coffee."

For the next half hour, we sat at the kitchen table, munching on jelly donuts and sipping coffee, freshly brewed out of Gram's old pot. The work ahead of me seemed far less daunting with my friend here. Valerie chattered on about work until she caught the pathetic longing on my face, then she switched the conversation to her last date with her boyfriend.

"Glen found this wonderfully quaint bistro downstairs from a Japanese market. A jazz trio was performing, and we sampled some miso soup with kelp floating around in the bowl, and they had several kinds of sushi. The latest news is, Glen got a promotion. He's now in charge of a whole new wing at the museum. He's planning to fill it with antiques and wants to sell some of them to the public."

A light bulb went off in my head, and I immediately knew what project Val and I could tackle.

"You drove here, right?" I said, raising my eyebrows.

"Yeah. I want you to know I rented a car. Then, I got up at the ungodly hour of 5 AM and hit the road by 6."

"I have the perfect job for you. You're gonna help me clean out my grandmother's attic. Some of the items up there have to be at least a hundred years old. Anything you think Glen can use in that new wing of his, we'll load it in your car and you can take it with you. He might need to restore a few things, but, who knows, some valuable antiques may be mixed up in all the junk."

Twenty minutes later, Val was wearing a pair of designer jeans and a silk blouse.

"So much for work clothes," I mused.

She gave me a whimsical shrug.

We mounted the stairs to the attic, lugging empty boxes with us. At the top, Val gasped for air. We opened the two windows, then we stood there, hands on hips, feet planted firmly, trying to decide where to begin.

I pointed at the bags of clothing. "Forget those. I'm gonna donate all of that to the community theater or to the church's thrift store."

I moved past the bags of clothing to a pile of household items where Gram and I had rooted around years ago.

"Let's look through there," I said. "If you find things Glen can use, set them aside. Everything else we'll stick in one of these boxes for the thrift store."

We plunged ahead. It wasn't long before Val found a Tiffany lamp, a pair of pewter wall sconces, several framed oil paintings, and a crystal vase. "This is Waterford!" she cried out. "Look!" She held it up to the light and pointed toward a gold sticker embossed with a green seahorse. "That's how you can tell." She raised her eyebrows and pursed her lips. "Of course, you may be able to sell it yourself. It could be worth a lot of money."

I shook my head. "Take it. I don't know where to market the thing. It could end up in a yard sale."

Val grunted at me. "Not on your life. It's going to Glen."

She set the vase in a safe place and went back to rooting around.

Meanwhile, I came up with a box of old baseball cards, a metal Batman lunchbox, and a wooden rocking horse with mane and tail made from beige yarn.

"What about that?" Val asked, gesturing toward Gram's old trunk. "No telling what we'll find in there."

I shook my head. "Sorry, the trunk is off limits."

She raised her eyebrows in puzzlement.

"Gram left some personal memorabilia inside, but it's for my eyes only," I explained.

Like always, Val didn't pry when I put up the wall. She'd find out soon enough, but for now, the trunk was all mine.

We went back to sorting, examining, and boxing, and every now and then one of us let out a shriek over a *treasure* of sorts.

We agreed that Glen might not show the same level of excitement we displayed, but that didn't dampen our spirits. In the end, Glen would benefit from Val's hoard of antiques.

By the time we finished, Val's automobile trunk and backseat were full of her treasures. All except the Waterford vase, which Val wrapped in a soft towel and carefully placed on the front seat.

We ended up with six boxes of leftovers, which joined the tower of boxes in the laundry room.

"Tomorrow we'll deliver all of this stuff," I announced.

"Okay," Val agreed. "If we can have lunch out. After that, I'll have to hit the road. I have three assignments waiting on my desk."

I smiled inwardly. The girl couldn't have known how much her visit had meant to me. Before she arrived I was beginning to feel very much alone.

We ate roast beef sandwiches and potato salad for supper, then we sat in the living room with steamy cups of herbal tea. She asked about Brian. I confessed I'd been growing fonder of him.

"Fonder?" she gasped, her eyes wide. "Fran, you grow fond of a puppy or an old grandmother. You must feel something stronger than fondness for the guy. You've been seeing him for over a year."

I nodded. "I'm afraid to go to the next level," I admitted. "Brian proposed a couple of times, but I keep putting him off."

"It doesn't have to be that way. For one thing, you have to get over that thing that happened with Jeff. He cheated on you fifteen years ago. It's time to let it go, don't you think?"

"I ran into him the other day. Just seeing him again revived the painful memories."

"That was in the past, Fran. You're a different person now. You're stronger and wiser. Like I've told you before, you need to forget about that jerk and get on with your life.

"I wish I could. It's not as easy as you think. Ever since Jeff, I've been sabotaging relationships. Either I leave, or I send the guy running. Sabotage.

Val let out a sarcastic laugh, then she shook her head at

me. "You're not sabotaging relationships, my friend. You're sabotaging *yourself*."

I lurched back in my chair. "Huh? What are you saying?"

"What I'm saying is, no one has been affected by your sabotage but you. Only you. *You're* the one who's still alone. *You're* the one who can't make up her mind. *You're* the one who's going to lose Brian if you're not careful."

I realized my mouth had dropped open, but I couldn't speak. Val's remarks had struck my heart like never before. In the past, she'd always joked about my inability to commit. Now she had stunned me with the truth.

We cleaned up our dishes without speaking. Val simply smiled and kept humming a tune I didn't recognize, like she had a secret and was waiting for me to beg for it. I refused to give in. I was still thinking about what she'd said about sabotage and how it was up to me to change everything.

Ultimately, we took turns using the bathroom. Then, both of us, exhausted, headed for bed, but not before Val gave me another one of her unspoken, disappointed shakes of her head. Then she disappeared inside her room and quietly shut the door.

I lay for a long time thinking about Val's words. She'd rarely been so blunt with me. I wasn't angry. Rather, I felt relieved that my friend had told me the truth about myself. I fell asleep comforted to know someone cared that much.

CHAPTER NINE

As promised, Home Depot's delivery men showed up early Wednesday morning. Val was still sleeping in one of the spare bedrooms. I hurried down the stairs in my PJs and let the delivery men inside the kitchen. While they installed the new stove, I went back upstairs to dress.

I peaked in on Val. She looked like she needed a little more sleep, so I quietly shut her door and hurried back downstairs. Slightly larger than the former stove, the new one fit the space with only millimeters to spare. The two men stacked the farmhouse sink and faucets in a corner and departed with Gram's old stove on a dolly cart.

I examined the new stove, tried the knobs, checked out the oven. Satisfied, I placed Gram's iron skillet and her tole painted cookware on a shelf above the stove, and I set her ceramic tea kettle with the floral design on one of the burners, ready for brewing.

My next step was to hire someone to install my new purchases, someone who could also measure the kitchen for new countertops. I checked out the two business cards, one bearing Fred Amati's name and the other belonged to Jeff Petrino.

It was no contest. I called Fred.

He answered on the fourth ring.

"Is this Fred Amati?"

"Sure is." He had a high, squeaky voice and sounded distressingly young. I needed a qualified builder, not a high school dropout.

"I tried to call you before, left a message."

"Yeah, I was gonna call you back today."

I told him about the work in the kitchen and asked if he could measure for a new countertop.

"Sure, no problem-a," he said with enthusiasm.

"I'll need you to come out and give me a price," I said, though I had misgivings. "How about tomorrow morning?"

"Sure. I can juggle some things around. I can be there around 10 AM, okay?"

"Sure," I said, using a word he seemed to understand.

With that settled, I started to put together a breakfast of ham and eggs, brewed a pot of coffee, and poured orange juice in two glasses with a red rooster design that matched Gram's clock. She'd had those glasses for as long as I could remember, had lost only one when my cousin Clara dropped it, spilling orange juice and shards of glass all over the floor.

Gram never got upset over such things. She mopped up the spill, then grabbed a broom and dustpan to sweep away the glass.

"There. All gone," she said as she wiped tears from Clara's cheeks.

I learned later that she'd inherited those glasses from her mother along with the rooster clock on the wall. Enzo had sent the package to Catherine during his time in France. With that kind of image running around in my head, Gram's reaction to the broken glass told me a whole lot more about the kind of person she was, someone who placed other people's feelings over material possessions. It served as a lesson for me, as well. How many times did I fret over a broken glass from the set of ten I had in my cupboard? And what about the time Brian dropped one of my good plates on the floor? How I'd like to take back the remark I'd made.

But what did Gram do? She dumped the shards of glass in the trash like they had no value. But she'd doted over Clara as though she treasured her beyond anything in the world. Gram was gone now, and she was still teaching me.

Val must have smelled the ham frying and the coffee brewing, because seconds later she was at the table, fork in hand, a look of mock impatience screwing up her face.

"Some hostess," she blurted out. "Makes her guests starve while she dilly-dallies over her brand new stove."

I made a face at her and set her plate on the table, then poured her a cup of coffee.

"How's *that*, your majesty?" I quipped back at her.

We bantered back and forth for a few seconds while I fixed a plate for myself, then our conversation settled around our plans for the day.

Val gestured toward the sink and the box containing the new faucet. "Are those on our agenda?" she said, frowning.

"No, I have someone coming tomorrow morning to install them."

She nodded. "So, we take the boxes we filled to the thrift store?"

"That's the plan. We may need to make several trips. Two of the bags of clothes need to go to the community theater. And we can drop the books at the library."

We finished breakfast and spent the remainder of the morning making deliveries. The thrift store was next door to Saint Agnes. The volunteer staff eagerly received our boxes, offered me a receipt for tax purposes, which I graciously refused, and, after receiving our third carload, they invited us to a church picnic on the following Sunday. I had no doubt my parents already had planned I would go.

For lunch, I took Val to Marco's Seafood House, where we enjoyed bowls of linguine with red clam sauce, antipasto salad, and spumoni for dessert.

Val's time to leave came too soon, but I knew I had to stay on schedule, which meant a ton of work still awaited me back at the house. Though I wanted to leave for the city with Val, I wasn't about to quit halfway through the renovations. We parted on the front porch, where I remained long after she drove away, like I'd been super-glued to the wooden floor.

There went my best friend, back to the life we both enjoyed, while I'd been relegated to the roles of painter, washer woman, and amateur carpenter. I was no good at any of those tasks. I was tackling them for only one reason. My dear departed grandmother loved me so much she'd chosen to dump it all on me.

Next on my agenda, I needed to tackle the wood floors and the ceramic tiles. I drove to what had become my shopping Mecca of choice. Not Macy's or Nordstrom's, but Home Depot. I had never expected a home improvement store could lure me inside its doors day after day. I'd been there so many times, my car could find the place on its own.

Of course, I had to ask the man in the orange apron what products I needed to spruce up the wood floors. Once again, I dug into my wallet and watched a couple of $20 bills take wing. I returned home with a gallon of the recommended hardwood floor cleaner plus a bucket and supplies to clean the tile flooring in the bathroom.

It took the rest of the day and part of Thursday to move furniture out of the way and bring Gram's wood floors up to a suitable shine. I gazed with satisfaction at the finished job. True, I was no Bob Vila, but even *he* might have been impressed. The downstairs glowed like a showroom, and a wonderful lemony smell permeated the atmosphere. Though the old aromas of garlic and tomato sauce had dissipated, the resulting freshness was a welcome change.

Here I was, a newspaper journalist, doing a job that was alien to me. No longer was I wielding a pen and reporter pad. I stepped completely out of my element and actually did a good job, if I must say so myself.

By now my back and upper arms ached something awful. I took an ibuprofen, then I soaked in bath oils for fifteen minutes. I went to bed that night exhausted but exhilarated. I discovered I'd been sleeping better with the bedroom window open and a soft, evening breeze tickling my face.

The next morning, I arose feeling rested, and it struck me that I never slept that well in New York. Most nights in the city I arose around 2 AM to use the bathroom or to get a drink of water. Or maybe a gunshot or blown tire shocked me out of bed. But not here in Gram's house. Nights were quiet in this part of New York State. Instead of the roar of a motorcycle or a noisy party next door, the only sounds were crickets mating in the bushes or an owl hooting in the maple tree outside my window. It was the kind of natural freshness poets write about. *No wonder I've been sleeping through the night, every night.*

I also found I'd been eating better. None of that quick cup of yogurt and out the door to work. I'd been having bacon, pancakes, and big bowls of cereal smothered in strawberries, just like when I sat in Mom's kitchen as a little girl.

Still a little achy from the hard labor I'd endured moving furniture around, I dressed in a pair of loose slacks and a T-shirt. I made a simple breakfast of scrambled eggs and coffee, and I'd barely finished eating the last piece of toast when Fred Amati came knocking on the door—10 AM, as scheduled. Impressed by his punctuality, I figured his work might measure up after all. As I had expected from his high-pitched voice, Fred looked like he'd barely gotten out of high school. He was a skinny thing, about my height, and he looked like he was swimming inside his overalls. Stringy hair hung to his shoulders and the hint of a blond goatee had begun to show.

"I work for my father," he squeaked. "He's a builder, taught me most of what I know."

I raised my eyebrows but chose to trust him with my kitchen anyway. What harm could he do? And his father was only a phone call away.

I showed Fred where everything was, then I retreated to the front porch to wash down the wicker furniture and sweep the floor. I used the broom to catch spider webs and mud daubers that had taken up residence in the rafters. Then I dropped onto Gram's front porch swing, nudged my toe against the wood slats, and set the swing in motion.

I breathed deeply of the fresh morning air. So far, I'd had excellent weather. I couldn't help but think maybe Gram was up there cheering me on and putting in a good word now and then. Maybe Salvatore and Rosanna were up there too, keeping an eye on how I took care of their original work. And Catherine and Enzo might have been watching to see if I would ever bring their garden back to life. I reveled in the realization that perhaps I wasn't doing all this alone after all. Perhaps my ancestors were up their guiding and prodding me into action.

At one point, Fred came out and announced he had installed the sink and the disposal, and he'd taken measurements for the wrap-around countertop. It was time for a break. I offered him a ham sandwich and a glass of milk, which he heartily accepted. While he ate, I told him about the upstairs bathroom.

"You'll have to pick up the double sinks, new toilet, and walk-in shower," I finished.

I expected him to say, "Sure."

But he shook his head. "I don't do bathrooms. My pop hasn't taught me yet. Plus, I drive a Mazda minivan, got no room for that kind o' stuff."

I puffed out a disgruntled sigh. "All right. What about your father?"

He looked sympathetic. "Too busy."

I released a sigh. "Okay, Fred. Let's just finish up in here, okay?

He nodded, ate the rest of his sandwich, and got back to work cleaning up the mess he'd made in the kitchen. The good thing was, he'd cut a perfect opening for the sink and disposal, left no unsightly margins, and had everything connected within the hour. I tested the faucets, tried the disposal, and was satisfied there were no leaks or any other problems. Too bad the kid wasn't bathroom qualified.

I handed him cash for the job and had him sign a receipt.

"Can you recommend someone to install the bathroom items?

Fred responded with the last thing I wanted to hear. "The only other handyman I know—other than myself—is Jeff Petrino."

I pressed my lips together and nodded, too disheartened to speak.

After Fred left, I grabbed a mop, filled a bucket with warm water and a splash of disinfectant, and got to work cleaning the tiles in the kitchen and laundry. Like Gram used to do, I found myself humming along with the *swish, swish, swish* of the mop. For Gram it had been Glenn Miller favorites, or her church music, like "Amazing Grace" and "How Great Thou Art."

For me, however, it had to be Mariah Carey's "We Belong Together" or Kelly Clarkson's "Since You Been Gone" both of which had me thinking about Brian.

In almost no time at all I finished the kitchen floor. The whole room smelled like lemons. It left me with a bittersweet sense of accomplishment. While disinfecting everything, I'd almost completely annihilated the essence of my dear, sweet Gram.

I could have wallowed in regrets, but I kept reminding myself that I had no choice but to get the house ready for a prospective buyer, and that meant I had to eliminate any vestiges of the people who had once lived there.

Setting my mind on my next goal, I phoned Home Depot and asked the guy who answered if he could recommend a handyman. He also said, "Jeff Petrino." I suppressed a curse and hung up.

I went online to see if I could search for one myself. Jeff's name kept coming up, as did his ads, and even a YouTube video of him promoting his business. He looked like a used car salesman with his hair slicked down and a phony grin on his suntanned face. But he wasn't selling cars—he was selling himself.

As a last attempt, I did another online search but this time I went outside Cittadina and checked for handymen/contractors in Syracuse and Rochester. I made several calls but kept getting the same answers. Full schedule, too far, and not worth the trip.

Reluctantly, I grabbed Jeff's card off the counter and stared at it, anger boiling up inside me. I couldn't believe he was the number one choice of handymen in Cittadina. But considering the size of the town, it made sense. I punched his number into my cell phone and held my breath.

A big part of me hoped he wouldn't pick up.

He answered on the second ring. Disappointed, but having no other choice, I got right to the point and didn't give him the opportunity to turn my phone call into a personal chat.

No surprise, he was willing and able to do the work. My throat seized with anxiety as I forced myself to hire him.

Ten minutes later, he was at my door. It was like he'd been waiting down the street, watching my house. The thought gave me the creeps, but I let him in anyway. I was struck dumb when he strolled inside, acted like a professional, and without saying a word got busy measuring and making notes in a tiny pad he pulled out of his shirt pocket.

We discussed price. Jeff was right about one thing. The other day when we met at Home Depot, he'd told me he was cheap. He wanted only $200 for a job that could take five hours or more. Plus he still had to pick up the supplies. I immediately got suspicious, but I didn't quibble about the price.

Without another word, he hurried out the door, got into a big, white monster truck, and sped off to Home Depot to pick up my entire order, plus PVC pipes and glue, and whatever else he figured he'd need to install everything. Two hours later, he came back with a muscular, teenaged helper named Russ, who assisted him in carrying the fixtures upstairs. The shower came in sections, which made it easier to handle, but the toilet had to weigh 100 pounds or more. Jeff lugged it up the steps like it was made of feathers. Somehow, everything made it into the bathroom without any damages to the products or the door frames.

The next step for Jeff was opening up the closet to expand the bathroom. I stood in the doorway and envisioned a glorious spa with a walk-in shower and maybe some candles all around like I'd seen in the movies.

While the two guys pounded and sawed upstairs, I got to work polishing Gram's furniture in the dining room and living room. The solid oak shone like brand new. Gram had taken excellent care of her things.

I spent some of my free time reading more of my

great-grandparents' correspondence. Not much had changed. Catherine was still working the garden and visiting with her sisters-in-law. Salvatore spent much of his time sitting on the front porch, rarely speaking, just reading his Bible. And Enzo was becoming more impatient to get to his first campsite.

My reading was interrupted when Jeff came down the stairs and told me they'd finished the bathroom, and did I want to take a look?

I waited while the two of them hauled the old fixtures out to Jeff's truck, then I hurried up the stairs. Like a kid playing house, I turned all the faucets on and off, checked the hot and cold water flows, flushed the new toilet, and slid the glass shower door back and forth. Then I ran my hand over the rim of the tub. It was a true master suite. I had to admit, Jeff was worth every penny.

At that moment, I sensed his presence close behind me. I felt his breath on my neck and shivered.

"I can picture you in a tub full of bubbles," he whispered in my ear.

I backed away, then I shoved past him and went downstairs for my purse. Jeff and his helper followed close behind me.

Still fuming, I dug out my wallet and thrust four fifty-dollar bills in his hand.

I glared at Jeff's smirking face. "I wouldn't have used your services at all if I'd been able to get anyone else," I snarled.

He simply laughed.

Poor Russ stood gawking at us, like he was trying to decide if I was unhappy with the work. Jeff tucked the money in his pocket and grabbed his tools. As the two of them left, I stood seething in the doorway. When Jeff got to the sidewalk, he turned like he was about to say something. I slammed the door and flicked the lock with a loud click.

I needed to get my mind off of Jeff Petrino and onto the work that still lay ahead of me. The man had ruined my life once. I wouldn't let him ruin it again.

Now that the kitchen was sparkling, the hardware on the cupboard doors seemed dated and dull. I wanted to change it out to something brighter. Of course, such an addition required another trip to Home Depot. The salespeople had begun to call me by my first name. No problem, I'd be gone in a few weeks, and they'd soon forget about me like I'd forget about them.

I walked the aisle with a female salesperson who seemed to share my taste in hardware. We picked out black knobs and handles that had a farmhouse feel to go with the big sink.

I was back home, in the middle of swapping out the old hardware for the new, when the front doorbell rang.

I began to pray. *Please, God, don't let it be Jeff. Please, don't let it be Jeff.*

By the time I reached the door, I had psyched myself into a frenzy. I was primed to scream in Jeff's face and tell him to get lost. But when I opened the door, I stood in shock for a few seconds as I tried to place the young woman who was standing before me. Then I focused on her blue/violet eyes, and I let out a shriek.

"Penny!"

CHAPTER TEN

Like an apparition from the past, my best friend from high school was standing in front of me. It took a few seconds for the reality to sink in, then I pulled her close and gave her a hug. Breathless, I backed away, my hands resting on her shoulders. I shook my head in awe and looked her over.

She was wearing an ankle-length flowered skirt and a peasant blouse, so out of character for the girl who once lived in blue jeans and T-shirts. Her brown hair now glowed with blonde highlights and hung to her shoulders. Her round dimpled face hadn't changed much, except for smile lines at the sides of her eyes. Her irises fluctuated between blue and purple as she held my gaze. I've never known anyone else who could captivate people with her eyes like Penny Boticini could.

I blurted out the first thing that came to mind. "I thought you moved to California. Why on earth did you come back to Podunk?"

She responded with a bubbly laugh that used to get everyone chuckling along with her. She shrugged. "I came home."

I regretted having lost touch with her. My move to New York did more than sever bad memories, it alienated me from people I loved—namely, my family and my closest friend. Shame washed over me. I had failed to appreciate the people in my life. I'd taken them for granted, didn't think twice about them when I walked—or rather *ran*—away from my hometown. For the first time in nearly fifteen years, I rued the day I'd left the best parts of my life behind in Cittadina.

I ushered Penny inside the house and guided her into the kitchen. Her eyes widened as she surveyed the room's transformation.

"You've done wonders with this place," she crowed. "I heard you were renovating your grandmother's house, but wow!" She paced around the room and ran her fingers over the new stove and sink, then bowed to get a better look inside the oven.

She straightened and smiled. "Remember those afternoons when we barged in here after school expecting your gram to feed us the treat of the day?" she said, her eyes sparkling with the memory. "That woman never disappointed us. I can still taste those Italian confections."

She stood in front of me and crossed her arms. "So you inherited this old house, huh? What do you plan to do with it?"

I told her the truth. "I'm gonna fix it up, sell it, and go back to New York."

Disappointment washed over her face. "Really, Fran? I thought maybe you were here to stay."

"Not a chance," I said firmly. "What about you? Are *you* here to stay?"

Her rosy cheeks spread in a coy smile. "Maaaybe." "She drew out the word. "I might have a good reason to stay."

"Why don't you buy Gram's house?" I offered. "I'll give you a price you can't refuse." I took her arm. "C'mon, I'll show you the rest."

We went through the downstairs, and I soaked up her *oohs* and *aahs*. She seemed to like Gram's old furnishings, the wood floors, the narrow staircase leading up to the second floor.

We hit every room, including my new bathroom spa, then we made a complete circuit back to the kitchen.

"Want to have supper?" I said. "It won't be much, just a salad and some garlic bread, but it's free."

"Sounds perfect."

She went to the sink and washed her hands. "Let me help."

While Penny assembled a salad, I prepared the garlic bread and set the table. Our conversation transitioned to the past. We laughed over the dumb, childish things we did as teenagers, like the time we went up on the roof of the high school and had a midnight picnic of cold pizza and warm beer. Penny made a few cracks about the nerds in our class, people who years later had moved into high paying careers while the rest of us were still trying to figure out what we wanted to do with our lives. Then she told me about the challenges of trying to break into the Hollywood scene.

"I tried acting," she said, smirking. "Couldn't get an agent or an audition." She shrugged. "Tried singing—off-key most of the time. Then I fell back on the one thing I knew how to do well—set design. I messed that up, too, the day I placed a vase of chrysanthemums in front of an actor who was allergic to them. After five years of one disappointment after another, I came back to the place where I was loved and appreciated. I took a boring job answering phones in the hair salon. But, at least here I can be involved in community theater, and if I make a mistake, I'm forgiven. In fact, in Cittadina, mistakes are expected."

We laughed over her last remark. Then our mirth turned to sadness as we ran through the names of classmates and favorite teachers who'd passed away. In less than an hour, Penny and I had reminisced over the past fourteen years. Our talk had a cathartic affect on me, a sort of cleansing of the heart, as I also opened up about my own successes and failures. One thing was certain, I could always bare my soul to Penny and not fear judgment.

We finished our meal and cleaned up, then retreated to the living room with cups of hot herbal tea. Penny grabbed Gram's rocker, so I moved my great-grandparents' letters to the fireplace mantle. I settled on the sofa, content to yield my favorite chair to my friend. I was so glad she'd come to call.

I gingerly sipped the hot tea. "When did you get back in town?"

"A few years ago." She ran her hand through her streaked hair. The strands dropped like threads of fine gold to her shoulders. I had to admit the look was quite becoming on her.

"I missed my folks," she said, and a sadness clouded her eyes.

"I no sooner got back to town when they packed up and moved to Florida. Can you imagine?" Her bubbly giggle returned. "They couldn't wait to get out of here." She shrugged. "They gave the house to my sister, Chris, and me."

"So Chris stayed in Cittadina?"

Penny nodded. "Yeah, she's a confirmed bachelorette."

"And you?"

She sipped her tea and eyed me sheepishly over the rim. "While I was in California I married a wanna-be actor. Like me, he never made it, hid his grief in booze and other women." Penny let out a sigh that had twinges of pain laced within it. "Turns out I married a worthless cheater. After we divorced, I didn't want to stay in L.A."

Jeff came to mind, and my heart froze. "I know what you mean," I said. "If you remember, I went through a similar trauma. After what Jeff did, I didn't want to stay here either. Too many bad memories." I paused for a second, then added, "He stopped by here the other day. Against my better judgment, I hired him to install my bathroom fixtures. Had no other options."

She grinned. "He's the only decent contractor in town. He does a good job."

"Well, the toilet flushes, and the faucets work, that's all I know."

She smiled like the Cheshire Cat, and I knew she had a secret she wanted me to pry loose.

I tilted my head. "Okay, what?"

She lowered her eyes and squirmed a little. I frowned in puzzlement.

She looked me in the eye and snickered. "I'm dating him."

"What?!" I straightened. "You're dating Jeff? Please say it isn't so."

"It's true. I like him, Fran. A lot."

"Have you forgotten what your ex did to you? Have you forgotten what Jeff did to *me*?"

She nodded and a pathetic wrinkle crept across her forehead. "He's different now. He grew up."

"Right." My disbelief cut through the air like a knife. My best friend had fallen for the guy who'd made my life a living hell, the one I trusted with my heart and then left me wondering if I'd ever trust anyone again.

"I thought you were smarter than that, Penny."

She cocked her head to one side. "He's the one who told me you'd come home, that you inherited your grandmother's house and were fixing it up." She glanced around the living room and changed the subject. "I like the floors. Why don't you stay? We can hang out again." She smiled and raised her eyebrows.

"Penny, we were talking about Jeff."

"I know, but we've both said enough. I'm dating him and that's final."

I couldn't believe she'd forgotten about the man's past, how after me, he didn't even last with Denise. Went from one girl to another. I shook my head. "I'm not staying, Penny. I don't want to be that naive little girl again." I set my jaw. "I'll stay long enough to get this place ready for sale, and not a day longer."

"Okay, then, I'll help." She perked up a little, and dimples reappeared in her cheeks. "We can have a painting party or something."

I began to relax. "That might be fun," I agreed. "I still have the upstairs to do." Perhaps with Penny helping, that was one thankless job I wouldn't have to do alone. "Come back Monday in your dumpiest clothes, and I'll get you started painting walls on the second floor."

I smiled. During our senior year, Penny had turned her own bedroom into a showplace.

"As I remember, you had a knack for decorating," I reminded her. "I'd love for you to help with that, too."

Unlike most of us girls, Penny had taken her high school home economics classes to heart. While we settled for making potholders and aprons to give out as Christmas presents, she created fancy pillow shams for her bed and curtains to match, a hand-woven rug for her floor, and cross-stitched artwork for the walls. She even took worthless items, like pieces of plastic, tissue paper, and pipe cleaners, and created beautiful flower arrangements for her dresser and end tables. Stepping inside Penny Boticini's bedroom was like entering Martha Stewart's showroom.

A sparkle had filled Penny's eyes, like she couldn't wait to get started. She shared several ideas she had for Gram's living room, then, in a flurry, she was gone.

The time we'd spent together had resurrected old feelings of fun and fantasy. But I had to remind myself that our visit was temporary. In a few weeks I would leave for New York City, Penny would stay in Cittadina, and we'd probably never see each other again. She was in a relationship with a man who'd treated me like the dirt under his shoes. It would be best if I could move on and forget about both of them.

My thoughts then turned to Brian. With my boyfriend coming to town, I could enjoy my weekend and forget about Penny dating Jeff.

I was sitting up in bed still reading my great-grandparents' letters when my cell phone rang. It was 11 PM.

"Sorry if I woke you," Brian said. "You didn't wake me. I was reading."

"What'cha readin', Fran?"

"Old letters."

"Huh?"

I explained about the trunk in the attic and the memorabilia my Gram had left.

"Sounds fascinating," he said. "Wish I could read some of those letters with you."

"Well, I'm not going to throw them away, so maybe you *will* read some of them. They're extremely old though, about ready to fall apart. The blue notepaper has yellowed, the edges have frayed, and some of them have stains all over, like someone dripped coffee on them or was crying when they wrote them." I paused, then turned my attention to Brian. "So, how are *you* doing?"

"Great. I'm almost done with my classes. Mr. Judd, the owner of the firm, has agreed to foot the bill. Everything's going fine, but I miss you a lot, Fran. It's not the same here without you. I keep worrying that you might discover you like your old stomping ground and maybe never come home. After all, you sublet your apartment."

"It's a month-to-month sublease," I reminded him.

"For now."

I chuckled. "Brian, there's no chance I'm gonna stay in this place. I only want to get this house ready for sale and then it'll be, *Adios, amigo.*"

He chuckled, but I detected a hint of concern. "We'll see," he said, as if he knew something I didn't.

"What do you mean?" I could hear him breathing, but he didn't answer right away. "Brian?"

"Yeah, I was trying to decide how to say this. Okay, here goes. It's commitment, Fran. You've never committed to anything. You see your job as a stepping stone to better things. The same with your apartment. From the day you moved in you said it was temporary, until you can afford something better. I don't know, maybe you feel the same way about me."

Brian's remark pierced my heart and sent me reeling for a moment. Had I really said those things? Had I been thinking like everything was temporary. Including him?

That wasn't how my great-grandparents viewed life. Everything they said and did seemed to center around each other. And permanence. I frowned with concern.

"You're wrong, Brian, but I'll consider what you're saying."

"Remember, I'm driving up there tomorrow, and I'm planning to help with the renovations."

"Really? The guy who doesn't know one end of a hammer from the other? The guy who sits at a desk all day and reads law books?"

"Okay, so I never got my hands dirty that way, but I can pound a few nails. I can handle a paintbrush as well as the next guy."

"The painting's almost done. I already finished the downstairs, and my old friend, Penny Boticini, offered to help with the upstairs painting next week."

"So, you don't want me to come?"

"Of course I do. But I don't know what you'll do when you get here. Maybe *something*."

"Then something it is." He breathed a heavy sigh. "I guess we'd better hang up for now. I need to rest up for the drive tomorrow."

I think we both said goodbye. At any rate, he was gone before I knew it. As always, I'd done a great job of pushing him away. My usual sabotage routine. Protect my heart at any cost.

At that moment, Jeff came to mind, his black mop of hair and winking dark eyes, and the eternal smirk on his lips. He'd be thrilled to know I was brushing off another relationship, and all because of him. The guy had turned my heart to stone, and I didn't know how to soften it.

But Brian's not Jeff. I had to keep reminding myself of that. Otherwise I might lose the greatest guy who'd ever walked into my life.

I fell asleep thinking how lucky I was to have found someone who was more like my great-grandfather than anyone I'd ever known. Brian had dropped out of college to serve in the Marines. After his stint was done, he'd resumed his education and then interned at the firm where he now had an office. He was the kind of guy who committed to something and then followed through to the end.

Apparently, unlike me.

Besides all that, he'd never given me any reason to doubt his love for me. So why was I holding back? Why couldn't I say, "I love you?" like Catherine and Enzo did, over and over again, in every letter. And like Brian did, every time we talked.

CHAPTER ELEVEN

The next morning, I went right to the shower, enjoyed the hot spray for several minutes, then wrapped myself in one of Gram's giant body towels. I was busy dressing when a dripping sound caught my attention. I went back to the bathroom and checked the faucets on the shower. They were off.

The dripping continued. I followed the sound down the stairs to the kitchen. There, in the center of the ceiling, was the beginning of a giant water spot. I clenched my teeth. It had to be coming from the drain Jeff had installed.

I grabbed my cell phone and dialed his number. I got voicemail.

"What's going on, Jeff? There's a huge water spot on my kitchen ceiling. You need to get back here and figure out where the leak is coming from."

The dripping sound had stopped, but something wasn't right. I wouldn't be able to take another shower until Jeff fixed the problem. But should there even *be* a problem? Everyone around here said he was the best.

Still fuming, I telephoned Brian and asked if he'd left New York yet. With a lilt in his voice, he informed me he *had* left the big city behind and had entered a whole different world.

"The air is so clean and fresh—quite different from the haze and smoke the city traffic stirs up," he raved. "I could get to like this part of New York State."

"Come on, Brian. You've been away from the city before."

"Sure I have, and I've loved it every time. But I normally leave by plane and travel to some far off place where they do zip lining and rock climbing. I've never driven to Upstate New York—never had a reason to until now. It's beautiful up here."

A surge of pride came from somewhere deep inside my heart. My great-great-grandfather must have felt the same way as Brian when he left the city and purchased his little plot of land. I tried to imagine the first time Salvatore caught sight of Upstate New York. Then Enzo had lived there with his bride, Catherine. They loved it so much, they'd enhanced the property with beautiful gardens. The property had passed on to Gram and Poppa. They kept the gardens going and made a few modern changes of their own to the house. My father grew up in the house on Maple Street. Then he moved a few blocks away to Almond Lane and the Victorian home where I grew up. My family not only settled Cittadina, every one of my ancestors had contributed in some way to the town's growth.

Now Brian had reminded me what a wonderful, wholesome part of the state I had lived in.

"How are things going with the house?" he said.

"I'm afraid the handyman left me with a problem," I told him.

"Really, what's wrong?"

"Just a leak. Nothing he can't fix, if I can get him over here."

"Maybe I can help."

I stifled a laugh. Brian hadn't repaired anything in all the time I'd known him. Like me, he always called the super of his apartment building.

"I'll show you when you get here," I said, with tongue in cheek. "For now, just pay attention to your driving. And be careful."

Brian was coming to visit. Butterflies stirred in my stomach. I felt like a teenager getting ready for her prom. I stood for several minutes in front of the open closet, tying to decide what to wear. I finally chose a yellow sundress and white sandals. I fixed my hair the way Brian liked it, with a part on one side and falling to my shoulders in neat waves. A pair of pearl earrings finished the look. I used minimal makeup. Neither Brian nor I cared for that caked-on look. And false eyelashes were out. Those embellishments were okay on Val. She was fashion model material. But me? I would have looked like a little girl playing dress-up.

While I waited on pins and needles for Brian to arrive, I tidied up around the house. With thoughts of lunch, I checked the fridge and pantry. They looked like Mother Hubbard's cupboard.

I made a list—it seemed I was living with lists these days—grabbed my purse, and headed for the supermarket.

Strolling the aisles at Cittadina's Food A-Plenty took me back to my youth and various shopping trips with my mom. The segue back in time had me filling the cart with items my mother might have purchased—lemon pepper chicken, macaroni salad, peaches and plums, and, if dad had been there, a killer dessert, something like black forest cake or apple pie.

I had to laugh at myself. I'd grown up and moved away, yet here I was, regressing back to my childhood and no longer fighting the influence my folks had on me. In fact, I was kind of enjoying it.

I took my purchases home, stored everything in the fridge, and set the dining room table with Gram's good china. Then I went out to the front porch to watch for a silver blue Toyota Corolla.

Thoughts of Catherine waiting for Enzo to come home from war swarmed into my head. Though our situations were different, I experienced stirrings within my hear, the kind that strike when a loved one has been far away and suddenly reenters your life.

To fill the remaining time, I went for the letters and took them out to the porch swing where I could continue to watch the road for Brian's car while reading.

The next two letters came from Catherine, dated *June 20* and *June 25, 1917*. I opened the first one. The ink was smeared in several places.

My dear Enzo,
I can no longer bear the emptiness I feel in your absence. Your

brothers' wives all have their children to keep them busy. I don't have that kind of distraction. Your papa doesn't require much care. Salvatore does well on his own, except he still misses your mama something awful. Rosanna's passing left him with a dark emptiness I can't seem to penetrate. He spends most of his days tending our little garden, which helps to keep us in fresh vegetables. I wish I knew how to get him to smile again.

I don't know how long the bank will hold your position. Without your income to pay the bills, I have taken a job in town. The money will help, and I'll stay busy. So, starting tomorrow, I'll be manning the post office desk every morning, and I will spend the afternoons volunteering at the local Red Cross auxiliary. We're preparing bandages and other supplies to be shipped to our troops overseas. In that way, I can be a part of the war effort, which should keep me close to you, my love.

I think of you all the time—when I cook your favorite foods, like pasta e fagioli and spaghetti carbonara, when I enter our empty bedroom, when I sit on the porch and look at the stars like we used to do. I wonder where you are, if you're at sea, or if you've entered France yet. I have so many questions. Are you well? Are you safe? Do you have everything you need?

I try not to think about the war. Though your papa gets the paper every day, I avoid reading it. I want to know, yet I don't want to know. It's crazy.

Anyway, I don't mention my concerns around your brothers's wives. Nor do I want to keep dwelling on the situation. But you have to know, my life has changed drastically since you left. I miss you so much.

Please take good care of yourself. I wouldn't be able to go on without you.

Yours always,
Catherine

My own tears fell on the page and blended with those likely left by Catherine. The thought of someone hurting that much overwhelmed me. What if Enzo hadn't made it back? What if Catherine had to go on without him?

For that matter, what would my life be like without Brian? I'd never considered it before

I took a moment to check the street. No sign of the blue car yet.

Catherine's next letter was equally heart-rending.

My dearest Enzo, my love,

Annette stopped at the post office yesterday morning. She said she has not heard from Franco since he left. I tried to console her, but it was like one fretful woman trying to soothe another. All we could do was cry together. I didn't tell her you had written, but I did say the mail is slower going back and forth between the Army camps and those of us waiting at home. That wasn't a lie. Your first letter took almost two weeks to reach me.

If you're able to find out where your brothers are and how they are doing, let me know and I'll pass the information to their wives. Other than that, we are all doing as well as can be expected.

I like my job at the post office. It keeps me busy and doesn't give me time to fret about the war. My Red Cross duties have been a godsend. I've met so many women who also wait for their husbands and sons to return from the war. We have a lot in common and we often talk about our men. We comfort and support one another. We don't have to hide behind a false smile. We cry together and laugh together. And a small group of us gather for prayer at the end of the day. Because of them I'm able to face every day with fresh hope.

Please remember, Enzo, You are in my thoughts and prayers all the time. I'm longing for the day when I can wrap my arms around you again.

Love and Kisses,
Catherine

As I read their letters, it became easier for me to imagine them as real people, young and passionately in love with each other.

What a shock! They were exactly like my parents. Maybe even a little like Brian and me.

Brian and me.

The realization struck me like the blast of a cannon. I couldn't deny I was missing Brian in much the same way Catherine was missing Enzo. Oh, he wasn't in any danger. Nor was I. Neither one of us had traveled overseas. But the distance between us was as pronounced as if an entire ocean had come between us. I began to admit the truth. I'd been missing Brian from the day I'd arrived in Cittadina. Perhaps some of the tears I'd shed for Catherine and Enzo were really about my own loss.

Until now, my great-grandparents were images in old photos. Now they'd come right onto the front porch where I was reading what they wrote to each other. It was as if they'd come home—Enzo returning from war and Catherine rising up to meet him.

I shook my head, as reality sank in. How many of us young people think of our parents and grandparents as if they came out of a mold already old and gray, having no past and no future? How many of us forget that inside each of those wrinkled foreheads lies a world of wisdom and experiences beyond anything we could ever imagine? If only we opened our hearts to whatever they might say, perhaps we could actually learn something. And maybe what we learn might make our own futures a whole lot better.

I began to consider this also from a reporter's viewpoint. How many times had I avoided speaking with elderly people at the scene of an accident or some other occurrence and instead sought out the voices of the young? What had I missed? I determined right then and there that I needed to change my interviewing preferences to also include the elderly and the infirm.

I reached for the next letter, but took a second to look down the street. No sign of a silver blue Toyota.

I turned my attention back to the letter. This one was dated *June 28, 1917* and it was written by Enzo.

Dearest Catherine,

Our journey across the Atlantic took several days, two of them were quite rough. Lots of guys got sick and tossed their breakfasts over the side. We all joked about it. One soldier claimed he was feeding the fish and got the rest of us laughing. I cut back on eating and tried to stay on deck as much as possible. I breathed in the fresh sea air and waited for the waves to settle down.

We arrived in France two days ago. More than 14,000 of us split up into different units in various parts of the land. Our arrival had an amazing affect on the French. When we marched through the towns, people spilled out of their doors into the streets, smiling and shouting for joy. They came bearing flowers and sweets in their hands. They thanked us for coming. It was a good feeling to receive such a welcome.

When we set up camp, we each received a gas mask, wire cutters, and a three-day ration pack containing a can of meat, hardtack, coffee, sugar, and dried fruit. Each of us has a "Soldier's Small Book," so we can record our service record and any personal notations. Whenever I add a note to these pages, I always think of you, dear Catherine, certain that you will read my words someday, hopefully with me at your side.

It took about an hour to put up our tents. They're huge pieces of thick canvas that will certainly keep out the rain. I'm bunking with three other guys—Philip, a mason from Ohio, Jack, a dock worker from Boston, and Matt, a college student who dropped out to serve our country. We're sitting inside our tent now, writing letters home and listening to the steady pelting of raindrops on the canvas above our heads. It's almost musical.

Already, Corporal Minton has assigned us our duties. I ended up with meal detail, which means I'll have to get up at the crack of dawn and help out at the big mess tent. That was okay by me. I'm used to getting up early so I could tend our gardens before heading off to work. So mess turned out to be the perfect detail for me.

The other guys will rotate on guard duty, with each of them taking four-hour shifts. Jack got midnight, the poor guy. He'll be walking up and down past the tents while everyone else is snoring.

I think of you often, Catherine. When I'm peeling potatoes, when I'm cleaning up scraps of garbage, when I'm cleaning my rifle or shining my boots—whatever I'm doing, I'm thinking, I'm doing this for Catherine, so she'll be free and safe, so she'll be proud of me. And, to be honest, I'm doing it for America, and for France, and also for Italy, my Papa's homeland. Please tell my father I said that. It might mean a lot to him to know I haven't forgotten our heritage. He's a proud old guy, always talked well of the old country. Even though he loved his life in America, he always impressed upon us boys the importance of our ancestry.

I'll write again soon and let you know as much about our mission as I'm allowed.

With much love,
Enzo

I was sobbing now. No one ever told me I should be proud of my ancestry. If they had, I didn't hear them. Maybe I didn't care. Well, I cared now. I had immersed myself so deeply in my great-grandparents' lives, I wanted to keep going, wanted to dig deeper into the hearts of Catherine and Enzo.

I struggled with whether to pick up another letter or get ready for Brian's visit. It was almost 12 o'clock. He might show up at any moment.

I eyed the rest of the weathered stack of old mail. Then, breathing a long sigh, I took the pile inside the house and put them in the hutch beside Salvatore's daybook.

The sound of a car pulling into the driveway caught my attention. Suddenly, nothing else mattered. Not the letters in the hutch, not whether there was enough food in the refrigerator, not even the work that still remained. I ran to the front door and down the porch steps, and lunged into the arms of Brian Kelly.

Brian eased out of our embrace and surveyed the front of the house. His lips broke into a broad grin, and his brown eyes shone with approval.

"It's exactly what I pictured," he said. "A charming vision from the past."

I giggled with delight. A deep sense of pride swept over me. Why did I feel that way? I hadn't planned to own the place for more than a few weeks, nothing more. After that, it'll be, *So long, charming vision from the past.* Yet, I felt pleased to hear Brian's praises.

"How about some lunch?" I said. "I have a refrigerator full of food."

He shook his head. "There's no need to cook. I want to spend every minute with you. And I'd like to take a tour of your town while we still have daylight. Let's eat out at one of your favorite restaurants."

I gave him the choice between Marco's Seafood House and Luigi's Italian Eatery.

"Luigi's, of course," he said, smiling. "We're in *Little Italy*, aren't we? Let's go Italian all the way."

I laughed and poked his arm. "Not so fast. Let's put your bags inside, and you can freshen up."

He nodded, and, suitcase in hand, he trotted behind me up the porch steps and into the house. Inside the living room, he stopped walking and swiveled his head from side to side.

"This is nice," he said with sincere admiration. "I was expecting a dilapidated, old collection of boards ready for the junk pile. But this place feels solid." He stomped one foot. Except for a slight groan, not a board rattled or sank beneath his step. "Real solid," he repeated.

I beamed with pride. "My great-great-granddad knew what he was doing when he built this house."

"He sure did; can't wait to see the rest of it."

I beckoned him to follow me up the stairs, then got him situated in the room Val had occupied during her visit. I'd already changed the bedding and had placed a flickering candle on the dresser.

I took a minute to show him the new shower stall and pointed out where I thought the leak might be coming from.

"Hmm," he said, as if he understood. I knew better.

He bent close to the drain. "I'll bet your handyman didn't seal the pipes. Did you call him back?"

I nodded. "Right away, but he hasn't returned my call, yet."

"Hmm," he said again.

I chuckled to myself. My boyfriend, powerhouse in the courtroom but all thumbs in home repair. "Why don't we just get something to eat?"

Since I knew my way around town, I decided to drive and let Brian gaze out the window. His comments reminded me of a child seeing Disney World for the first time.

"I love these old houses," he said as we meandered up and down the tree-lined streets. "I grew up in the city and never had the chance to know what small-town life was like. So far, all I knew about quaint little villages came from movies like *Peyton Place* and *Doc Hollywood*."

"Believe me, you didn't miss anything."

I made a few turns and ended up on Main Street.

"How awesome!" Brian cried out. "A genuine striped pole in front of the barber shop. And look, there's an ice cream store, and an old-fashioned pharmacy, and a tiny jailhouse. The whole downtown area looks like a real-life Mayberry."

I tried to see what he was seeing, but I came up empty. I shook my head and kept driving.

"You got to walk everywhere," he rambled on. "I had to take a bus or depend on my mom to drive me. You must have had, what—seventy-five kids in your class? My grade had 1,500, and I made two friends before I graduated. You knew everyone in town, while I met only strangers on the streets of New York."

Brian's praises for Cittadina caused me to take a second look at the place where I'd grown up. How had I missed all of that? And now that I called New York City my home, did I even see the difference? I pondered this as we drove on and turned toward Lincoln Highway and Luigi's Italian Eatery.

We shared an antipasto consisting of chunks of lettuce, sliced tomatoes layered with mozzarella cheese, rolled up ham, prosciutto, and salami, plus an assortment of pickled olives, artichokes, and pearl onions. We still had an entree coming, and if I knew Brian, we couldn't leave the place without first having dessert.

For a main course, I settled on Luigi's specialty, spaghetti and meatballs. Brian chose stuffed manicotti and a serving of fried calamari. I ate slowly and enjoyed watching my boyfriend scoop up heaping forkfuls of each selection.

During lunch I filled him in, detail by detail, on everything I'd done to the house.

"Now if I can only get Jeff to fix the leak in the bathroom shower," I grumbled.

"Wasn't he the guy who jilted you?" Brian asked. Then he winced and quickly added, "Sorry, honey, I didn't mean to bring up a bad memory."

I shrugged. "Yeah, he jilted me all right. Over and over again. But, I'm fine now." I raised my chin with forced confidence.

Brian smiled at me over a forkful of manicotti. Then he went on savoring each bite of food.

I eyed Brian with concern. Somehow, I needed to come up with the most logical job for the two of us to do together. There was no way I'd ask him to paint the upstairs ceilings. He was the kind of guy who'd get more paint on himself. Nor was there any need to have him check out the condition of the roof. I didn't want to have to pick up broken pieces of Brian on the front lawn.

"Why don't we wash the windows?" I suggested. "You can do the outside, and I'll take the inside. Of course, it means you'll have to climb a ladder to reach the upstairs windows."

He nodded in agreement.

"On second thought, you should do something else," I conceded.

"Listen," he said, like he'd read my mind. "I can handle this. Don't forget, I go rock climbing at least twice a year."

"It's not the same."

"I can climb a ladder, Fran. I've done it before."

He shoveled manicotti into his mouth and managed to smile at me. "Have faith," he mumbled and took another bite. Then, catching my look of skepticism, he set down his fork. "You obviously don't know my hidden talents, Fran. I didn't grow up in a law office. I was once a little boy who went to camp and climbed a thirty-foot oak tree. And guess what? I survived."

He picked up his fork and resumed eating.

I laughed. Like I'd done with everyone else in my life, I'd put Brian in his own little box, and I hadn't expected him to get out. Now, Brian had challenged me to believe in him beyond what I already thought about him. He wanted to prove he could do more than look over someone's legal papers.

We finished lunch and went home with a couple of take-out boxes—one holding a large slice of chocolate cake, and the other filled with my leftover spaghetti.

We went upstairs to our individual rooms and changed clothes into something more fitting for washing windows. I couldn't help but admire Brian's rugged new look. Though I'd seen photos of him in his climbing gear, I'd never been face-to-face with him in work clothes. I smiled with admiration. This was a side of him I could learn to like.

While Brian got the ladder out of Gram's shed and positioned it next to the house, I filled a bucket with soapy water and vinegar, then handed it to him along with a handful of soft rags. He got right to work on the outside, and I took a spray bottle of window cleaner and started on the inside. Occasionally, we met up at the same window, made faces at each other, threw kisses, and then moved on.

When we finished, we put the ladder away and stuffed the dirty rags in the washing machine.

Brian put his hands on his hips. "Okay," he said, his energy still up. "What next?"

I suggested we see what we could do with the landscaping. I could sure use his help with the outdoor projects.

As we strolled around the property, Brian kept shaking his head. "What a disaster," he said, and I thought for a minute he was going to back out.

I let out a sigh. "Gram had been ill for a long time and let everything go," I said. "My folks kept checking on the house and mowing the lawn, but they didn't have time to keep up the flower beds or Gram's vegetable garden. Their own house needs plenty of tender loving care. Dad still works as an accountant, albeit mostly from home. And Mom is busy with charity work in town."

I had to admit, Catherine and Enzo would have been appalled at the state of the gardens they had lovingly planted decades ago. The two of them had created a floral wonderland. And Gram had added her own touch of color to the property. I wasn't sure we could make much of a difference.

"I can't wait to tackle it," Brian said, his face aglow.

His reaction sparked a flame in me. Maybe we *could* do something worthwhile. "The plants in the front can use some serious pruning," I suggested. "And the circular flower bed around the flagpole has gone to seed. We can revive that little plot of ground."

We walked to the back yard and passed the crippled wooden bench and the two maple trees Catherine had planted a hundred years before. The flower beds had lost their vivacity, and a pitiful wisteria vine still clung to the crumbling wooden trellis.

"We can fix this up," he said, undaunted. "Think about it, Fran. We can be backyard artists."

As the sun began its descent in the west, we went inside the house. I grabbed the shower first so I could start supper while Brian cleaned up.

I donned a soft blue sundress and sandals, pulled my hair back in a ponytail, then went to the kitchen to warm up the lemon-pepper chicken I'd purchased that morning. By the time Brian finished dressing, I had set the table with the chicken on a platter, the pre-made salad in one of Gram's bowls, two glasses of red wine poured and ready, and two tapered candles flickering in the center of the table.

Brian bounded into the room, a big smile on his face. How could someone climb up and down a ladder and work on windows for two hours and come away looking like he'd been to a spa? It seemed to me country living agreed with him.

Once again, I took small helpings of everything while Brian heaped his plate with several slices of white meat, both drumsticks, and most of the salad.

While we ate, I tried to think of something we could do after dinner. This wasn't my New York City apartment. We didn't have the entire metropolitan scene to draw us outside for the evening. The best I could offer was a couple of hours of watching fireflies from Gram's front porch swing. And going downtown? Not a chance. This was Cittadina, where the streets folded up at 9 o'clock, and except for a few scattered street lamps, the downtown area went dark.

Then I remembered my great-grandparents' letters. Brian had said he wanted to read them. Though they'd been meant for me alone, I believed Gram would want me to share them with my boyfriend.

After cleaning up our dishes, I retrieved the stack of letters from the hutch and invited Brian to join me on the sofa. We sat close, shoulder to shoulder, and I opened the next letter in the pack.

It was signed by Catherine, and dated *July 5, 1917*. We read it quietly together.

My dearest Enzo,

I wish you could have been here last night to celebrate the Fourth of July with me. Everyone in town had a flag hanging from their front porch or flying from a pole in the yard. As always, Salvatore went out and raised our own flag.

You'll be happy to know our rose bushes are in full bloom. They smell wonderful. The blossoms on the azaleas lasted for a little while, and the holly bushes already have red berries popping out all over them.

To celebrate Independence Day, Salvatore and I fried some hamburgers and hotdogs at home. I made potato salad. And we drank lemonade. When it grew dark, we walked together to the town park and watched the celebration. Father Petrie said the opening invocation. Then Mayor Barnati stepped up to the podium and read through a list of names of the men of our town who had gone off to war. I choked up a little, and I felt a deep sense of pride when the mayor called out your name.

After the ceremony, a local band played the anthems of both America and Italy. The trombones and accordions and cymbals could be heard from one end of town to the other. A sensation of patriotism took over the crowd. It was like medicine for the lonely hearts who wait for their beloved soldiers to return. Children ran around with huge webs of pink cotton candy in their little hands, and we older folks kept our spirits up by singing along with the band.

Your brothers' families came to the park. They spent time with your papa. About halfway through the fireworks, Salvatore said he was tired, so I helped him walk back to the house. It was only a couple of blocks, but it was the farthest he'd gone in a long time, and it seemed to take forever.

My greatest regret was having to spend the Fourth of July without you, my darling. Hopefully, we'll have next year and many more years after that.

Go with God, my love, and be safe.
Eternally yours,
Catherine

I looked at Brian. His eyes were filled with something akin to fascination. He coughed once, then he struggled to speak, like there was a lump in his throat.

"Your great-grandmother's letter has opened up a whole other era for me," he said, his voice taut. "Back then, life was simpler. An afternoon at the park was the highlight in a person's day. No rush hour traffic to contend with, no cell phones or internet to distract a person. Catherine had me wondering if perhaps I'd been born at the wrong time."

I nodded. "There's something fascinating about the early 1900s. Life must have been easier back then. Catherine didn't have to pay megabucks for a crowded seat at a concert or a stage play. On the Fourth of July, she walked to the park and enjoyed free entertainment. And the food? Back then it was hot dogs and cotton candy, which probably satisfied the appetite as much as any New York style grilled steak or seared fish."

Brian nodded and gently ran his finger over the delicate note-paper. "Reading this letter has worked magic in me. It's taken me away from the competitive, non-stop lifestyle I've been living." He turned and looked at me. "Don't get me wrong, Fran. I love the challenges connected to my job. But for a moment, I escaped, and to be honest, it was hard to come back to reality."

I understood. Reading my great-grandparents' letters was like visiting another time and place, one that I, too, had found it hard to leave. Though I'd kept telling myself this was a temporary journey into the past, I would cherish those images for the rest of my life. I slipped my hand in Brian's. We sat quietly and stared at the pile of letters. For the first time since we met, I felt as though I could build a life with this man.

oincidentally, Enzo's next letter, like Catherine's, was dated *July 5, 1917*, the day after Independence Day. It was as if those two hearts had connected in some mysterious way, like they could pick up each other's thoughts without having to speak them aloud.

Catherine, my love, he began, and my heart went out to him. He'd traveled away from home to live in a tent on foreign soil and had subjected his life to imminent danger. Despite his decision to physically serve his country, his heart still remained at home. As Brian and I read on, I became even more aware of the difficulty Enzo faced in making such a decision.

How I wish I could have been with you on the anniversary of the birth of our nation. I'm sure the people of Cittadina put on a great celebration. Me and my buddies, we took a walk into the nearest town to enjoy the nice weather and the fresh air away from the stale odors of camp. The tents, damp from recent rains, smelled moldy. The cook fires left a residue of ash in the air. And the odors from our makeshift latrines were beginning to gag us.

It was good to walk through a normal countryside where the whitewashed houses glowed in the sunlight and flower beds burst with many colors and pleasant aromas. They reminded me of my own home and garden far away.

Nearby is a little country village with few men, except for the old ones and the little boys. Like in America, most of the men have gone off to war.

Though the Fourth of July is our own special holiday, these women and children came out of their homes with their arms loaded with fresh baked breads and fruit that grows everywhere around here. They can't speak a word of English, and only a couple of us could speak a little French, but we didn't need verbal communication to know how much they appreciate our being there.

Apart from those welcoming moments, the women keep their distance from us soldiers, which is probably for the best. I don't have a problem staying faithful to my one true love, but some of the guys have made unsavory comments. I caution my tent mates and pray for God's intervention. It won't be good for the cause if our soldiers cross the line of decency.

Though it's nice to venture out in public once in a while, we pretty much stay in camp most of the time. We share books some of the guys brought with them, sit around smoking cigarettes and telling jokes, and several of us gather after supper for a time of prayer.

An amazing thing happened just before sunset, yesterday. A French Army band came marching along those winding back roads past our camp. You can't imagine how wonderful it was to hear those bugles playing the "Star-Spangled Banner." Though slightly off-key, it was the most heart-warming rendition I've ever heard. They followed up by playing several bars of their own "La Marseillaise."

What a great time we had, shaking hands, hugging, and patting one another on the back. The French also have this custom where they kiss you on both cheeks. I wasn't the least bit offended when one soldier after another planted kisses on my face.

At night, we had our own "fireworks," put on by enemy forces that had come too close for comfort. Though we were not in the midst of the fighting, I was amazed at how near we had gotten to the front. We could hear the crack of gunfire off in the distance. Sparks and flares rose up fifty miles away, and once we could see a fire glowing on the horizon. The muted rumble kept us awake throughout the night. I lay there with my rifle by my side. None of us spoke or slept until the gunfire ceased and everything went dark.

I wish it didn't take weeks for your letters to arrive. Sometimes

I get three in one day, then I go for days without a word. I suppose it's the same on your end.

My dear Catherine, I'm missing you more than ever.

I will see you soon.

All my love,

Enzo

The next few letters were short enough for us to read quickly. While I handled the fragile stationery, Brian leaned over my shoulder. We'd become engrossed in my great-grandparents' romance while gradually fueling one of our own.

Most of the letters said pretty much the same thing. Then, we came upon one special letter from Catherine, dated *July 10, 1917.*

Dearest Enzo,

Not much has changed around here except for one thing. I may be expecting a baby. I made an appointment with the doctor for next week. Think about it, Enzo, when you come home you will have a child waiting for you. I couldn't be happier.

In the meantime, I'm going to keep working at the post office and volunteering with the Red Cross. I've also started planting seeds for a fall crop of vegetables in our own backyard, plus flowers that will bloom at different times of the year, so we'll always have color in our yard. Salvatore promised to help me with the vegetable garden, and I intend to do some canning, so we'll have plenty for the winter months.

I put in a row of forsythia along the rock wall at the edge of our property. It's already bursting with a glorious spray of yellow. It looks like a bright golden waterfall tumbling down the wall. I also planted several chrysanthemums around the base of the front porch. They'll add a touch of softness to the old house, don't you think?

The town officials began erecting street signs last week. Every cross street is named after a different tree. We now live on Maple Street and our address is 122. In honor of our street name, I have planted three maple seedlings, one in the front yard and two out back. By the time you come home, they will have grown taller than you.

I can get home delivery of the mail if I want it, but since I work at the post office I will hang onto the box for now. Well, my darling, I can't wait for you to come home and enjoy our outdoor garden. For now, keep these images in your mind and dream about the day when you'll return to me.

Longing for your strong arms around me.

Love,

Catherine

Enzo's letter was dated a month after Catherine's.

My dear love,

I can't tell you how happy I am at your news. Please, keep me informed and let me know how you're doing. Don't do too much, my darling, and listen to your doctor. I want you healthy and strong for the birth of our little one. Tell me, have you thought of any names yet? I like Alberto if it's a boy and Monica if it's a girl.

Meanwhile, things haven't changed much here. They've been keeping us busy with duties and drills. The enemy draws closer, so we have to be on the alert for an attack. I'm watching and keeping my rifle by my side.

I love what you and Papa are doing with the gardens. I can't wait to taste those homegrown vegetables and walk among your flower beds.

For now, I try whenever possible to get into town where the country roads and cow paths wind past the gardens planted by the peasants who live there.

You mentioned the rose bushes. They have them here too, bright red, the same color as the poppies that grow wild in the fields. The women also seem to like peonies and daisies. They're everywhere. A tremendous amount of greenery covers the countryside. Ferns and moss and grass go on for miles and miles. I hope the war doesn't burn away the beauty of this place.

We received a Red Cross package today. Plenty of toothpaste and soap and other important things we keep running out of. Maybe it didn't come from Cittadina, but I like to imagine it did. Perhaps your loving fingers touched this bar of soap. I can only dream.

Anyway, I have to go now. I pulled guard duty tonight.

Love,

Enzo

Those colorful images the two of them painted in their letters swirled around in my head. Enzo and Catherine had a deep respect for God's creation, actually favored the natural world over man-made products that rust and fade away. I appreciated the fact that they worked hard to create a beautiful setting for the house I had inherited. Their landscaping had turned a basic house into a fairy tale cottage.

When I arrived a couple of weeks ago, I noticed that the vegetable garden had died off, and most of the plants had gone to seed. Only dried up vines and weeds remained. And the flowers? Here it was the middle of summer, and the place should have been bursting with color. Except for three thriving maple trees, and the lawn, the property looked like it had died with Gram.

I turned to Brian. "I have a plan. We can revive the landscaping around the house. Maybe it won't measure up to the beautiful gardens Catherine and Enzo created, but we can add our own touch of color, maybe plant some flowers and bushes, restore the old trellis and salvage whatever still has life in it."

"I'm in," Brian said, beaming. "Nothing like putting the old green thumb to work. I don't get to do that much in the concrete jungle I call home."

"It'll make the house more sellable," I noted. "Realtors tell you first impressions make a huge impact. They call it *curb appeal*. It can make the difference between whether someone walks inside or just drives by."

Brian nodded with enthusiasm. "That settles it. Tomorrow after church we'll go out and buy some plants, and we'll spend the rest of the day beautifying your Gram's property. Maybe it won't match what Catherine and Enzo did, but it will look a whole lot better than it does now."

I was getting ready for bed when my cell phone rang. I rushed to it, hoping Jeff was ready to make good on the shower. It was Fred.

"I told my pop about your problem," he said. "We'll be out first thing in the morning to fix the drain. Probably a simple mistake. Anybody could mess up."

He'd made a lame excuse for Jeff, but it didn't matter. At least *someone* was coming out to fix the leak.

I lay in bed that night with Brian a wall away, yet I felt closer to him than I ever had before. We now shared a desire to bring Gram's garden back to life. Such intimacy goes far beyond the touch of a hand or a kiss on the lips. In a way, we were like Catherine and Enzo, an ocean apart but their love continued to blossom with the gardens they'd planted.

The thing was, in two brief days, Brian and I had become so intertwined with my great-grandparents' lives, I no longer knew where their story ended and ours began.

Sunday morning, the paperboy dropped off the Cittadina Gazette, like he'd been doing every day since I arrived. I assumed Dad had ordered it for me, one more ploy to get me to want to stay. I picked it up off the front porch and brought it inside to show Brian.

He was sitting at the kitchen table with a plate of scrambled eggs and toast in front of him, a cup of coffee in his hand.

"Look at this," I said, laughing. I opened it to the front page. "The worst crime in Cittadina. A shoplifter arrested at the five-and-dime." I flipped to the B section. "These pages are filled with fluff—a fashion show, renovations of the local park, school kids raising funds for their mission trip to Belize—nothing but small town news."

With an air of disgust, I tossed the paper onto a nearby chair.

"Can you imagine? My dad wants me to write for this rag. In the city, we have *real* news, the kind that sets your teeth on edge. In New York we tackle more important issues. We track down famous people. We uncover political scandals. Our pieces often hit the national wire. Tell me, Brian, who in San Diego or Chicago would want to read about a petty theft in Cittadina?"

Chuckling, he reached out and stroked my arm. "Come on, Fran. Whoever said you *had* to write for the—"he glanced at the crumpled paper on the chair—"Cittadina Gazette?" His eyes sparkled with mirth. "Nobody's twisting your arm. Not even your father. He merely made a suggestion."

My response was interrupted by a knock on the door. It was Fred and a man who looked exactly like the boy, only older. Instead of blond hair, his was gray, and he had a few extra lines on his face, but he definitely was an older version of Fred. They were carrying my countertop. Fred Jr. got to work removing the kitchen sink so he could install the butcher block I'd requested.

"Thanks for coming out on a Sunday morning," I greeted them. Then I led Fred Sr. past Brian on the way upstairs to the bathroom.

Fred's father gave a sideways glance at my boyfriend then grunted as if to say, "What? Can't *you* fix a leak?"

I left him upstairs in the bathroom and went back to the kitchen, poured myself a cup of coffee, then dropped into the chair across from Brian. Between sips of the steamy liquid, I huffed and puffed out my frustration. Brian went back to his eggs.

I grabbed a piece of toast and spread marmalade on it, took a bite, and began to relax. Brian was right. I was making a big deal out of nothing. Nobody was twisting my arm. So why the internal conflict? Had I been defending something that didn't need defending? I was a big girl. I could do whatever I wanted, go wherever I wanted, work wherever I wanted. I tasted victory along with another bite of toast.

Fifteen minutes later, Fred's father returned to the kitchen, wiping his hands on an old rag.

"Job's done," he said. "Your installer failed to glue the drain pipes in place. Easy fix. I used a fast-drying glue. You should be able to use the shower tonight."

"Right," I said, then added, "How much do I owe you?"

Five more twenties left my purse, and I let the two of them out the door. Though a hundred dollars poorer, I breathed easier for the moment, knowing I wouldn't have to let Jeff back in my house.

The rooster clock said 9 AM. Time to start getting ready if we wanted to make it to church before the service began. My stomach did a flip-flop. Brian was about to meet my folks for the first time.

CHAPTER FOURTEEN

Though my parents already knew I had been dating some-one named Brian for more than a year, they were about to get a first-hand look at the guy. True to his heritage, my dad had been hoping for an Italian son-in-law. Mom was a little less demanding. She'd be happy as long as Mr. Wonderful agreed to live in Cittadina. I hated to break her bubble, but that wasn't going to happen.

When the time came for us to leave the house, Brian was decked out in a pair of tan linen pants and a navy blue golf shirt. I came down the stairs in a red and white print dress that got him whistling when I entered the kitchen.

This time, Brian drove and I navigated from the passenger seat.

When we arrived at the church, my parents were already standing out front. I made the introductions. Mom embarrassed me by gushing all over Brian, saying how wonderful it was they'd finally met, and what a nice looking young man he was. Then Dad left me mortified by asking if he might be Italian.

"Dad," I griped. "His last name's Kelly. It's Irish."

I caught Brian screwing up his mouth to keep from laughing. I grabbed his arm and led him up the stairs. I suffered through another few moments of discomfort as I introduced my boy-friend to Brother Pat. The kind priest graciously welcomed my friend to the service and asked no awkward questions.

I settled into the coolness of the sanctuary, grateful to have gotten through the tough part. I held Brian's hand through most of the service, and when it was over, he gave a hearty nod of approval.

At my parents' request, we met for lunch at Marco's Seafood House. Over plates of seared fish and bowls of broccoli with rice, Brian gave his thoughts about the mass.

"I liked your priest," he said directly to Mom. "I'd been expecting an old, no-nonsense, pulpit-pounder breathing coals of fire at us, but Brother Pat was nothing like that. The service was quite refreshing, and he gave an excellent sermon. I have to say, he's more like the non-denominational preachers I've been listening to. He speaks *to* the people, not *at* them. And his message of salvation was right on. By grace are we saved, not by works."

Mom was beaming. "I agree."

"But works *do* have a place," Dad cut in. "Like Pat said, works should be a result of our faith, not the other way around."

Brian nodded. "You're so right," he said, drawing a huge grin to my dad's face.

Lunch went better than I'd expected. Brian interacted with my parents like he'd known them all his life. He had a gift for setting people at ease. No wonder he'd been a success as a lawyer in such a short time. He definitely had chosen the right profession. He seemed interested in people, listened more than he talked, and was able to take control of the conversation when he needed to. He had Dad laughing and Mom swooning. I couldn't have asked for anything better.

Brian also picked up the check, claiming he wanted to thank us for the wonderful vacation he was having. But I knew better. The man wasn't on vacation. He had committed to helping me with a backbreaking chore that might put him in bed with a bottle of ibuprofen when we finished. If washing windows hadn't debilitated him, digging ditches, planting shrubs, and cleaning up the backyard might do the job. I pictured him fleeing back to his comfortable apartment in New York and to a job that didn't require more of him than lifting a pencil.

After a lingering farewell to my parents, we left the restaurant and headed for home where we changed into gardening clothes. We took both cars to Noni's Plant Nursery on the highway, five miles outside of town. After making our purchases, we loaded Brian's car with potting soil and mulch, plus three flats of flowering petunias, begonias, and impatiens, and we used my hatchback and back seat for azalea bushes, rhododendrons, and a healthy wisteria vine to replace the dying one still clinging to Gram's trellis.

Back at Gram's place, the two of us unloaded everything onto the driveway, which ended up looking like an outdoor plant nursery. Then we got to work cleaning up the backyard. We pulled up all the dead plants, taking care to leave anything that still had life in it, which meant the wisteria at the base of the trellis definitely had to go. My great-grandparents' rose bushes had survived the months of neglect and merely needed a little pruning.

While Brian demonstrated his prowess with a hammer and nails by repairing the trellis, I grabbed a hose and washed down the brick patio and the outdoor furniture. With spades and claws in hand, we prepared the front and back yards for their beautification. Working together, we arranged the plants according to their need for sunlight or the lack of it. Out front, Catherine's original forsythia along the rock wall had been replaced by each succeeding generation, but the current version definitely needed some TLC. We pulled away the dry pieces and pruned it back. Within months I expected it would return to its previous splendor. And the circular plot for the flagpole came back to life as we filled the space with pink and white begonias. We added potting soil where needed and covered everything with cedar mulch.

As I worked beside Brian, with both of us digging our fingers into the soil and bending our backs to plant the shrubs, I couldn't help but think of Catherine and Enzo doing the same thing a hundred years ago. Though my great-grandparents had planted the gardens, Gram and Poppa had kept them up. Now it was my turn.

I looked at Brian, sweat pouring from his brow, a determined grin on his lips, and I marveled at how well he'd made the transition from law office to backyard garden. But hadn't Enzo done the same thing? My great-granddad worked in a bank, yet he'd gladly discarded his teller's suit and tie and had donned overalls to help Catherine plant flowers. He'd gotten down on his hands and knees, like Brian was doing right now. Together, we were restoring the original beauty of the place. I marveled that the house on Maple Street had become more than a piece of property to me. It was a wonderful part of my ancestry.

It was then I discovered that Brian and I had moved past the level of dating we'd maintained over the last year. Our relationship had drawn close to what I'd imagined my great-grandparents had enjoyed. I was beginning to trust him with my heart. Near or far. Like Catherine and Enzo. It didn't matter if Brian was in New York and I was in Cittadina. I knew now that the miles wouldn't interfere with the feelings we had for each other. For the first time in my dating life, I could picture a long and happy future with someone, and I was no longer afraid.

When the flower gardens were finished to our satisfaction, I suggested we return to the nursery and buy a few plants for the withered vegetable garden.

"Who's gonna eat the vegetables?" Brian said, a skeptical look on his face. "You won't be here."

I shrugged. "Whoever buys the house."

He acquiesced, and within the hour we'd come home with two mature tomato plants and enough flowering squash and zucchini clusters to fill a couple of three-foot rows. Brian did the hoeing, and I did the planting. We rearranged the chicken wire to make the enclosure smaller than the one my great-grandparents had created. Then we stood back and admired our creativity.

We had finished our labor of love mere minutes before the sun dipped below the horizon, and a subtle gray aura settled on the property. Brian chose that moment to kiss me, and despite the dirt and sweat on both of us, I didn't resist.

He gallantly insisted I go up and use the shower first, while he cleaned up the debris and put it all in a trash can. I didn't argue.

A hot shower sounded too inviting. After I finished getting dressed, Brian took over the bathroom, and I went downstairs to prepare supper.

I didn't want to make peanut butter and jelly sandwiches. Not tonight. A memory came to mind of Gram putting together a meal from whatever she found in the pantry. So I rooted around and found a box of fettuccine. I ended up copying her recipe for Alfredo sauce using a little flour, milk, and butter, plus nutmeg as a seasoning. Then I put together a romaine salad and added croutons, olive oil, and lemon juice. In the end, I roasted some peppers and garlic that I found sleeping in the fridge. Within minutes, the kitchen erupted with aromas that took me back twenty years.

Brian entered smacking his lips and rubbing his hands together. "Mmmm-mm," he declared. "What is that wonderful smell?" He peered over my shoulder at the pot of fettuccine, now coated with sauce. I sprinkled parsley over the top and handed him the bowl, which he eagerly carried to the dining room. While I added breadsticks and salad to our setting, Brian opened a bottle of wine.

We dined by candlelight, with Brian still uttering lip-smacking compliments and me reveling in his accolades.

"I don't know what happened," I admitted. "I never cook like this. You know that. But a part of my grandmother must have rubbed off, I guess. All I know is, I felt quite at home in that kitchen."

Brian gave me one of his appreciative smiles and kept eating. When we finished, he suggested we read more of the letters. I didn't need much persuading, for they'd been on my mind, too.

Like before, we snuggled together on the living room sofa with the letters on my lap.

As I peeled an envelope from the pile, I took a closer look at my hands. My finger tips were raw, my nails chipped, my skin rough, looking distressingly like the hands of a washer-woman.

Those couple of weeks of hard labor, plus the garden work

Brian and I had done, had taken their toll. I shook my head at my own shame, and admitted how pampered I'd been. For years, I'd worked at a job that required little more than writing in a notebook and typing on a computer keyboard. Then there were my weekly manicures, half-hour sessions in a steam room, and a bathroom full of creams and lotions to keep my skin soft and smooth. I eyed my hands with concern, fearing the hangnails and scales might damage the fragile notepaper I was about to open.

I hesitated and cast a worried look at Brian. He followed my gaze to my raw hands. He seemed to understand, because he smiled and nodded.

"Don't worry about your hands," he said, kindness filtering into his voice. "Catherine would be pleased at how hard you worked to restore her garden."

Comforted, I carefully slipped the notepaper from the envelope and began to read.

I miss you so much, Enzo, Catherine wrote. *The garden keeps me alive. I nurture our tender plants as though they were our children. I prune with care, weed out the bad stuff, and I feed and water them, never giving too much, but just enough.*

While I care for our garden, I find I also need to give more care to Salvatore. He's aged over the last couple of months, and he grows more frail with every passing day. He sits for longer hours on the front porch and just stares at the flowers and raises a hand to wave at neighbors passing by. I bring him his meals. He rarely finishes anything, not even his favorite pasta dishes. I fear we may lose him before you return.

She then wrote about the Red Cross projects and the increasing lack of materials for bandages and slings, and then the miraculous influx of linen, gauze, and tape, so the team of women could make more of the needed aids.

Enzo's letters were guarded. He couldn't say much about the war effort. He mentioned a secret rendezvous of troops, which didn't make sense, because by the time Catherine received his letter, the event had already taken place.

Brian and I chuckled over Enzo's letter at the end of November. He wrote about camping out in a frost-bitten foreign country that didn't celebrate our Thanksgiving Day. The French had their own annual celebrations. Bastille Day, for example. But Enzo seemed to find comfort in every little recognition the French villagers bestowed upon him and the other men in his unit. Though they didn't have a turkey, they had something else.

One of the farmers butchered a cow and brought packages of broiled beef to our camp, Enzo wrote. *It had been weeks since we had anything but canned, tasteless imitations. But this was our Thanksgiving Day. We devoured their gift like ravenous wolves. And we gave sincere thanks to God, though we hadn't expected such a treat in this cold and distant land. All I could do, my dear Catherine, was hope your own rations had not gotten so scarce you couldn't share a hardy Thanksgiving meal with my father.*

Another letter told of a change of their location, which sent a chill through me. I'd been hoping Enzo never got any closer to the fighting. But that was not realistic. He'd gone there with one purpose, to win a war and come home.

We pulled up camp the other day and relocated closer to the front. We ate an evening meal of hard tack and cured beef when a team of American soldiers came marching through. They held guard over three German aviators, their hands bound, their ankles tied with long ropes extended between them. The three prisoners of war were

young men, like us, except they were battered and bruised from the plane crash, while we didn't have a scratch on us.

Our clean and safe appearance wasn't our choice. We wanted to get in on the action. We'd come there to fight, but we hadn't shed one drop of blood, nor had we suffered anything more painful than a hangnail.

The prisoners marched on over the hill to a place where the Allies had set up a temporary holding place where they kept prisoners of war until they could figure out what to do with them. As they passed by, one of them looked me in the eye. I couldn't read his message, but it didn't appear to be friendly.

Brian and I continued to open envelopes, eager to read through the pile of correspondence. Then, one, written by Catherine, stood out from all the rest. It was postmarked *August 20, 1917.* Frowning, I looked closer at the date. Somehow this letter had gotten out of sequence.

Dear Enzo,
I lost the baby today. I'm fine, darling. I'm resting at home feeling sorry for myself. Don't worry about me. The doctor said I can have more babies. We'll have a child in God's timing.
Yours always,
Catherine.

I collapsed in Brian's arms. Sobs erupted from my throat. My dear boyfriend held me close and stroked my hair. I turned to look up at him and saw his eyes were moist. The two of us had connected so deeply with Catherine and Enzo, we also felt their pain.

And their love.

CHAPTER FIFTEEN

Monday morning arrived too soon. When I came downstairs, I found Brian pacing between the living room and the kitchen.

"I don't want to leave, Fran. It seems I just got here, and already I have to get back to the city."

I wrapped my arms around his waist and rested my head on his chest. The pulsing of his heart warmed me.

"And I don't want you to go," I murmured.

We stayed that way for several minutes until Gram's rooster clock sounded the hour—8 AM. Brian backed away. I gazed into his face, a picture of sadness.

"If I start out now, I can get a few hours of work in," he said with remorse in his voice.

I nodded. "What about breakfast?" I offered.

"I'll pick up something on the road," Brian replied.

His suitcase sat waiting at his feet. With noticeable reluctance, he picked it up and started for the front door. We shared one last kiss, then, with tears streaming down my cheeks, I stared after the silver blue Toyota until it disappeared from view.

I let out a long, dejected sigh. Thankfully, I wouldn't be alone for long. Penny had promised to take the day off from work and help paint the upstairs rooms.

I fixed myself a bowl of cereal and had just finished washing the dishes when I heard a gentle knock on the side door. It had to be Penny. I hurried over, but I wasn't prepared for what I saw when I opened the door. Jeff Petrino stood like a big hulk behind my friend, his face beaming with a familiar arrogance in his eyes. I greeted him with a scowl.

"My shower leaked into the kitchen. I'm going to have to repaint the ceiling."

"So, I'll fix it," he said, his eyebrows raised in an arrogant slant.

"No. I had to pay someone else to fix it."

He shrugged. "No problem. I'll paint your ceiling, then."

Penny didn't seem to notice the scowl on my face. She barged into the house, laughing and chattering about getting to work and how three can get a lot more done than two.

I was about to tell Jeff to hit the road, when I thought about the high ceilings and my aching neck from having tackled the kitchen ceiling only last week. I offered the two of them coffee and breakfast but they declined, saying they'd stopped at a fast food restaurant on the highway before coming over.

With an air of submission, I trudged up the stairs to the second floor. Whether I liked it or not, I was stuck with Jeff helping out. I pointed out the painting supplies I had deposited in the hallway. Penny and I donned painters' hats and got to work applying tape to the appropriate areas. Jeff grabbed a roller and pan and went downstairs, presumably to touch up the kitchen ceiling.

Afterward, he joined us upstairs and got started painting the ceiling in the hallway. I began to give him the benefit of the doubt. Like young Fred had said, anybody could make a mistake.

I wanted to turn my back on Jeff and leave him to work on the ceilings while Penny and I tackled the walls in the bedrooms. But Penny was giggling and pointing at Jeff.

It was a comical sight to be sure. The two of us fell into hysterics as we watched the 6-foot, 2-inch hulk pacing back and forth, his right arm extended overhead pulling the roller behind him. I had to admit, he was doing a good job, and he'd taken the most difficult part of the project away from me.

Chuckling and shaking my head, I guided Penny into the room where I'd been sleeping.

"Let's start in here," I told her. "That way the smell of paint will have dissipated by the time I go to bed tonight."

The two of us moved the furniture to the center of the room. Some of the pieces slid easily across the wood floor, while heavier items had to be walked over, like children guiding an oversized baby doll, step by waddling step.

We covered everything with drop cloths and started pulling down the aging flowered wallpaper, which came off as easily as it did in Gram's dining room. Within the hour we were ready to paint.

Since Penny was two inches taller, she took charge of the upper half of the walls, while I started halfway down and also took care of the baseboards.

The entire time we worked, Penny bored me with stories about the fun times she'd been having with Jeff.

"We went to a carnival in Rochester last month," she giggled. "Jeff won a large panda bear for me at the shooting gallery—did you know he had joined a gun club?" I was still scowling when she let out a pathetic sigh. "The Ferris Wheel was so romantic," she went on, her voice soft. "I made him take me up three more times. We finished the evening dancing at a local nightclub. The band played our song, "Can't Help Falling in Love with You." Do you believe it, Fran? After all these years, that song still speaks to couples in love."

I stood in shock. Had she forgotten Jeff and I had dated for a year, that we'd done a lot of those same things before he broke my heart? Like a tidal wave, sweet memories came flooding back. The afternoon we rode the Ferris Wheel, Jeff with his strong arm around my shoulders, my head resting on his chest next to his heartbeat. The Teddy bear he'd won knocking over wooden milk bottles. There also was the dancing. Our song was "Unchained Melody," another classic that never seemed to die. Though I never wanted to hear that song again, it was still hitting the airwaves.

As Penny went on and on about the amazing Jeff Petrino, I

wondered how many other young girls had fallen prey to his charm? How many had been kicked aside when someone better—or faster—came along. I looked at my friend with concern. She was humming away, oblivious to the harm she had inflicted on me, unaware that the same thing could happen to her. I wanted to say something, to warn her, but I didn't know how to begin.

I took a deep breath and summoned the courage. "Penny, have you forgotten that Jeff and I once dated?"

She stopped humming and her hand froze with the roller firmly planted against the wall.

"Oh, my goodness, Frannie. I'm so sorry." She lowered her arm and gazed at me, her face a picture of despair. "I assumed you'd gotten over him a long time ago. Don't tell me you care."

I swallowed my pride and gazed at her with compassion. "It's okay, Penny. You can date anyone you want, even Jeff. I just don't want to hear about it."

Regret filled her eyes, changing the purple hues to a soft blue. "Forgive me?" she said, raising her eyebrows.

"Of course." A sympathetic smile tugged at my lips. "And I'm sorry for my reaction."

"No, no, Frannie," she said, shaking her head. "You had every right. I was so insensitive."

I stepped back and shrugged. "Let's forget about it, okay?"

She nodded as if she agreed, but the shifting colors in her eyes told a different story. They spoke of a sudden meeting with reality, a rising fear of heartache, and a need for truth.

I sought for the right words. My best friend from high school had gotten into a relationship with a man I was certain could not be trusted. I wanted to protect her.

"You remember what Jeff did to me, don't you, Penny? I mean, you caught him with Denise, right?"

She tilted her head to one side and frowned. "He's different now," she mumbled, but her response was weak.

"I don't know." I shook my head, wanting to believe he had changed but suspecting he had not. "All I can say is, be careful."

She shrugged and let out a nervous giggle. "Don't worry. I'll be all right." Then she turned back toward the wall and resumed painting.

I had nothing more to say, so I pressed my lips together and went back to the task at hand. Still, thoughts of Penny and Jeff together, the way we used to be, kept me concerned—not because I was dwelling on the past, but because I didn't want my friend to suffer as I had.

I could still remember the deep, sharp pain of a heart being torn apart, the initial nausea, my entire body cramping up in the fetal position, like I wanted to return to the womb or die. The next morning, I walked on trembling legs into class. A cold wave engulfed my face and brought me to the floor in a dead faint. Then I awoke to the pungent odor of smelling salts. For hours after, the smell of ammonia swirled around in my head. I lost my appetite, couldn't even hold down my favorite foods. For days after, I refused to eat a full meal. I lost weight, couldn't sleep, and cried almost nonstop.

Mom knew something was wrong. She asked but didn't press the issue, almost as if she was afraid to know. Or perhaps, she knew. I found comfort in one place. Gram's kitchen. As I sat at her table with a plate of almond cookies, I looked up at her sharp blue eyes and I bared my heart.

Despite Gram's age, she seemed to understand. "First love can bring a ton of emotions," she said. "It can fill your heart with joy, give you a purpose for living, and offer hope for the future. But first love also can bring pain. And shame of having been deceived. And it can leave you with a future that seems empty."

She drew close. I wept against her tiny frame, found comfort in her arms.

"Once you survive a painful experience like the loss of a love, you will come out stronger and wiser, my dear," Gram went on. "But, don't let that new strength destroy you. Don't let it take away your chance to find love again. Next time it could be the right one."

With those words Gram had left me with a tiny ray of hope. I looked for it in every relationship that came along after Jeff, but never found it until now. Brian had done more than win my heart. More importantly, he'd won my trust. I thanked God for bringing him into my life.

This was my comfort and strength as I continued painting the bedroom walls with Penny, while Jeff was only a few feet away in the hall. There was no doubt in my mind, I'd gotten over him long ago. Last night was another breakthrough for me. I finally admitted I was in love with Brian.

When Penny and I reached the halfway point, Jeff came in to do the ceiling. I didn't want to stay in the same room where he was working, so I nudged Penny.

"Let's go downstairs and figure out something for lunch," I said, as I wiped my brush clean.

We headed downstairs to the kitchen, washed our hands, and pulled all things edible from the fridge. By the time Jeff came down, the kitchen table was laid out with egg salad, sliced ham, cheese, potato chips, and several cans of soda pop.

Needless to say, I sat through the most uncomfortable lunch I've ever eaten. So uncomfortable, in fact, I had trouble swallowing, kept sipping my root beer, and ended up leaving half of my ham-and-cheese sandwich on the plate. Penny seemed to have drifted off to another land. Here was the most loquacious girl on our high school debate team, and she didn't say much except, "Pass the salt, please." She took small bites of her egg salad and stared starry-eyed at Jeff. I wished she would remember what he looked like with his arms around Denise. Perhaps the memory might raise some red flags before it was too late.

Jeff was beaming, like a bull moose overseeing his herd of cows. I couldn't help but wonder how much of our conversation he'd heard outside the door of that little bedroom.

One thing was certain, he hadn't lost his appetite. He ate all of his sandwich and the other half of mine. Little did he know how much I still resented him. Didn't he see the fire in my eyes? There was no telling what kind of ego trip he was on. He kept smiling, and every now and then he let out a chuckle, like something funny had struck him, though he never shared what it was.

I was glad when lunch was over, and we could get back to work. I sent Jeff out for two more cans of paint, and Penny and I finished my bedroom and moved on to the bath.

Our conversations from then on centered around our families. I filled her in on what was happening with my brother Tom, that he was comfortably settled in Boston with a high-paying job, a wife, and a new baby. Penny told me her parents had found a nice place in Florida and had invited her to come down for a visit with a friend. I knew with some degree of certainty that she would ask Jeff instead of me.

Then she spoke about her own ups and downs in the working world. "After I left California, I took classes in home decorating. I wanted to open my own business right here in Cittadina, but this definitely ain't the place to fulfill such a dream."

"Come to New York," I offered, more out of spontaneity than desire. "You'll find plenty of job opportunities, shops that need someone with your talent. You can share my apartment. I can show you around—"

She was already shaking her head. "I don't know. Maybe later," she said with a sigh. "For now, I'll stay in Cittadina."

I stopped painting and turned to face her. "Penny, listen. This is your friend speaking. I'm not a jealous rival who wants to take you down. I'm a person who really cares about you. What Jeff did to me he could do to you. There's a saying, a leopard doesn't change his spots."

"I've heard that before," she said, tossing her head. "That's an old wives' tale. People do change. Or at least they can. And, he *does* seem different. Haven't you noticed?"

I released a sigh. "Whatever. You have to make up your own mind. But please be careful, okay? Promise me?"

"I promise."

I sensed danger was lurking ahead of my poor, naive friend. Penny had always acted on impulse. Didn't the trip to California prove that? She'd met up with one disappointment after another. About the time we stopped writing she was still out there, reaching for the brass ring. Now, this thing with Jeff....

I loved Penny. We'd bonded as teenagers, almost like sisters. I didn't want any harm to come to her, didn't want her heart to break the way mine had.

As if on cue, Jeff returned with the two buckets of paint and picked up where he left off on the ceilings.

I continued to paint my part of the bathroom, but every now and then I glanced at my friend. The smile on her lips and her soft humming sent shivers of anxiety into my heart.

As we worked, Penny joked about how Jeff's muscular build often got him in trouble when we were kids. Like the time he sat on a playground swing and brought the entire set down. He was sixteen years old and built like a halfback. Then there was the day he walked down the aisle in the five-and-dime and knocked over one of the counters, strewing novelties across the floor.

"He's like a bull in a china shop," Penny said, laughing.

I couldn't help but laugh with her. Our tittering sent Jeff into a clown act. He picked up his step and began to prance back and forth, pulling the roller against the ceiling. The louder Penny and I laughed, the more Jeff kicked up his heels.

I'd forgotten what a card he could be when his friends goaded him into action. Not only had he been one of the best looking guys in school, he'd also been one of the funniest. No one could deny the personality and charisma of Jeff Petrino. No wonder so many girls had fallen for him, including myself, Denise Conn, and now Penny. There was something magnetic about the guy.

Too bad he doesn't use those qualities for good, I mused.

Jeff finished all the ceilings, and Penny and I completed the walls in another bedroom. That left one more bedroom, which I assured them I could finish myself the next day.

Nodding his agreement, Jeff ran out to buy two large pizzas, and Penny and I cleaned up our paint supplies. Then I crossed my arms and stepped back. Penny stood beside me, and together we admired our finished work.

"It would have taken me three days to do what we accomplished in one," I told her. "It looks great, Penny. Fresh and clean and ready for the finishing touches. Next comes the fun part—the decorating." I turned to face her. "Wanna help?"

"I'd love to, but I'll be working the rest of the week. How about Saturday?"

"I gave her an encouraging smile. "Of course, Saturday's perfect." If anybody could bring those bedrooms to life, it was Penny.

The rest of the evening went fairly well. Over a supper of pizza and salad, the three of us chatted about life in Cittadina. Penny and I drank sodas, and Jeff finished off a six-pack of beer.

"Why don't you let Penny drive?" I suggested.

They both laughed like I had said something ridiculous.

"I mean it, you two. You've had too much to drink, Jeff."

Penny leaped to his defense. "Relax, Frannie. Jeff's fine. I've seen him in worse condition. Anyway, it's just beer. It doesn't contain that much alcohol."

"Six of them do," I countered.

But my argument fell on deaf ears. Jeff climbed into the driver's seat of a black-and-green Jeep Wrangler, and Penny slid in beside him. So, the guy had a huge monster truck *and* what looked to be a brand new Jeep.

On his salary? Exactly how lucrative is a handyman job in a town like Cittadina?

I stood in the doorway and suppressed a growing anxiety that one of my dear friends was putting herself in grave danger, not only physically during the drive home, but also emotionally, having put her heart in the hands of a man who could crush it without a second thought. I didn't want her to suffer the kind of pain I'd endured at the hands of that self-centered, narcissistic playboy.

But I didn't know how to rescue her.

CHAPTER SIXTEEN

The next day, Jeff and Penny returned to their jobs, and I tackled the walls in the remaining bedroom. By late afternoon, all of the rooms gave off the aroma of fresh paint. I scratched a major item off my list then walked around the house noting what else I needed to do—very little beyond staging the place for sale.

The thought struck me, *I have almost finished the renovations. Soon, I'll return to New York City and to the life I left behind.*

I should have been excited about it, but a sense of loss entered my heart. During the time I'd been working on Gram's house, I'd grown attached to the walls I'd painted, the furniture I'd polished, the outdoor garden Brian and I had planted.

Over a supper of leftover pizza, I phoned Valerie. She apologized for not having called in several days. She and Glen had taken a trip to the Poconos, and after they returned she'd spent every waking hour catching up on her work.

"I'll do better," she promised. Then, after a pause. "Anyway, you're coming home soon, aren't you?"

I didn't answer, didn't know what to say.

"Hello? Are you there?" Val sounded impatient.

"Yes, I'm here," I managed. "To be honest, Val, a change has come over me."

"Change? What change?"

"Well, I've begun to imagine what it might be like to live in Gram's house—to keep cooking on the new stove, to sit on the back patio with a morning cup of coffee and admire the gardens, to stroll through town with nothing to do except talk to the locals. It's such a simple life—so different from the fast-paced lifestyle I've gotten used to in the city. But you know what? I like it."

"Whoa, girl." Val sounded like she was about to lecture me. Instead, her voice softened, and she said, "Are you serious, Fran? Do you really like small-town living?"

"I'm starting to," I admitted.

"Granted, it's a quaint little house and a charming town, but I think you should take a step back and think clearly. Once you consider what you'd be giving up, you might change your mind."

"Maybe." I knew I sounded weak. "I haven't made up my mind yet, just trying to imagine what it would be like to stay."

"Look." Val's tone was firm, kind of like a big sister might sound when talking to a teenage sibling. "Finish the job. Come back to New York and clear your head. Once you get back to work and settled in your own apartment again, you're gonna think more rationally. Then, you can decide."

"We'll see," was all I could say.

We hung up with the issue unresolved and more conflicting thoughts running around in my head.

That night, though exhausted, I went to bed with what was left of my great-grandparents' letters. I looked forward to reading them. It was like someone was telling me a bedtime story every night. Though they wrote pretty much the same thing over and over again—how they missed each other, and how much they loved each other, and how they longed for the day when they could be together again—I envied what they had.

As usual when I was reading those letters, Brian came to mind. I picked up my cell phone and punched in his number.

After our initial warm greetings, I brought him up to speed on what I'd accomplished on the house.

"How are the flowers and plants doing?" Brian said.

"Still alive," I assured him.

"Don't forget to water them every day."

"I will. I promise."

"The boss has set a date for my trip to California," he said with noticeable enthusiasm. "That negotiations class will help me move into litigation law."

"When do you go?"

"Sunday. The class starts Monday."

With Brian's job in New York looking even more secure, I grieved for a moment over what might happen to our relationship. *What if I stay in Cittadina?* I decided not to mention the conflict that had been running around in my head.

"I'm getting ready to read the rest of my great-grandparents' letters," I said instead. "Want me to read some of them to you now?"

He released a sigh. "I'm tired," he said, and I could hear it in his voice. "I might fall asleep while you're reading. Do you mind if I get some sleep, and you can share them with me at another time?"

"No problem." I felt a twinge of disappointment. I had enjoyed reading the letters with Brian at my side, snuggling together on the sofa and basking in the love of Catherine and Enzo. Their loyalty to one another had seeped out of the pages and into my own heart, and I'd found myself wanting what they had.

"Why don't we talk on Saturday, when you get a break from work?" I suggested. "If you're leaving Sunday evening, we may not get another chance to talk until you're done with the class. Two weeks, you say?"

"Yeah, two weeks, and it's supposed to be intensive. There will be homework."

"I understand," I said, though I didn't. Was I losing Brian? Had something happened during his visit to Cittadina to put doubts in his head?

After we said our goodbyes, uncertainties returned tenfold. Now that I had let down my defenses, I felt vulnerable again. A cold wave of doubt swept over me, and I shivered. My usual reaction was to back off before I got hurt. Dump him before he dumped me.

Then I caught myself. *I'm doing it again. The same old sabotage. Another relationship down the tubes, if I don't stop myself.*

With purposeful determination, I turned to the two people who'd been helping me escape that emotional see-saw. I turned to Catherine and Enzo.

Catherine had been writing twice a week, though most of the time she had little to say beyond what she'd been sharing in previous letters. She missed Enzo something awful. She prayed for him daily and was looking forward to the day when he'd come home.

Some of her envelopes also contained newspaper clippings about the Great War. Enzo's letters trailed so far behind those news reports, it must have been frustrating for Catherine. Much of the time, she knew what was happening over there before he had a chance to tell her. Worse, she didn't know if he was alive or dead. He could have been wounded in battle or maybe on his way home. Or he could have been lying in one of those miserable, unmarked graves in France.

Meanwhile, Enzo's last few letters were postmarked during the summer of 1918. By that time, his unit had relocated four times and had moved closer to the front. There was my great-grandfather, hunkered down in a watery trench, scanning the horizon for enemy troops. I was overwhelmed with pride and awe that one of my ancestors had come that close to getting himself killed for his country.

I opened the next letter, this one written by Enzo.

Darling Catherine,
Nothing much has been happening. I signed up for service more than a year ago, but I haven't yet had the chance to fight a real battle. So far, I haven't done anything of value. While we sit here safe and sound in our tents with the villagers showering us with gifts of food, our Allies have entered the midst of the conflict. Gunfire sounds all day in the distance. Fire erupts on the horizon. The wounded have

been coming through our camp in droves. The medics take them beyond our hill to makeshift hospitals and to airfields where they can get transportation home. And still, we wait.

I frowned in puzzlement. So Enzo was stuck peeling potatoes and taking nighttime guard duty, while what he really wanted was to be in the thick of the battle. I shook my head. *Men are strange creatures.*

I shuffled to Enzo's next letter, dated *October 1, 1918.*

Dearest Catherine,

I can't believe it. This morning, our captain told us to get ready to move out. We will follow the tanks and the heavy artillery as they inch closer to the front. My buddies and I, though we have some fears, we want to do our part in driving the enemy back. We need to protect our friends in the village. Even more important, we need to win this war and go home.

That was my great-grandfather! I wanted to cheer him on. How could I read his letters and not get excited about a war that was long past? At that moment I realized I needed to pay more attention to what was happening to our troops when they get deployed overseas. Some will never see their families again. Some come home missing limbs. Some in body bags. I needed to root for them just like I would for my great-grandfather. Every soldier deserved a cheering section.

I read on, my heart aching for the troops heading into battle.

We moved our camp inside the Meuse-Argonne region. The area extends a great distance, from Verdun, France, and on through Belgium to the English Channel. The rolling hills and thick forests form a kind of fortress for the Germans. But the Expeditionary Forces

should be able to penetrate those barriers. In time, they'll drive the enemy back. When that happens, my unit also will move forward.

I'm not afraid, Catherine. I only fear coming home without having taken part in this war. I am doing this for you and for our neighbors and for all Americans. I don't want to fail in that commitment.

But you need to know, the Germans are not our only problem. We've confronted another killer. A terrible influenza has swept into our camp, putting many of us out of commission for a while. Matt got it real bad. I had a mild case of it and had to stay in bed for a few days. Maybe the Germans will also suffer with this illness, which could be to our advantage if they are disabled by it.

Catherine's next couple of envelopes held newspaper clippings—this time, not about the war, but about the Spanish Flu. According to the articles, many of the deceased had to be buried there in France, both the soldiers who died from influenza and those who perished in battle. Catherine's notes contained pleas for Enzo to take care of himself.

I reached the bottom of the pile of letters. The final one was dated *November 11, 1918*. It was Enzo's last correspondence.

My beloved Catherine,
Word came in today that a general armistice has been announced. All advancements have stopped. The war has ended, my love. I am coming home.

By the time you receive this letter, you'll already know the war has ended. Who knows? I might be there before my letter arrives. No matter. I still want to talk about some things that happened. It's kind of therapeutic to write it all down.

After I'd been out in the trenches for a week, I took a bullet in my right leg. The medics carried me back to camp where a doctor removed the bullet and put me on bed rest. Of course, I wanted to get back out there with my buddies, but I couldn't even stand up.

My friend Jack did not fare as well. He was killed during a battle in the Argonne Forest. I'm not sure if I would have survived if I'd been by his side instead of on a medical cot nursing an injured leg. Our troops were overwhelmed, but they remained constant, moving ahead with tanks and mustard gas and phosgene shells. Thank God, the Allies pushed the enemy back. Now that it's over, we can all breathe easier again.

For me, it means I'll soon hold you in my arms. I'll return to my job at the bank, and we can resume caring for our beautiful garden. Together. And, we can try to have another baby. Would you like that, Catherine?

See you soon, my darling.

Love,

Enzo

That was the end of the letters. I gathered them together and replaced the red ribbon the way I had found it. I carried them to the hutch in the dining room and lay them to rest beside Salvatore's daybook.

I went back to the trunk in the attic. The little jewelry box still lay on the top of the pile along with a light tan booklet labeled *Soldier's Small Book,* which Enzo had mentioned in one of his letters.

I flipped through the pages. Most of them held particulars about his date of enlistment and his rank, instructions about caring for a soldier's equipment, and information to help the authorities connect with the next of kin. But Enzo, like his father had done in his daybook, also had added more personal feelings, similar to what he'd shared in his letters to Catherine. There was nothing new. Still, I clutched the book to my heart, knowing it had accompanied my great-grandfather into battle and then had come home with him. Perhaps, like he'd hoped, he and Catherine had read it together.

The jewelry box was the size often used to gift wrap a watch or some other piece of jewelry. I opened it with anticipation.

My heart nearly stopped. Inside was a red-white-and-blue ribbon with a 1 ½-inch gold star, engraved with a circular wreath and in the center a tiny, silver, five-pointed star.

"The Silver Star," I whispered. "My great-granddad was awarded the Silver Star."

I held the medal in both hands. Tears flooded into my eyes. Through a blur I caught sight of a folded slip of paper at the bottom of the box. I carefully lifted the brittle, discolored sheet which had been lying there for a hundred years. As I spread it open, a crisp crackle rose from the age-old paper.

Inscribed at the top of the certificate was the name
Corporal Enzo Capellini, United States Army
followed by the accolade,

*FOR CONSPICUOUS GALLANTRY
IN COMBAT ACTION
AGAINST ARMED HOSTILE ENEMY FORCES
ON 20 OCTOBER 1918
WHILE SERVING IN MEUSE-ARGONNE, FRANCE,
IN DIRECT SUPPORT OF
THE AMERICAN EXPEDITIONARY CAMPAIGN.*

"What a treasure," I murmured. "My great-grandfather was a war hero."

The small book and jewelry box with the medal inside also found a place in Gram's hutch. The collection was not finished. More treasures remained in the trunk. I had only to follow my grandmother's instructions and work my way through them.

That night, as I lay in bed in the silence of night in the country, I thought about the house and all the people who'd slept there before me. Salvatore and Rosanna, Catherine and Enzo, Gram and Poppa, my father and his brothers. Now it was my turn to inhabit the house, my turn to add some history to it.

I'd come to Gram's house often when I was a little girl, but back then it was only a house. Sure, I wanted to visit Gram. But

I never knew anything about my other ancestors. Why hadn't my father said anything? Why hadn't Gram allowed me to look in her trunk until now?

The truth was, I had been enjoying this little game of hers. It was like going on a treasure hunt, opening one surprise after another. As it turned out, those surprises had brought me closer to my ancestors and maybe a little closer to myself.

CHAPTER SEVENTEEN

Over the next two days I mowed the grass, watered the lawn and flowers, polished the furniture, and cleaned both bathrooms. I went about the house sweeping floors, polishing light fixtures, and changing bulbs where needed. Last of all, I laundered the throw rugs, quilts, and pillow shams.

On Friday morning, I took time for a long, luxurious bubble bath, complete with a cup of herbal tea and Agatha's novel, which I finished while lolling in the tub. When I emerged, luxuriously pampered, I dressed in shorts and a T-shirt and started out on a stroll through town.

I wanted to walk everywhere, like I did when I was a kid. I headed first to my old school yard. The building was gone, but the town officials had maintained the playground. It teemed with kids, running, sliding, swinging, hanging from the jungle gym. A little girl with blonde pigtails ran squealing away from another girl with long, brown hair. For an instant, I pictured Penny and myself playing a game of tag. My heart ached all over again for my dear friend.

I moved on to the old movie theater. It had been turned into a community playhouse. The marquee out front said, *Closed until Oct. 1. Don't forget the Harvest Festival this weekend.* I'd been in Cittadina for almost a month. During that time, the season had transitioned from summer to fall.

Like harvest festivals did in every small community, they kicked off other fall events—neighborhood yard sales, Thanksgiving Day parades, and Christmas pageants, every one of them drawing people to the center of town for a day of relaxation.

A twinge of nostalgia seized my heart. I had forgotten what those gatherings meant to me when I was growing up. All those years while I was away, I told myself I didn't miss them. But the truth was, I *had* missed them.

I proceeded down a couple more streets, turned a corner, and came face-to-face with St. Agnes Church. The cross at the top of its steeple glistened in the morning sunlight. I climbed the stairs and tried the door latch. To my astonishment, it opened easily. *Don't they lock church doors in this town?* They did in the city. Too much vandalism there. Too much looting.

I stepped inside and was greeted by a cool semi-darkness. An aura of light penetrated the stained glass windows, bathing the sanctuary in a diffused pattern of colors. No one was there, not even Brother Pat. I tiptoed forward and sat in a front pew facing the large cross that hung from the ceiling beyond the altar.

It had been a long time since I spoke to my Savior. Gram had led me to Christ when I was ten years old, but I'd somehow lost touch with Him since leaving home. Now, with my life in an unexpected upheaval, I wanted to reconnect, though I wasn't sure how. I sat in silence for a good ten minutes. Then overcome, I wept freely over my indecision whether to sell the house or move in. Did an answer come? Not immediately. But I knew from past experience that God sometimes answers prayers at unexpected times.

As I exited the church, bright sunlight stung my eyes. I donned my sunglasses and continued my tour of the town, passed the old library, the lone fire station, and the Cittadina Police Department, followed by a row of shops, some of them fairly new, many of them looking like they did twenty years ago and maybe long before that.

I sauntered inside Mama Mia's Coffee Shop, got a latte to go and continued my stroll. A couple of turns brought me into the residential section of the tree-lined streets where the towering plants matched their individual street signs. The trees on Elm Street had grown into large umbrellas that cast patches of shade on the sidewalk. Tiny spiked balls covered the ground on Sycamore Lane. And Lilac Court still had a few pink, purple, and white blossoms, though most of them were dropping from the branches and littering the lawns in a rainbow of color.

As I wove up and down the various trees, I noticed with concern that many of the homes I'd visited as a child had been torn down, and in their place stood prefabricated shells, not much bigger than what had occupied the lot before, but newer and cheaper looking. The older houses at least had character. The individual owners had included a little of their own personalities in the architecture. I recalled one of the former houses looked like an Alpine chalet. Another had displayed an Amish hex sign between the clerestory windows. Still another had window boxes its owner had filled with pansies and petunias. Those homes were gone now and so was their individuality.

Several houses on Walnut Place had been marked for demolition. Out front were signs that read, *Newman Bros. Properties*, and underneath in small print, a phone number and the words, *A New And Better Way Of Living.*

Before heading back to Gram's, I went two blocks out of the way and turned the corner. This part of town was known as the Historic District. A variety of architectural designs had dominated those streets for as long as I could remember. English Tudor, Greek Revival, Colonial, and several Victorian homes, like the stately dwelling where I was born and raised.

When my folks married about 40 years ago, Dad bought the house from a couple who wanted to retire and move in with their son. There was no telling how long it had stood there before that. All I knew was, it was already old when I entered the world.

It was just the two of them back then, and they didn't know for sure how many kids they might have. But Mom wanted a large house with many bedrooms, two fireplaces, and a wrap-around porch. She'd been hoping for a half-dozen kids, but it turned out, they only had two—my brother, Tom, and me. Nevertheless, she hoped relatives from afar would come and stay. It was an ideal setting for family reunions.

I gazed with a touch of smugness up and down the street. There were no Newman Bros. signs here. No chance of replacing any of those massive homes with a shoebox. They were all on a historic registry and would never be torn down.

I walked around to the back of my folks' home and entered the kitchen to the aroma of apples and cinnamon. Three apple pies stood cooling on the sideboard, and from the aroma rising from the oven, a couple more were baking. Mom, swathed in one of her frilly aprons, was filling an empty pie shell with apples dripping with sugar and spices. I had a nightmarish image of the *Stepford Wives* for only a moment.

Mom smiled and wiped her hands on her apron, then she gave me a hug.

"What's all this?" I gestured toward the row of finished pies.

Mom shrugged. "The usual. Sunday is the Harvest Festival. The bake sale will raise money for the children's hospital in Syracuse. I'm doing what I do best—baking apple pies for the sale. You're coming, aren't you?"

My eyes darted again toward the array of pies on the counter. My mouth had already begun to water.

Mom caught my hungry look. She shook her head and laughed. "Oh, all right. Your dad's been bugging me all morning for a piece. You'll find him in the living room. Get him in here."

I did as Mom asked, found Dad reading the *Cittadina Gazette*, and planted a kiss on his forehead, noting that there was more forehead to kiss these days.

I gestured toward the paper in his hand. "Any big news in the little town of Cittadina?" I'd kept my tone light. I didn't expect him to expound on the daily news. After all, what major catastrophes happened there?

But Dad was scowling. "Look at this." He shook the front page in front of me.

The headline read. *More houses topple as Newman Brothers Company gets another foothold.*

"What's going on?" I wanted to know. "I passed the demolition signs. Manny Carlino's house is gone. They're building a piece of plastic on the empty lot. And, it looks like they're getting ready to tear down the houses where some of my classmates used to live."

"It's a disaster," Dad grumbled.

I had a feeling he was about to drift into a lengthy denunciation about out-of-town contractors stepping in where they didn't belong. I stopped him before he began.

"Mom is cutting a slice of apple pie for you. But you need to hurry 'cause I'm planning to beat you to it."

I turned my back on him and bent over like I was at the starting line of a race. He rose from his easy chair with a groan, and the two of us sprinted to the kitchen. At the last second, Dad stepped back and let me pass through the doorway ahead of him. I squealed with delight, but when I turned around, I noticed he still had a strangle hold on the newspaper.

I tilted my head at him. "Dad?"

He took his eyes off the pie in my mother's hand and looked at me. I pointed to the crumpled newspaper in his hand.

He scrunched his lips. "I'll tell you all about it, Frannie, but it's best to let me have my pie first."

I nodded and took the plate Mom held out to me. Dad and I went to the kitchen nook. I slid onto the bench, and he moved in beside me. Mom pulled up a chair and joined us with a slice of her own.

"I figured, why not?" she said with a shrug. "I certainly can't take half a pie to the festival."

Dad waited until we'd eaten every last crumb, then he leaned back and unfurled the battered newspaper.

"A bunch of money hungry developers have come here and have bought up properties all over town. They want to raze the old homes and put up cheap imitations in their place." He shook his head and his eyes flickered with sadness. "They're tearing down Cittadina's history, Frannie."

I didn't know how to respond. My parents' ties to the village were a lot stronger than mine. I'd come there with one goal, to fix up Gram's house and leave. I didn't care if builders came in and changed things. I didn't have to be there to see it. But I cared about my parents, and the anxiety on Dad's face bothered me. He'd lived in this village all his life. Now someone had come in to change everything. Nicholas Capellini wasn't about to sit back and let it happen.

"What are you gonna do, Dad?"

"He's gonna complain to whoever will listen," Mom interjected. "After he gets it out of his system, he'll go fishing."

"Not this time," Dad persisted. "This is different, Roberta. I have to do something. I'll talk to Mayor Bosco, maybe the entire city council. They can put a stop to this building scheme. Those idiots from Texas have torn down perfectly sound homes and have replaced them with junk they'll sell at top dollar. This upheaval will lower the value of every property in Cittadina. They've already finagled several deals out of people who didn't know better. But it's not too late. This article says they've only just begun. There's still time to rally people. We need to get folks to say no when those money-grubbing brutes come knocking on their doors."

As usual when Dad discussed politics and injustices, his face turned bright red from his balding forehead all the way down to his collar bone. I reached out and stroked his arm. He raised his eyes from the article and caught my look of concern.

"I do get carried away, don't I?" he admitted with a sigh.

I leaned close and kissed his cheek. It was flaming hot.

"Dad, your heart," I reminded him. Two years before, he'd suffered a slight attack. The doctor put him on digitalis and insisted he keep the stress down.

He took a deep breath and settled back in the booth. The red on his face faded to pink and then was gone.

It was time I left. I didn't want Dad stressing again, didn't want to give him an audience for more ranting.

Mom stopped me at the door and handed me a Tupperware container that held a large wedge of the pie we'd assaulted. I accepted it with a smile and a hug.

It was time to go home. I'd read all the letters Enzo and Catherine had written, some of them twice and a couple of them three times over. With most of the work finished, I could contact a Realtor tomorrow and get the ball rolling. I still needed to sweep out the attic, but I could do that before the For Sale sign went up.

In the meantime, I had to finish emptying Gram's trunk, so I could move it out of the attic. Besides, I wanted to find out what other treasures awaited me at the bottom. After Penny and I completed the decorations inside, I could stay for the festival on Sunday and leave town on Monday. Like Val said, I only needed to get out of Cittadina and back in familiar territory to think clearly again.

After I left my parents' house, I rounded a couple of corners and approached Maple Street. I hadn't noticed before, but as I entered Gram's block, I caught sight of three parcels marked for demolition and new construction, with the Newman Brothers' signs out front. I approached Gram's house and stopped short of the property. In the driveway was a silver Dodge RAM, and on the side door was a decal with the Newman Brothers' logo.

My heart leaped to my throat. What could they possibly want with Gram's house? I'd already fixed it up nice enough to sell. It was far better than those shoeboxes Newman Brothers was building. Their idea of a single family home included a plastic, three-bedroom, two-bath, cubicle with a front stoop. Those Newman Brothers wanted to turn Cittadina into a sterile tract of housing clones. I frowned with distaste. Like Dad had warned, the town's old-fashioned atmosphere would fade away, and Cittadina would lose its historic charm.

I shook off the irritation. I wasn't going to stick around to see it happen, so why should I care? But another voice in my head said, *Ah, but you do care. You care because Gram cared.*

I ventured up the front walk and faced the man standing by the silver truck. He was tall—about six-foot, three—and slim. He wore jeans and a cowboy shirt, and his dark brown mustache matched the fringe of hair sticking out of his ten-gallon hat. So did his thick, bushy eyebrows. He was twirling a toothpick between his teeth, and he stared down at me with an air of superiority.

The back of my neck prickled with annoyance. Unflinching, I met his gaze.

"Are you looking for someone?" My tone came out strong, exactly as I had intended.

"Well, Miss, I'm looking for the owner of this house." He had a southern accent, maybe Texas, but I wasn't sure.

"I'm the owner." I didn't offer anymore information than that. I pinched my lips together and crossed my arms.

"I'm George Newman." He extended his right hand.

I stood firm, kept my arms crossed, and stared bullets at him.

He shrugged off the affront. Then he lowered his hand and faced me full-on.

"We're buying up properties in town, and we got word that you're getting ready to sell. I want to make a reasonable offer."

"I'm planning to work with a real estate agent. An agent can take care of all the paperwork and get me the best price."

"That's fine, but do you want to pay a commission? We can make a deal without involving a middleman. We work exactly like the agents do without claiming a percentage. We'll conduct a market analysis, find out how much houses sell for in your neighborhood, and make you a comparable offer. We take care of all the paperwork and the filing. You do nothing but put out your hand and accept the money."

I tilted my head and narrowed my eyes at him. "I've seen your signs all over town. Why are you doing this?"

"You mean you don't know?" His mocking tone sent icicles down my spine.

"Know what?"

He chuckled. "Walmart has negotiated a huge deal on several acres outside of Cittadina. They want to build a state-of-the-art store with multiple amenities and a warehouse that will serve all their stores within 50 miles. They'll be hiring a couple thousand employees. Their new hires will be looking for houses. They'll want modern homes, not rundown, old shacks.

More prickling hit the back of my neck.

"Newman brothers can provide the kind of houses that will sell to these people," he went on, hardly noticing the scowl on my face. "We've done this all over the United States. Our main office finds the locations and we head out and make the deals."

When I didn't respond, he shifted to his other foot, let out an exasperated puff of air, and pulled a card from his shirt pocket. He held it out to me.

"Think about my proposal. If you're interested or want to know more, give me a call. You don't want to miss out on a super deal. Not when all your neighbors are coming on board."

I accepted the card and turned my back on the guy. Before I reached the top step of the porch, his truck rumbled to a start and his wheels stirred up the gravel as he backed out of the driveway. I turned, expecting the silver truck to disappear down the street. Instead, it came to a stop beside another vehicle several houses away. Both drivers had put their windows down and were leaning toward each other in conversation. I gasped with astonishment. The other car was a black-and-green Jeep Wrangler, and sitting in the driver's seat was Jeff Petrino.

CHAPTER EIGHTEEN

As she promised, Penny returned Saturday morning with one hand clutching two large shopping bags bulging with pillows and pieces of cloth and the other hand pulling a yellow suitcase behind her. She was dressed in faded blue jeans and an old blouse. With her hair pulled back in a pony tail, she looked like the teenager I'd hung out with more than fifteen years ago.

She came alone, thank God. Without Jeff lurking around, Penny and I could enjoy a fun afternoon decorating Gram's house. The first thing we did was unload the pillows and hand-made throws, which we placed on the beds and chairs. Penny followed up with curtains—light blue sheers for the large bedroom, a green and blue panel for the room where I was staying, a violet and gold swag for the other bedroom, and a yellow valance for the bathroom. Somehow, Penny had matched the curtains to the existing bed covers, setting each room apart from the others.

She then flung her suitcase on my bed and began to unpack a wonderful array of vintage items—sepia toned photographs of Victorian children, artificial flower arrangements in porcelain vases, an antique ewer and matching bowl, an old leather Bible, and tons of dried leaves, silk flowers, and berries, which she then began to turn into colorful wreathes for the bedroom doors and decorations for each of the dressers.

I stood watching, a hammer and hooks in my hands, ready to assist when needed. It was like watching a professional decorator at work.

"You need to open your own shop," I told her.

She gave me one of those, *Get real* looks, then went about switching one item for another, flitting between the bedrooms, stepping back, and switching things again until she was satisfied.

So, that's how a decorator works, I mused. I'd always thought they brought some unique item into a house, placed it on a table, and left. But not Penny. She tried several different arrangements and settings, shook her head, and started over again.

It struck me now that what she was doing was no different from what I did every day at my desk. How many times had I written and rewritten articles until I felt they were ready to turn in? It's called self-editing. Artists do the same thing. They paint a picture, toss it out, and paint the same thing over again, only better. Penny was sort of an artist at work, and I was going to be the recipient of her meticulous artistry.

But while I needed complete silence when *I* worked, Penny chattered away the whole time. She reminisced about our school days, the fun we'd had at the beach, shopping at the mall, and sleepovers—so many wonderful teenage memories, even mistakes that should have remained buried. We laughed till we cried, and we cried till we were exhausted.

When Penny finished decorating, we walked about the upstairs and surveyed each room, then we both breathed a long sigh.

"Well, what's next on the agenda?" Penny said, breaking the silence.

"Haven't you done enough?" I chided her. "You've already given two days to help me."

She shook her head, swinging her ponytail. "There's still a lot of work to do. Surely, you can use my help somewhere else."

"Why don't we go to the five-and-dime and root around in there? We can add a little more color to the downstairs rooms."

"Sounds like a plan," Penny said, grabbing her purse. "I'll drive."

We hopped in Penny's Chrysler convertible, a shiny silver chariot with the top down. The five-and-dime had been there for as long as I could remember. Walking up and down the aisles of the humongous emporium was like shopping in a

Dollar Store, only better. This shop smelled of incense, and the shelves were covered with interesting items, like pussy willows, cattails, smoked glass, cheap china, washboards, wall hangings, and other novelties.

I felt like a kid in a fairytale, sorting through plastic flowers, sun catchers, tiny vases, and ceramic miniatures of animals. I trusted Penny to choose what might work in Gram's house, and I purchased matching hand towels and wash cloths for the bath and a couple sets of rooster towels for the kitchen to match Gram's red-and-yellow wall clock.

We went home with two bags of novelties. As expected, Penny turned the downstairs into a showplace. She put one of her multi-colored throws on the back of the sofa, then used some of the curios she'd purchased at the five-and-dime. A family of ceramic ducks lined up on the kitchen counter, a three-by-five-foot muted print of a Midwestern farm over the fireplace, and a short stack of old women's magazines and a bowl of Hershey's kisses on the coffee table.

I hung the matching tea towels on a rack by the sink, and fastened a sunflower sun catcher to the kitchen window pane.

In appreciation for Penny's hard work, I offered to buy dinner out. We took turns freshening up in the bathroom.

We went to Luigi's and dined on antipasto salad and baked ravioli. We each had a glass of red wine, and we finished off our meal with tiramisu and coffee. I had to admit, the Cittadina restaurants easily rivaled those in New York. Most of them were mom-and-pop establishments, which meant they served authentic dishes, straight from the coffers of Italy.

"Are you going to the fall festival?" I asked Penny, expecting to spend another day with my friend.

"Can't," she said, then puckered her lips. "I'd like to go, but they're cleaning the theater Sunday, getting it ready for the first show in a few weeks. I already volunteered to help."

"A few weeks? Is that enough time for the actors to rehearse?"

Penny laughed at me. "No, silly. They've been rehearsing

for two months. Sunday's their one day off, and we use it for housekeeping. Don't forget, it's a *community* theater. The whole community pitches in—including the actors."

"Well, the festival won't be much fun without you, but I guess I'll manage."

A mischievous twinkle entered her eyes. "Maybe you'll meet one of Cittadina's eligible bachelors. I think there are two." She burst out laughing.

"I have a boyfriend," I reminded her.

"You never know," Penny pressed. "You might find something better."

I shook my head. "Not a chance, Penny. I doubt anyone out there can compare with Brian. I'll go to the festival with my parents, and I'll go home alone. End of story."

As it turned out, I did go with my parents. After church, I helped Mom transport her pies to the festival and helped her and Dad arrange them on the sale table. Against my better judgment, I stayed, but I refused to sit in a lawn chair and listen to an Italian oompah band's clamoring instruments. Things hadn't changed much since I'd left. In addition to the sound of a bass drum, mandolin, French horn, and tuba blaring from the bandstand, the crowd buzzed with conversation. It was like being thrown into a giant beehive with music.

I strolled around the park, kept to the outlying sidewalks, and watched the children playing tag and clambering over the playground equipment. I could lose myself among the younger, innocent faces. They brought back snatches of my own past— memorable, cheerful times before pain entered my life. Instead of taking advantage of the opportunity to reconnect with people I once knew, I found solace in that temporary escape.

A special table of desserts had been set up to raise funds for the children's hospital. An assortment of cookies, donuts, and other Italian concoctions was going fast, including my mom's apple pies. Individual kiosks sold corn dogs, popcorn, and cotton candy. Casually dressed villagers milled about, chatting, laughing, and toasting with who-knows-what in paper cups. It was like it had always been, as if time stood still for the people of Cittadina.

When hunger pangs hit, I reentered the real world and joined the line at the hot dog stand. I started at the pressure of a hand against my shoulder. I can't say why, but I knew the touch. I spun around, my eyes flaming.

"What do you want, Jeff?" I brushed his hand off my shoulder.

His eyes widened, and he stumbled backward.

"H–how did you know it was me?" he stammered.

"Who else would it be?" I said, scowling. "I asked you, what do you want?"

"I thought you might want some company." He looked around. "I don't see anyone else with you."

My frown deepened. "Have you been watching me?"

Already, the tone of my voice had aroused the interest of others in the line. People turned around and looked at the two of us.

"Leave me alone," I said, before he had a chance to answer. I spun away from him and resumed my place in line.

"Look, Fran, I wanted to apologize, that's all. I wanted to tell you how sorry I am for what happened. But that was nearly fifteen years ago. You must have gotten over it by now."

I didn't respond, just kept my eyes straight ahead and stepped closer to the kiosk. I placed my order and dug in my pocket for some cash. Jeff reached past my shoulder and placed a five dollar bill on the counter.

"My treat," he said, then added, "I'll have the same."

The teenager inside the hot dog cart accepted the bill.

"A peace offering," Jeff whispered in my ear.

As I stepped away with my fully loaded hot dog, he followed.

"Let's sit over there." He gestured toward a vacant bench at the edge of the park. "We can talk."

Though I'd have preferred to go home, I sat on the bench but scooted to the opposite side away from him. I began to devour my hotdog.

"You know," he said between bites. "I never had the chance to apologize to you. It was always on my mind, just didn't know what to say. But you need to know, I've learned my lesson."

I glanced at him, my face like stone.

"I don't cheat anymore," he said. "I'm ready for a solid relationship. Loyalty. That's the key. No more cheating. No more broken hearts."

Disbelief flooded over me. I looked more closely at him.

He was wearing designer jeans, a black Ralph Lauren Polo shirt, and brown leather sandals. On his left wrist was a gold chain bracelet. To my untrained eye, it was real, but how could I know for sure? He was a phony, but he liked to appear prosperous. A pair of aviator sunglasses finished the *movie star* look, but they also hid whatever truth was lurking behind them. Like my mother said, *the eyes are a window to the soul*. I had no way to read the guy's soul—not with those reflective lenses blocking my view.

"Take off those sunglasses and tell me that," I said with a sternness that got him flinching. He removed his glasses.

I stared into his dark eyes, black enough to mask his soul.

I shook my head. "I don't know, Jeff. I don't trust you."

He rested his free hand on my knee. "Believe me, Fran, you can trust me."

I shifted my leg away from his touch and went back to my hot dog.

"Fran," he persisted. "I've never gotten over you. And now that I see you again, how beautiful you are—how mature—I have to say, I still have feelings for you."

"I'm dating someone," I shot back.

"I don't see a ring on your finger."

"That doesn't matter. I'm seeing a decent guy, someone I *do* trust."

"Listen, Fran, I'm not the same guy you knew back then. I was stupid. I'm different now, and believe me, I learned my lesson. I'm telling you, I am no longer a cheater."

I lurched back in shock. "No longer a cheater? What do you think you're doing now?"

I leapt from the bench and faced him. "You're in a relationship with Penny, and you just made a play for me. If that isn't cheating, I don't know what is."

I flung the rest of my hot dog at him and stormed off. I didn't look back, didn't stop to see him scrambling to clean the mustard off his expensive shirt. I searched for my parents and found them exactly where I'd left them, in front of the bandstand, holding hands.

"I'm going home," I shouted above the cacophony of instruments. "I have things to do."

They looked perplexed but nodded. As I started to walk away, Dad pulled Mom from her lawn chair, and they began to dance to what sounded like, "That's Amore."

Smiling, I followed the sidewalk in the direction of Maple Street. I no sooner turned the corner when a black-and-green Jeep Wrangler drifted past. Jeff was at the wheel. He turned his head in my direction. I looked away and kept walking. He revved the engine and sped off.

Another childish stunt, I mused. *That man will never change.*

My mind wandered to his designer clothes, his expensive jewelry, plus two high-priced vehicles. Where did a small-town handyman get that kind of money? Then I remembered the day he'd stopped on the street to talk to George Newman. My heart pounded with misgivings. If Jeff had been helping Newman find houses to buy, that would explain why he weaseled his way into Gram's house. I thought about the leaky drain in the bathroom. Had he been trying to sabotage my renovations? I decided to check around to see if he'd done anything else to the house when I wasn't looking.

CHAPTER NINETEEN

I slept fitfully that night. My mind kept running over what I might say to Penny about her so-called boyfriend and his infidelity. I must have drifted off sometime past midnight, and I woke up before the sun rose. My heart was breaking for my friend.

I wanted to leave Cittadina, wanted to get away from all the drama. The house was finished. I could put it in the hands of a Realtor and simply leave town.

Three weeks had passed since I started the project. The time had literally flown by. Now I could see the light at the end of the tunnel. Brian was standing in that light. So was my job at the newspaper. So was my apartment and the magical skyline of New York.

That morning, before making breakfast, I strolled through the house from top to bottom and surveyed all I had accomplished. I kept my eyes out for anything out of order, searched for things Jeff might have done to the bathroom. I found nothing.

It was time I hired a real estate agent and scheduled an open house. Once I had a sign out front, the offers would come in. I could go back to the city and wait for the sale.

The sale. The words stuck in my throat like a thorn. If I couldn't say it out loud, how was I going to *do* it?

While growing up, I'd always thought of Gram's house as the homiest, most welcoming place I'd ever visited. Memories surfaced. Gram greeting me after school with homemade cookies and milk. Gram watching old movies with me on her big, old TV. Gram sitting with me on the front porch swing, telling stories about a young woman who'd traveled to far-off places.

A sadness swept away the memories. With all the cleaning and painting and changes I'd made, Gram had slowly been disappearing. From the start, I had hoped a small part of her might remain within those walls, that somehow she'd always have a claim to the house, no matter who owned it. Now she was about to disappear forever.

It turned out Gram wasn't the only one who was disappearing beneath the coats of paint and the change in the decor. Salvatore and Rosanna also were vanishing. So were Catherine and Enzo. I'd built every one of my jobs upon the foundation set by my ancestors. Now I was about to eliminate their hard work once and for all. The truth struck my heart like a dagger. I hadn't merely fixed up a piece of real estate. I had slowly and meticulously wiped away my roots.

I was at the sink washing my breakfast dishes, when a car pulled into the driveway.

I stepped out the side door. It was Penny's Chrysler. Instead of climbing out, she ran her fingers through her hair and offered a big smile.

"Wanna go for a ride?" she called out.

I shook my head. My heart pounded with anxiety. I was going to have to tell her about Jeff making a pass at me. If she heard it from him first, he could distort the truth and make it sound like I had pursued him.

"C'mon," she urged. "You've been cooped up in that house long enough. Let's go somewhere fun."

"Aren't you supposed to be at work today?"

She shrugged. "I took a vacation day. Besides, I don't think I'll be missed. Things are kinda slow right now."

"I need to talk, Penny." I nodded toward the house. "Let's have a cup of coffee. If you want to, we can sit outdoors and relax on the back patio."

I read disappointment on her face, from the wrinkle across her forehead to the pouting of her mouth. She followed me inside and waited while I fixed our coffee.

We carried our cups out back to the patio and settled in two chairs beside the little round table. As we sipped our coffee, Penny gazed about the backyard.

"You made a little Garden of Eden back here," she said. "It's a paradise. Can you imagine living in this house, in this town, Fran?"

I ignored her subtle suggestion. "Penny," I said, with caution. "I need to ask you something."

"What?"

"How well do you know Jeff?"

"Jeff?" she giggled. "He's my boyfriend. I think I know him quite well."

"What I mean is, do you think you can trust him?"

Penny looked at the sky and shook her head. "Here we go again."

"Penny—"

"Let it rest, Fran. You're not gonna turn me away from Jeff. I don't care what you say."

"He made a pass at me."

She frowned at me.

"Penny, he approached me at the park yesterday, and he bought me a hot dog—"

"Oh wow! A hot dog. Now, that's romantic. Was it a candle-lit dinner?"

"Will you please listen to me?" I tried to remain strong. "Penny, he asked me to sit with him on a park bench, said he needed to talk, and he put his hand on my knee."

Penny's frown deepened. "What are you saying, Fran?"

"I'm saying he admitted he still cared for me."

Penny clenched her teeth. Then she stood and slammed her coffee cup on the little table, shattering Gram's china. "I'm outta here," she snapped, and started to walk away.

"Penny, please don't leave. For your own sake, you have to know the truth. Jeff hasn't changed. Face the facts, Jeff Petrino doesn't care about anyone but himself and his next conquest."

She shook her head at me, sympathy building in her eyes.

"I feel sorry for you, Fran. You're the one who's clinging to the past. The truth is, you haven't gotten over Jeff. It's obvious you're jealous. Jealous of me and what I have with him. Well, you lose, girl. You will not turn me against him. For your information, he called me this morning and said we'll get married next year. Swallow *that*, my dear *friend*." She spit out the last word, then she spun away and stomped off. Seconds later, she peeled out of the driveway.

A hard lump rose to my throat. Hot tears filled my eyes. I hadn't handled things the way I wanted to. I'd forgotten all the little phrases I'd rehearsed while trying to get to sleep last night, words of warning to help rescue my friend. Instead, I hadn't rescued her at all. I'd sent her running back to a man who couldn't be trusted.

And our friendship was over. I was certain of that. Penny had made up her mind. But isn't that the way of young women in love? They don't want to hear the bitter truth. Hadn't I done the same thing—blindly trusted a guy who broke my heart over and over again, a guy who knew exactly what to say to win me back? Like Penny, I hadn't accepted the truth until it was too late.

Once again, the monster had won. He'd deceived my friend into thinking he wanted no one but her, and all the while he was looking everywhere else—including my way. Not only had he broken my heart years ago, now he'd come between me and one of my best friends. Jeff had effectively destroyed our friendship, and I'd helped him do it.

I needed a diversion, anything to get my mind off the trauma I'd just experienced.

Gram's trunk. There were still several more surprises in there. Five minutes later, I was in the attic, reading Gram's next instructions, and hoping I could lose myself within the adventure.

Darling Fran,
For your next journey into the past, you'll want to read my

leather-bound journal. When you finish, you can look through the photo album lying beneath it. And finally, you'll find a large box near the bottom of the trunk. But read the journal first, then look at the album, then open the box. It's important you open them in order. Take your time and enjoy yourself. You're about to go on a few more of my adventures. Some of them will seem a little far-fetched, but please keep an open mind and an open heart.

Gripping the journal, I hurried downstairs to the living room, where I settled in Gram's old rocker. How appropriate to snuggle into the very chair where we sat together, and she first told me her wild stories. Now I was going to read more of them. At least, that's what her letter implied. I ran my hand over the leather cover, then flipped it open.

Inside was the name *Francine Maria Rossi*, Gram's maiden name, plus an address in Italy, followed by another address in Albany, New York. The first entry was dated *December 25, 1939*. Gram would have been seventeen years old.

We are spending our third Christmas in the United States. My mother gave me this journal when we left Italy, and she told me to write whatever I wanted to say.

I grew up in Milan, Italy, with an older brother, Carmine, and two older sisters, Angelina and Gabriella. That's right. I'm the baby of the family, and I deserve to be spoiled. (Just kidding)

I had to chuckle. Gram? Spoiled? I doubted it.

When Mussolini joined up with the Nazi's, my father said it was time for us to leave Italy and go to America. He sensed that terrible things were about to happen. My dream of climbing one of the

Alps was crushed. I had gazed for years at those snowcapped peaks, always from a distance, always wishing I could go there, but never old enough. Now we've settled in Albany, New York. There are no snowcapped mountains here. But I love the rolling hills and the trees and the vast acres of farmland.

My father works as a plumber and makes a lot more money here than what he received in Italy. My mother hired a tutor to teach the four of us kids the English language. We learned enough to attend one of the American schools.

There were a number of blank pages, as though months had passed between entries. Then, Gram's writing resumed.

Both of my sisters graduated from high school and took jobs in a big department store in town. Angelina already has met a young man and will get married soon. Gabriella said she prefers the life of a spinster. As for me? I'm undecided. After my last year of high school, I'd like to go to college.

I couldn't help but smile. I was a lot like my grandmother in some ways. There was another break between pages, and then a date—*Saturday, September 14, 1940.*

Three of my friends and I joined a bowling team last month. We wanted to try something other than ladies' softball. Except for Annie, who can pitch better than some of the guys, the rest of us really stank on the field.

Bowling gave us a whole other activity to enjoy. Our first time out we beat four other teams in a round robin competition. Betsy kept getting spares and strikes, and Julia rarely left a pin standing. Like always, Annie did the best of all four of us. She's a true athlete.

My own form is developing quite well. If we keep getting high scores, we might qualify for a state tournament in Rochester in January.

It was hard to picture my grandmother rolling a bowling ball and then leaping for joy over a spare or a strike, but anything's possible, and I had to remind myself, she wasn't always old and feeble. She was young once.

Page after page contained more details about the different competitions, plus score totals and notations about stance and swing. Then came the county-wide bowling tournament in which Gram won a trophy for Best Bowler of the Season. She was eighteen years old at the time.

A few pages of writing strayed from the bowling stories and focused on Gram's interest in a young man named Buck Johnson. More notations revealed that Francine's parents did not approve of the fast-talking, fast-driving young man. Then she revealed another side of herself I'd never seen before. The precocious young woman wrote:

They've forbidden me to go out with him. I'm going anyway. My bedroom is downstairs off the kitchen. I can sneak out the window without anyone knowing and meet Buck behind the malt shop. I love him. I can't imagine living without him.

I shook my head in shock. *That little rascal.* My grandmother, the one who preached moral living and quoted Bible verses to me, had defied her parents and was sneaking out of the house for a secret rendezvous. I snickered. *She was like the rest of us girls.*

In between her bowling team's continuing successes, Gram inserted more details about her secret dates with Buck. Each time her admissions got a little more steamy. Yet, she insisted she was a *good girl*, and claimed she knew when to draw the line.

Her last entry that year included a heartbreaking conclusion to her relationship with Buck.

That jerk cheated on me.

I nearly fell off of Gram's rocker. The next part was equally shocking.

I thought we were going to get married. I thought he loved me. I just want to die. How can I face my friends at school? How can I go on?

Gram's account revived my own pain over Jeff's infidelity. Tears flooded to my eyes, and I wept for myself and for Gram, a naive young woman who'd trusted the wrong guy—like I did. At that moment, I recalled what she'd said when I confided in her about Jeff.

"This, too, shall pass," she'd murmured, nodding her head as if she understood. "You'll meet someone else someday. Someone you'll be able to trust with your heart."

And Gram also had met someone else. My Poppa, Alberto. He was one of the nicest, most considerate men I'd ever met. He doted on Gram, brought her flowers and candy, gave her his full attention, right up to the day he died. Their loving relationship gave me renewed hope. *All things are possible,* I mused.

After losing Buck, Gram wrote that she needed a distraction. She ended up traveling with friends to Washington, D.C., where she toured the White House, stopped to admire the various memorial statues, and visited the Smithsonian Institution. She even claimed to have climbed the 896-step, windowless staircase to the top of the Washington Monument, a claustrophobic experience if there ever was one.

A few subsequent notations talked about graduation, girl-friends, parties, and plans to do more traveling.

Then came a series of emotional entries, beginning with *February 10, 1941.*

My brother, Carmine, received citizenship papers today and immediately joined the Navy. Mama cries all the time, but she can do nothing to stop him. Carmine will leave for training in two weeks.

A few months later, her notation was brief.

After a three-day pass and a visit home, Carmine left for Hawaii this morning. What a lucky guy. It will be like a vacation in paradise.

December 8, 1941. The Japanese bombed Pearl Harbor yesterday. We are all praying for Carmine.

December 14. Today we received confirmation. My brother Carmine is gone.

For some reason Gram's notations ceased, until *Friday, August 6, 1948.* This amazing entry showed me she had finally experienced her long-held quest for adventure.

CHAPTER TWENTY

Gram was 26 years old when she traveled back to Italy. It was the adventure of a lifetime.

A local tour agency has posted a trip to the Italian Alps, and I am going. I've been able to save up the $1,200 fee. Aside from what I give Momma for room and board, I've saved nearly every cent from my job at the department store. I'm still single, and I don't want to waste another year wondering when I'll be able to follow my dream.

The next two pages contained details about what she could take in the military backpack recommended for the climb. I could almost hear excitement in her voice as I read on.

The flight across the Atlantic cost $135 and took 12 hours on a Pan American DC-4. Then, a three-hour bus ride, with multiple stops, took me to the village of Cortina d'Ampezzo situated three miles from the Dolomite Mountains. If I hadn't slept on the plane, I would have been exhausted. But I was wide awake and jumping for joy when I caught sight of snow-capped, gray peaks beyond the line of trees in the distance.

Tonight I dined with other members of our group at a little cafe where they served red wine and bowls of green olives, then tapas and open-faced sandwiches, followed by espresso coffee and a wonderful fruit-filled zeppolle.

The town gives off an aura of old Italy. I love the cobbled streets, the gaslights, the quaint country cottages, and the shops. But I didn't come here to sightsee. I came to climb to the top of one of those mountains and to look down at the world from 10,000 feet up.

She then shared what she'd learned from the brochure and from the people who ran the inn where she stayed.

Three decades ago, those mountains were the scene of heavy combat during the Great War. We've been warned to watch out for broken rocks with jagged edges and barbed wire that may have fallen across the paths where we will be walking. Some of the steeper areas had been rigged with ropes and cables to bring supplies to the troops encamped on the ridges. In recent years, climbers have continued to maintain those riggings. They dubbed the trail Via Ferrata, which means the "Iron Way."

The next page was labeled, *The Morning of the Climb.*

We rose from our cots while it was still dark. We dressed quickly and ate a breakfast of muesli and dried fruit. I ate about half the bowl. I had butterflies in my stomach. It felt like an electrical charge was racing through me. Except for hiking the lower Catskills of New York, I'd never attempted anything like this. It was quite daunting, to say the least.

Our group numbers 30 people, plus three guides, one for each team. Some have climbed the Alps before, but many, including myself, are novices and will depend on the expertise of the more seasoned climbers.

Before starting out, we broke into three separate teams of ten people.

My team includes seven males from different European countries, myself, and two other women—one an American named Ginger, and the other an Italian girl named Maria. Fortunately, our guide, Donato, speaks five languages, but everyone in our group also spoke English, so that became the language of choice.

Before starting out, Donato lectured us about staying together, assisting one another over the rough spots, and watching each other for signs of disorientation or altitude sickness.

Then, he asked if anyone wanted to quit. After getting a unanimous "No," he handed us our gear—a harness to fit around the waist, a helmet, and a set of ropes with two carabiners.

At that moment, I tried to envision Gram in her climbing gear—khaki pants and shirt, backpack, leather gloves, a helmet crowning her tiny head, plus ropes slung over her arm and carabiners in her hand. I had to remind myself she wasn't a white-haired old lady back then. She was a plucky twenty-six-year-old woman, and she was about to climb a 10,000-foot mountain of rock and ice.

Gram's descriptions were so vivid, I felt like I was on the journey with her. It appeared she had written them whenever she paused during the climb or after she returned to the village that night. I smiled as I remembered she'd told me a modified version of the climb in one of her fantastic tales about the girl who went on adventures. Now the story I heard when I was a young child came back in full bloom.

Gram's notations continued, with even more detail.

We walked the three miles to the base of Via Ferrata and began our climb, single file. As Donato had instructed us, we hooked our carabiners to the cable which was attached to the rock face by heavy bolts, spaced about ten or twelve feet apart. As we approached each bolt we needed to unhook one carabiner from the cable, while keeping

the other one hooked for safety. Then, we reattached the loose one on the other side of the bolt. In this way we always stayed linked to the security line. Nevertheless, during those moments when I unhooked one of my carabiners, my heart fluttered a little. Thank God, I never lost my footing, never missed a handhold, and our guide remained close, ready to help when needed.

We moved slowly and smoothly up the mountain, reached for knobs and indentations in the rock face, clipped and unclipped carabiners. In the crisp mountain air, the pings and snaps of our carabiners became more pronounced along with the heavy breathing of the hikers.

At times, our route became easier as the trail leveled off, and we easily walked along narrow paths and over wooden footbridges. As we continued to ascend, my team developed a smooth rhythm, like a well-choreographed company of dancers.

I was amazed by the transformation of the terrain. From a distance the mountain had looked like sheer silver, but up close, we found patches of grass intermingled with dirt and ice. Our climb went up one side of the mountain, and the way down was in a separate area on the other side. As a result, those who went up never met those who were coming down.

We reached the top as the sun was arcing overhead. I gazed out over the breathtaking view below. Numerous little villages dotted the landscape. I breathed deeply of the sharp, fresh air. I was so awestruck I couldn't speak. Nor could I move. I wanted to absorb the moment and never let it go.

Then Donato gathered our team for a lunch break. I tore my gaze away from the spectacular vista and joined the others squatting on the ground, but I made sure I chose a spot where I could still see the vast panorama below us.

Each of us had packed sandwiches and a thermos of black coffee. We chattered excitedly. After all, we had just climbed one of the Dolomites. We stood at the top of the world. We'd left all our cares behind, and, for me, at least, this was only the beginning. There on the top of Via Ferrata, I began to envision the possibility of more adventures. My appetite had been whetted, and I knew I couldn't stop.

Gram's account was so beautifully describe, I began to believe *she* was the adventurous young woman of her stories. Meanwhile, my common sense continued to argue that she was simply a very good storyteller.

The entries on the next few pages of Gram's journal teemed with more escapades, though none as exciting as the climb in the Alps. She went sailing on Lake Placid, walked a trail in the Canadian wilderness, and visited a Native American reservation. Then one of her accounts became more personal.

I met him at a USO dance at Fort Drum. His name was Alberto Capellini.

I immediately perked up. Alberto Capellini, my grandfather, my Poppa!

A group of us girls traveled there by bus. The Saturday night dances were organized to entertain the servicemen, many of them slated for overseas deployment.

There I was, a young woman who had climbed a mountain. Yet, I trembled with fear at the thought of meeting young men. I entered the great hall and nervously looked around. To one side was a huge table loaded with snacks and soda pops. To the other was a long row of metal chairs. The sound of Glenn Miller's "In the Mood" poured from a record player manned by one of the soldiers at the front.

Some of the girls had been there before. I decided it would be best to do whatever they did. They went to the row of metal chairs. I did the same, took a seat, and pulled my skirt down to my ankles, all the while uneasy about the group of men who stood in a line, staring at us like we were being auctioned for sale.

One by one, the soldiers ambled over and asked the girls to dance. I chewed my lip, afraid I'd be the one wallflower left sitting alone, and even more fearful of being led to the dance floor. Then my heart pounded as one of them approached me and extended his hand.

He was of average height and build. But what captured my attention was the non-threatening smile on his lips. He wasn't as handsome as Buck Johnson, but he had a pleasant look. His nose had a slight bend to it, like he'd been in a fight and lost. His dark hair matched mine, thick and wavy. I took his hand. His touch was gentle. He didn't pull me against him, like some of the other guys had done with the girls they had selected. He easily guided me into a foxtrot and circled the dance floor, gazing into my eyes and still smiling.

And when the music slowed to a waltz, I rested my forehead on his shoulder.

After several dances, he asked if I'd like to have something to eat. We filled a couple of plates with snacks and retreated to the metal chairs. He said his name was Alberto, and that he had two more years to serve before he would receive his discharge.

He asked where I lived. When I said Albany, his thick eyebrows slanted in disappointment. Then he told me he was born and raised in Rochester. After he gets out of the Army he plans to work as a plumber.

Gram's subsequent notations revealed that she'd returned to the base for each of the monthly dances. Every time, she danced only with Alberto. Every time, they got to know each other better.

When Alberto was deployed overseas, Gram filled the lonely weeks by satisfying her craving for another adventure.

First, was her account of a white water rafting trip on the Arkansas River in Colorado. For that trip she donned a life jacket and a helmet and joined a half-dozen other daredevils in a big, orange, rubber raft. Somehow, while maneuvering through rapids and plunging over a series of perilous waterfalls, she managed to take note of the majestic scenery well enough to describe it later in her journal.

Though I still had doubts about Gram's veracity, I read on with eagerness. Her next entry told about a deep sea fishing trip off the Florida coast near Fort Lauderdale. Gram claimed she had joined a dozen people on a boat ride out on the Atlantic, though it was mid-October in the midst of hurricane season.

We boarded the Southern Keys Charter Boat. The crew took us out a couple of miles from shore into deep water. The waves were exceptionally rough that day. It turned out a hurricane was building near Haiti and it was heading our way, which meant we had about an hour to haul in our fish before the captain would decide to take us home. Several men showed off a nice pile of fish. A few of the passengers appeared disappointed with only a bare hook and empty cooler to show for their efforts on the sea.

Then, without warning, our boat began to lurch about like a wild bronco ride at a rodeo. Several of the men became ill. But the rough seas didn't dampen their spirit. They set aside their gear, wretched over the side, and then grabbed their poles and resumed fishing. I shook my head in awe of those die-hard fishermen.

The waves didn't trouble me at all. I walked about as if I had sea legs, even ate a ham-and-cheese sandwich, and kept casting my line in the water.

The captain had found us a good spot. Some of the men began hauling in grouper, redfish, and the ever-present sharks. Those sharp-toothed monsters flopped around on the deck. We stepped cautiously around them, guarding our ankles, until the crew could either put them on ice or toss them back into the sea.

At one point, I felt a tug on my line, and a member of the crew helped me bring in a five-foot-long shark. He took it off my hook, grabbed it by the tail and slammed its head on the deck, stunning it long enough for me to get my picture taken with it. Unlike some of the other "fishermen," I chose to throw my catch back to live another day.

In addition to the fishing, I sure enjoyed the boat ride, in spite of the angry waves—or maybe because of them. As it turned out, the hurricane changed course, like they often do, turned into a tropical storm and meandered around the Gulf, doing little damage.

I spent the next couple of days sightseeing in south Florida. The tropical atmosphere was a refreshing respite from the chilly weather that awaited me back home in New York.

Gram then mourned the fact that when Alberto was discharged, they'd be living hours apart. I mused that their relationship paralleled the one I had with Brian.

What if I decide to stay in Cittadina? I might never see Brian again. All the more reason I need to go back to New York.

Eager to learn how my grandparents worked things out, I read on.

Alberto was discharged from the Army on January 10, 1951. As he planned, he moved to Rochester and began his career as a plumber, a trade he learned while in the service. Six months later, I left Albany and also moved to Rochester, found an apartment, and went to work as a seamstress in a factory where they made men's suit coats.

Alberto and I dated for a couple of years. Then he approached my father and asked his blessing. Both Mama and Papa welcomed him with open arms, and we began to plan our wedding.

I grunted. *Why can't life be that simple?* People used to meet and fall in love, pretty much at first sight. They married and stayed together for fifty years or more. It's like the Bible says, a man leaves his father and mother and marries one woman. Gram and Poppa remained committed to each other through good times and bad times. So did Salvatore and Rosanna, Enzo and Catherine, my parents, my aunts and uncles, and pretty much everyone from their generation.

Not like today. People love each other one year, and the next they're getting a divorce. I didn't want that. I wanted what my parents and my grandparents had. But don't most people go into a marriage thinking they'll be together *until death do us part?* What guarantee did I have if the man I chose to marry didn't share my commitment?

I searched the next few pages for an answer. Gram wrote about life as a married woman, how she'd given up seeking adventures for a little while in order to focus on starting a family. She even insisted she loved being a wife and mother as much as she enjoyed climbing the Alps—maybe more.

That's commitment, I thought. *That's what people do when they're in love. They make sacrifices. They consider the needs of the other person.* Gram was quite clear about what marriage meant to her. She wrote:

It's a different kind of exhilaration. One that fills a woman's heart with purpose and unexplainable joy.

Then one-by-one, she mentioned their three sons—my Uncle Giuseppe, their firstborn, round bellied and the laziest kid she'd ever seen, but a real joy; my father, Nicolas, the studious sort, good with numbers and straight-A student; and their youngest, Paulo, a little soldier, playing with GI Joes, and coming home with dirty hands and torn pants from tumbling about with his friends.

Alberto made a terrific father. He keeps the boys in line and has taught them to respect me, never allows them to talk back to me. Al and I seem to agree on everything that counts. I have no doubt, I married the right man.

If Gram had stayed with that guy Buck, she might have had a miserable life. That's what happens when a person hooks up with a self-centered narcissist. They make decisions for themselves, with little concern for anyone else.

Like Gram, I had been spared such a nightmare with Jeff. I now had an Alberto of my own. My one problem was deciding where I wanted to live. I was beginning to feel torn between my fast-paced, big-city life and the hometown feel of Cittadina. If I gave up New York, would I also lose Brian? And, if I chose New York, would I lose all the wonderful experiences I'd had since coming home? Would I forget about my ancestors? Would I let go of my personal heritage? How easy was it going to be to walk away from the house on Maple Street?

CHAPTER TWENTY-ONE

Monday morning, I took a break from Gram's journal so I could get with a real estate agent. I wasn't about to sell her house to the Newman brothers. A Realtor could market it to someone who wouldn't tear it down, someone who would live in it and appreciate its history.

As for me, I'd chosen New York. I'd made up my mind to get out of Cittadina, away from Penny and Jeff, away from the pressure my Mom would surely put on me, and I'd get my freedom back.

I headed for the center of town where two banks, a law office, and a real estate firm had set up shop a block away from the courthouse. How convenient. People could handle an entire transaction, from start to finish. They could arrange to sell a house, get a lawyer to check the paperwork, file a deed, and put the money in the bank, all within easy walking distance.

As I exited my car, I chuckled over the miniature version of a large city business district. The biggest difference was everything had slowed down to a crawl. A few people in dark suits strolled along the sidewalks like they had nowhere special to go, and a woman pushing a stroller crossed in front of me at the light, stopping halfway across the street to give her baby a pacifier. I found the lazy atmosphere refreshing. But while a part of me appreciated the laid-back ambience of my former hometown, another part longed for the hustle and bustle of New York's busy sidewalks where nobody ever strolled.

Unlike the slow-moving snails who lived in Cittadina, I

trotted over to the real estate office, then stopped to peruse the flyers taped to the plate glass window out front. The home prices ranged from the low $100,000s to $2 million for a horse farm with 50 acres a few miles outside of town. I estimated Gram's house might bring in $130,000 or more.

I entered the storefront to the aroma of polished walnut and oiled leather. A row of padded chairs hugged the area near the window. Along the back wall stood a row of metal filing cabinets. And in the center of the room stood two massive desks, each manned by an agent with a computer. The desk on my left was home to a gray-haired antique of a woman with a sharp nose and dark, beady eyes. She was on the phone, so I quickly turned my attention to the smiling young woman seated behind the desk on my right.

Her name plate said *Beverly Strong, junior agent.* Though a little plump, she had a fresh, youthful glow that set me at ease. She blinked innocent, sky blue eyes at me, then she stood and extended her right hand. I already felt comfortable with this young woman, like I could trust her to get Gram's house on the market and sold within a matter of days. I shook her hand and settled into the chair across from her.

She welcomed me with a musical southern accent, which struck me as odd. No one in Cittadina had a southern accent. Nearly everyone had Italian roots in this town. Some spoke with such heavy broken English I could barely understand them.

"Where are you from, Miss Strong?" I boldly inquired. "I couldn't help but notice your accent."

"Oh, don't call me Miss Strong," she sang. "It makes me feel old. You can call me Beverly. Ahm from Dallas, Texas. Ah moved here six months ago to take this job."

I smiled in puzzlement. "What? They don't have real estate offices in Dallas?"

She giggled. "Oh, yes, but Ah couldn't ignore the job offer. Anyway, small-town life intrigues me. Don't you agree?"

"No. I was born and raised here, but I live in New York City now, and I prefer the faster lifestyle."

She hadn't lost her smile once during our brief visit. She nodded and leaned back in her chair. "Tell me, did you come in here to buy a home or to sell one?"

"To sell one. Believe me, that's all I want to do."

It took a half hour to explain my situation, starting with Gram's death and ending with the renovations. Beverly raised her eyebrows several times, ran a hand through her honey colored bob, and said, "Um, hm," more times than I could count. Throughout my monologue she made notes on a yellow pad. I suspected she might be doodling.

When I finished, Beverly skimmed over her notes, and with amazing accuracy, she read back many of the details, word for word. The renovation sounded more sugary sweet on her lips, and I had confidence she could entice a slew of serious buyers.

Her smile broadened. "It sounds like you've done a fabulous job on your grandmother's house. Of course, I'll want to take a look. If you haven't already done so, we'll need to order an inspection. Most sales require them, unless the buyer waves the process. I don't expect that to happen in Cittadina. Too many decrepit, old houses in this town."

Her last remark irritated me, but I shrugged it off. "My father ordered an inspection before I came here," I told her with confidence. "They found my grandmother's house to be quite sound. It may be 132 years old, but it was built by my great-great-grandfather, an experienced craftsman who was up on the latest techniques. Like many men of his generation, he took pride in his work. My great-grandparents landscaped the property with plants and trees. And my grandfather was a plumber. It looks like he changed all the corroded pipes for PVC, and he also created a full bath upstairs. I've turned it into a master suite," I added with a touch of pride.

"When can Ah see it?" An eagerness had filtered into Beverly's voice.

"How about right now? That is, if you're not busy."

"Not at the moment." She opened a desk drawer and pulled out her purse. "Let's go," she said, rising. "Your car or mine?"

"I'll drive," I told her and led the way to my car.

On the way I meandered down the prettiest streets, hoping the ambiance might make a difference in our asking price. Didn't agents do a market analysis of the neighborhood?

When we drove up to the house, Beverly let out an admiring gasp, and a sudden flush of pride colored my cheeks.

"I've done what I could to restore the dying landscape," I told her. "I tried to copy what my great-grandparents had done."

"How wonderful," she said, her eyes taking in the flowering shrubbery, the immaculate front porch, and the trellis and park bench, visible to anyone who drove up the driveway.

"Why, you have created a lovely wonderland," Beverly cooed. "Are you sure you don't want to stay here and live in this quaint little house?"

"I'm sure," I said with an air of finality. "I have a job and a boyfriend and a whole other life waiting for me in New York."

"Well, Ah can guarantee, Ah'll find the right buyer. This place is ve-e-e-ry charming."

The way she strung out the word *very* had me picturing dollar signs.

Before going inside, we walked around the property to a concert of Beverly's *oohs* and *aahs*. She needed to touch everything—the trellis, the park bench, the patio furniture. She even ran her hand over the rose bushes and stirred up a hint of their aroma.

Our tour of the inside brought more accolades from my enthralled guest. She continued making notes but asked few questions. I steered her away from the rocking chair where Gram's journal lay waiting. My grandmother had meant those words for me to read and no one else.

I also kept our tour to the two floors and avoided the attic. There was no reason to get her asking about the old trunk. She already knew too much.

I drove Beverly back to her office and followed her inside. Our conversation centered solely around Gram's house. She asked a few questions, made some notations on her computer, then read through the file. It didn't take long for her to put together a listing agreement.

I squirmed a little under the watchful eye of the older woman seated at the other desk. Her nameplate read *Peg Atwater, senior agent.* It struck me that she wasn't Italian. But then, lots of other people of different nationalities had settled in Cittadina.

She stared back at me with piercing dark eyes. I got a strange feeling that she was trying to convey a message. A chill traveled down my spine. Though I made every effort to ignore her steady gaze, it troubled me that she found my transaction more interesting than the pile of documents on her desk.

Beverly continued to make notes and shuffle papers, behaving like she hadn't noticed Peg Atwater's eagle eye. She printed out a listing agreement—twelve pages in all. I assumed most of those pages were duplicates of what every other client received, with a few particulars related only to my house.

She leaned toward me and arched an eyebrow. "Have you thought of an asking price, Miss Capellini?"

I nodded. I'd had a figure in my head since day one, but I took a chance and went higher. "I think $150,000 sounds fair."

She tilted her head and frowned. "I don't know. That sounds a little high for 1,300 square feet of living space, and no garage." She gestured toward her computer screen. "I completed a market analysis of your neighborhood. Similar homes have been selling for a lot less. Some haven't even topped the $100,000 mark."

I thought about George Newman and the kind of deal he'd likely been offering. He could bring down the value of every house in the neighborhood.

I matched her frown with one of my own and sat back. "I've put a lot of money into the renovations," I noted. "I've been working nonstop for almost a month."

She sighed pensively and pressed a finger against her cheek.

"After walking through your grandmother's house and property, I tend to think $90,000 may be more of a logical starting point."

I shook my head. "I don't know—"

"Tell you what. We can hold an open house. A price of $90,000 will draw more potential buyers to your door. Higher offers might come in. In the end, you may even get your price, though I doubt anyone will go that high."

I chewed my bottom lip, thought, *Maybe I should call Dad*, then discarded the idea. I was supposed to be doing this on my own. Then I thought about perhaps seeing a lawyer. I could even email the information to Brian. He was trained in real estate law. Surely he could decipher the mumbo jumbo in this girl's listing agreement, maybe give me some sound advice.

I squashed that idea too. My boyfriend was sitting in a classroom at UCLA, finishing up a course in negotiations. He'd be too busy to take my call.

Anyway, at my age, I was still trying to prove that I could handle such decisions on my own. Though I wasn't above asking for advice, I cringed at the thought of running to Mommy and Daddy, or even to Brian. And for some reason I couldn't explain, I wanted to show Beverly Strong that I could check out a simple listing agreement without calling a lawyer.

I read over the agreement, page by page, even the fine print, and kept nodding my head like I understood the terminology. Then clenching my teeth, I picked up the pen and signed the first page, then I scribbled my initials on every line marked by a red arrow.

One notation in small print troubled me. Something about giving the agent full power to finalize a deal with a buyer of her choice. I'd actually frowned when I read it, then brushed it off as real estate jargon and nothing more.

Fifteen minutes later, I left the real estate office with a copy of the documents. I drove to the little grocery store three blocks away and picked up a few essentials. Then I went home, convinced I had left the sales transaction in the hands of a competent agent.

But the older woman's unnerving stare continued to bother me. Though Peg Atwater hadn't said a word, something about her manner kept me wondering if something was up. Call it sixth sense or women's intuition, whatever, I couldn't shake the uneasiness. If there'd been another sales office, I would have made a switch, but as far as I could see, I had no other choice. The tiny office seemed to be the only one in Cittadina.

I walked around the kitchen like a zombie, putting away groceries. Then I fixed a cup of tea, sat at the kitchen table, and read over the documents for the third time, and then the fourth. The agreement was for six months. Of course, in the best scenario, the house would sell within a few weeks. I didn't intend to wait around. I had considered a few more enhancements for the house, which I could do in a couple days.

I also needed to finish emptying Gram's trunk before I left for New York. Suddenly, out of nowhere, a twinge of guilt seized my heart. I had raced off to the real estate office with so much determination, I hadn't stopped to consider if this was what Gram might have wanted. *Why does anybody give someone a whole house?* I asked myself. *To sell?* I doubted it. *Or to live in?* That made more sense.

Gram didn't leave her house to my brother or any of my cousins. And, why not? Because she knew they would have sold it without ever touching it with a paint brush. They would have unloaded it, as is, no repairs, no loving care.

So, why me? Why the single granddaughter living the high life in New York City? The one with a career and a boyfriend and a future plan that didn't include living in an old house in Cittadina. The one who had left her hometown promising herself she'd never return.

Why, Gram? Why did you choose me?

Then I knew. She had chosen me because she could trust me. She knew I wouldn't let her beloved home fall in the wrong hands. Like George Newman. She knew I would love the house because I loved her. And for the same reason, she'd left me that secret trunk in the attic and everything it held, knowing it would draw me closer to my roots. As a newspaper reporter, my curiosity had taken over. I dove into the lives of people who had permeated those walls from the day the house was a drawing on a blueprint to the present time.

My great-great-grandfather built the house. My great-grandparents had filled the property with color. My gram had permeated the inside with the flavors and aromas of Italy. So, was it *my* turn now? My turn to move in and leave a part of myself here?

It struck me then that 122 Maple Street was more than a house, more than a piece of real estate. It was my heritage. And less than two hours ago, I'd signed it away for good.

Still troubled by my indecision, I went back to Gram's journal if only to escape from reality. I picked up where I'd left off. It was like reading a novel, every page led to another adventure.

I expected to read another of Gram's fantastic stories in which she was supposed to be the main character, when her journal entries took a surprising leap into the everyday life of a busy mom. She now spoke of christenings, birthday parties, and holiday get-togethers.

It was 1965, and she was volunteering at a veterans' hospital in Rochester, where she helped with feedings, sponge baths, shaves, and bandages. As enthusiastically as she'd spoken about her climbing team, she talked about the soldiers in her care.

Those Vietnam veterans have the lowest self-image of anyone I've ever seen, she wrote. *My heart goes out to them. I can do little to lift their spirits. They've come home to a society that either rejects them or fears them. People spit in their faces or they avoid them completely. I ask myself, how can I make a difference? Sometimes, I read a few verses of scripture to one of them. Some lap it up like a thirsty animal. Others don't want to hear what God has to say. They feel abandoned by their fellow man. They're fighting a different kind of war. Only the location and the enemy have changed.*

When I look at them, I can't help but think about my brother Car-mine. He was in the Navy, stationed at Pearl Harbor, Hawaii. He went down with the Arizona. Someday I want to visit his watery grave and pay tribute to my big brother.

I can't explain why Gram's words had me choking up. She'd lost two relatives to senseless wars. Her brother and her son, who perished in Afghanistan. Through her writing, Gram had drawn me into her own heart so deeply, I'd discovered a whole new world of emotions there. Even though she was gone, we were now developing a bond I'd never known before.

I was about to read on when the doorbell rang. Reluctantly, I put down the journal and went to open the front door, shocked to find Peg Atwater standing on the porch.

I stood speechless for several seconds. *Peg Atwater? At my front door? But why?* Though confused, I stepped back and welcomed her inside.

The woman still wore the same scowl I'd seen at the real estate office, like it had been permanently etched on her face. Her slight frame shuffled past me, and she waited while I shut the door. I invited her into the kitchen with a wave of my hand. Neither of us had spoken a word yet. I, because I was stunned silent, and Peg, for reasons unknown to me. I braced myself for whatever tirade might spew from those pursed lips. Perhaps Beverly had overstepped her position, taking a client without first checking with the boss.

Or maybe she had bad news about the potential sale of my house.

"Would you like a cup of tea?" I offered, breaking the silence.

"Tea would be nice." Her voice was surprisingly soft, the antithesis of her sour expression. She settled into a kitchen chair and folded her hands on the table.

I turned on the teakettle and put together a plate of Mom's cookies, set them on the table with cups and sugar, and went back for the teapot. All the while, neither of us spoke. I didn't mention the nice weather we'd been having or the great time everyone had at the festival. None of the usual small talk. I poured the tea and took a seat across from her. Then I waited. It was Peg Atwater's party.

"I suppose you're wondering why I'm here," she began as she dunked her teabag.

She gazed at my face, like she was waiting for a response. I nodded, then tended to my own tea.

"I wanted to stop you," she said. Then her shoulders tensed a little as she transferred the tea bag to the saucer. "You made a deal you might live to regret, and I didn't know how to prevent it from happening."

An uneasy frown had crossed my forehead and I stared open-mouthed at the little woman.

"If you recall, I was on the phone when you entered my office." She took a careful sip of the hot liquid. "You approached Beverly and there was nothing I could do. Nothing I could say."

I found my voice. "I had the feeling you wanted to tell me something. Are you saying I shouldn't have signed with Beverly?"

The stern shadow returned to Ms. Atwater's face. "That's *exactly* what I'm saying." Her voice had a sharp edge. "Without knowing it, you may have sold your grandmother's house down the river."

She let out a sigh, then continued. "Last year, the main office transferred out the young man who'd been working with me for five years. They replaced him with Beverly, brought her up from Texas about the same time the Newman Brothers came to town. I'm certain that girl is helping them acquire properties in Cittadina, and for mere pennies. They're demolishing the old homes, and in their place they're erecting prefab houses and selling them for top dollar."

I thought about the homes I had passed during my walk through town. The piles of rubble on some lots, the shiny new constructions that had gone up seemingly overnight, and the signs out front boasting *A New And Better Way Of Living*.

"Don't look so shocked," Ms. Atwater said. "Those people

want to destroy the historic ambiance of Cittadina, one house at a time."

"My grandmother's house included?"

"Yes, your grandmother's house, too, if you agree to the sale." She breathed a heavy sigh, sipped her tea and ignored the cookies. "I knew your grandmother well," Ms. Atwater continued, her voice pensive. "She was my babysitter when I was growing up. She was like a second mother to me, fed me well—oh, my, those Italian concoctions—I must have gained ten pounds that first year she sat with me."

The prune face had broken into a wide smile, and Ms. Atwater's eyes began to water.

"I attended your grandmother's funeral, though you must not have noticed me for the huge crowd that filled the little church."

She reached across the table and gently grasped my hand. "Your grandmother was one of the nicest people I've ever known. She loved her town. She loved the people. And I need to tell you, she loved her house. I would hate to see anything bad happen to it."

Ripples of anxiety coursed through my veins. I narrowed my eyes, not in offense to Peg Atwater, but out of fear that I'd made a grave mistake. I needed to know more. Unlike my New York apartment, the house on Maple Street was meant to be more than a place to eat and sleep. It had meant a lot to Gram and to my ancestors before her, and it should have meant more to me than I had allowed. At that moment, I wasn't sure I wanted to sell it at all.

I came right out and asked the question that had been preying on my mind. "What can I do, Ms. Atwater?"

"Please, call me Peg."

I nodded. "Is it too late to break the deal I made with Beverly Strong?"

"I think there might be a way, although she may have included an iron-clad clause within the fine print, perhaps wording that gave her more control than you might want her to have. She called it a listing agreement, but I'm thinking it was more of a contract."

"I guess I picked the wrong agent," I conceded.

"If you'd come to me, there'd be no problem," Peg assured me. "I never make those pre-sale arrangements. My work with the folks of Cittadina has always involved a handshake and a commitment to search for a buyer. Nothing more. Until I make a sale, I refrain from shoving binding papers in front of my clients."

I nodded but didn't comment. My heart was pounding so hard I couldn't drink my tea.

She chewed her bottom lip for a moment and the prunish wrinkles returned to her face.

"Let me do some digging, and I'll get back to you. Perhaps it's not too late. And remember," she said, unscrewing her face and raising her eyebrows with optimism. "You can always refuse any offers that come in. Especially if they come from Newman Brothers." She shrugged. "You can simply tell Beverly you've changed your mind."

She thought a minute then added, "Of course, those hustlers may find a way to sweep this house right out from under you simply by using a false name for the sale."

I frowned at the thought. "The listing agreement is for six months," I informed her.

"I'll see what I can do," was all she said.

I stood at the open front door as Peg Atwater drove away. Her warning left me wondering how forceful Newman Brothers might get if I refused their offer. What kind of group was that, anyway? I doubted they would give up before trying everything they could to get my gram's house.

I needed to talk to some of the neighbors. For sure, I'd have to tell Dad about what happened. Maybe we could approach the city council together, get some officials involved, perhaps run Newman Brothers out of town on a rail, like folks did in my great-great-grandfather's day. Tar and feathers seemed appropriate. I snickered over the image.

My work at the newspaper had uncovered similar scams in the big city. If the battle became rigorous enough, I could call on my contacts in New York and find out what to do. Getting up a petition might help.

It had become a natural course of events for me to escape into Gram's journal. For a month I'd been consumed by my work on a 132-year-old house I owned but didn't want. With all that had happened over the past couple of days, I needed to immerse myself in Gram's journal—whether the tales it told were true stories or not.

So, with lunchtime looming, I made a peanut butter-and-jelly sandwich, poured myself a glass of milk, and settled in the old rocker. Then I steeled my imagination for another trip into Gram's wild fabrications.

The next entries had me laughing out loud. Gram had concocted an assortment of sensational journeys into fantasyland. Now I was certain they were false.

In one entry, dated *April, 1970*, Gram swept me away with her escapades at the world's fair in Osaka, Japan. With unmasked delight she described the unusual and elegant pavilions. She wrote about the Rainbow Tower, the Tower of the Sun, pagodas, pavilions, and a real Japanese garden filled with cherry blossoms and huge bonsai trees. She raved about the advancements in technology—the unveiling of the first mobile phone, the premiere of the first IMAX movie, robotics, airplanes of the future, and household appliances unlike anything she'd ever seen, but commonplace in my day. She mentioned a Japanese pavilion that was run completely on gas, from the air conditioner to the film projector that showed a comedy on a huge screen.

Then, in a moment of prideful reflection, she wrote about the United States pavilion.

The exploration of space display included a moon rock brought back by the Apollo 12 astronauts. That was the highlight of my time at

the fair. The shows were entertaining, the rides were thrilling, and the cuisine was delicious, but that moon rock took my breath away. Oh, if only I could make that trip and pick up one of my own.

Gram also claimed to have visited an underground disco following a high velocity train ride from Osaka to Tokyo.

They call it the "bullet train. It travels ninty miles an hour and is never late.

I had to chuckle. I'd recently read that the fastest train in the world today is China's Maglev magnetic railway that travels 180 miles per hour, literally double the speed of Gram's supposed ride.

I couldn't help but wonder where Poppa was all this time. If Gram really took all those trips, she'd done so alone, for she made no mention of anyone accompanying her. One more reason for me to think of her escapades as mere fantasy.

I shook my head and moved on to her entry of *March, 1971,* which turned out to be one of her most fascinating accounts yet.

For her next trip, Gram went to Israel's Sinai Desert, where she claimed to have stayed overnight in St. Catherine's Monastery at the base of Mount Sinai.

Sure, I said to myself. *And, what brochure did you read to concoct this story?*

Gram told a reasonably believable tale about eating a thick stew she'd assumed came from a camel and was served to her by cassock-clad monks. She slept on a narrow, uncomfortable cot, rose the next morning while it was still dark, then dressed in many layers of clothing for a journey up the mountain where Moses was said to have received the Ten Commandments directly from God.

I wore shorts and a T-shirt, then added khaki slacks, a long-sleeved shirt, and a heavy jacket. Our party of two dozen people gathered outside of the monastery, where our guide gave us the option of climbing Mount Sinai on foot or by riding one of the camels. I chose to ride, but several folks shied away from the restless animals.

A Bedouin driver helped me climb onto the wooden saddle. I grabbed the horn and kept my balance as the animal rose to stand, rear end coming up first and then his front. What a precarious spot up there, with the ground far below and a huge mountain looming in the blackness before me.

Still, I wasn't sorry I'd chosen to ride. The journey uphill took two hours in near total darkness with our sure-footed beasts navigating the trail. About halfway up, we reached a place too steep and rocky for the camels, so we dismounted and prepared to go the rest of the way on foot. By this time, the sky had turned a light gray and revealed the uneven face of the nearly vertical elevation. I was grateful I'd worn hiking boots, which made my uphill ascent more secure. But I couldn't help but wonder how Moses did the same climb in sandals.

By the time I reached the top, my leg muscles ached, and I was shivering from the cold. Our guide ushered us into a wooden shack where a large kettle of black coffee simmered over a rock-hewn fire pit. He filled paper cups with the thick, dark liquid and passed them out to our group. Though I like cream and sugar in my coffee, none of those condiments were available up there on the brink of nowhere. Cold as I was, I sucked up the hot, bitter liquid like it was a fountain treat. The shivering subsided, and we soon were joined by folks who had decided to make the climb entirely on foot. I heard many regrets and complaints about tired legs and aching backs.

With the camels long gone, all of us had to walk down. By this time, the sun was directly overhead. We began to shed our outer clothing until most of us ended up in shorts and T-shirts. As I made my way over each rocky ledge, I caught my breath at the sight of sheer drop-offs beside the narrow trail we had traversed in the dark on camelback. In broad daylight those precipices had me quivering at the thought of how close we had come to falling off the side. Thankfully, our camels must have had night vision or something, because they made the climb flawlessly.

The rest of our trip to the desert brought us by bus up Mitla Pass on our way back to Jerusalem. Two guards armed with Uzis accompanied us, and our driver wore a shoulder holster with a pistol. Hundreds, maybe thousands of deserted tanks lay broken and ravaged along the sides of the road, remnants of the Six-Day War. Camels grazed on clumps of grass nearby. Most of them had been hobbled and couldn't move about much. Our guide told us they were being protected from stepping on the many land mines buried beneath the soil near the road. Needless to say, none of us stepped off the bus.

I lowered Gram's journal to my lap and breathed a long sigh. What an imagination that woman had. But she'd given facts that could only be told by someone who'd been there. Or someone who *knew* people who'd been there. Or someone who'd *read* about people who'd been there. I decided to withhold judgment.

More stories Gram told me when I was a little girl came flooding back with each account I read. Her written notes were merely abridged versions of the detailed stories she'd recited to me back then. As I turned my innocent eyes up to her face, she'd gone on and on about the dangers poor imaginary Francine had encountered.

Now I shook my head, fascinated that she'd sucked me into her delusions and had me believing Francine the Adventuress was real.

I went back to the journal. Gram's concluding entries on her *trip to Israel* centered around the holy sites in Jerusalem and Bethlehem. She shared the thrill of placing her hand on the gnarled trunk of a 2,000-year-old olive tree, the sadness that swept over her while standing on Calvary, the shock of seeing teenage boys and girls in uniform with rifles slung over their shoulders, and the disappointment of being approached by hawkers selling plastic figures of Jesus and Mary outside the shrines.

Her next paragraph had me nodding in agreement.

If a person can look past the commercialism and ignore the wars that left their debris nearly everywhere, it's easy to disappear into the past and imagine how things were when Israel's prophets walked the earth and, better yet, when Jesus came here in the flesh. I will never forget the intense joy of having walked where Jesus did.

I took a break then and brewed myself a cup of coffee. Then I ambled out to the front porch. Sitting there, on Gram's wicker swing while enjoying my coffee, I allowed my thoughts to drift back to another day and time when my ancestors sat on that very porch and waved at folks who walked by. They must have sipped their coffee or tea or lemonade and talked about the simple things of life, like what time the postman would come with the morning mail, or whether to mow the lawn tomorrow, or should we visit the widow across the street to see how she's doing. Their entire lives revolved around family, church, and the tight, little community around them.

I began to relax after the throes of yesterday. Fifty to a hundred years ago, small town life was less complicated. Residents of Cittadina either worked during the week at white collar jobs, or they strained their backs in the rail yard, the grist mill, or on one of the many farms that skirted the countryside. They took pride in their work, rarely strove for something better or more lucrative. People were contented back then. None of this climbing the corporate ladder or breaking the glass ceiling like people want to do today.

Maybe for Gram, excitement came through one of her overseas trips—if they really happened. Maybe her stories helped her escape from the daily grind.

Like so many people of my generation, I'd taken a different road. A road that drew me away from small town life and took me to the excitement and pressures of big city life. The truth was, I had dedicated the past ten or fifteen years to the so-called rat race. Since coming to Cittadina, I had temporarily gotten off of that merry-go-round.

Working on the house and reading Gram's journal had given me a whole different perspective. Walking around Cittadina had drawn me back to my youth. It really wasn't that bad.

I stopped short and began to lecture myself. *Don't get caught up in the fairytale. Your place is in New York. You know you could never be happy anywhere else.*

Again, an internal battle raged within me. In a few days, I needed to go back to the city. Yet, part of me wanted to take down Beverly's For Sale sign and cancel the deal. I felt tormented. One minute I was determined to go back, the next I was dreaming about what it would be like to live in Gram's house. When I was in New York, I didn't struggle with such uncertainty. I had a job I did well, followed all the rules, and set my goals. I had a comfortable relationship with a man I might even marry one day. I had friends, coworkers, people I met with on a regular basis. What more could a single, unattached woman want?

I returned to the house and looked around at what I had accomplished. The renovations were nearly complete. I had nothing else to do but finish cleaning out Gram's old trunk. Then, it would be time to go. I returned to her journal, knowing when I finished reading it, I'd be nearly done.

Moments later I was once again lost within her stories. Real or false, they had grabbed my attention. I'd become an addict of sorts, looking for the next upper. Gram's stories had served as an escape. When I was reading her journal, I didn't have to think about real life, didn't have to make a decision or worry about Newman Brothers or think about what was going to happen to the house.

I flew through the next few entries. They included a variety of excursions—sky diving in Zephyrhills, Florida, a zip line adventure in Brown County, Indiana, ice skating on a lake in Canada, a ski trip in Salt Lake City, and a cruise to the Bahamas. Summer of 1978, Gram wrote about a motor scooter tour around the island of Taiwan. Her flowery descriptions painted beautiful pictures of Keelung Harbor with its turquoise water, Yehliu Park with its amazing natural rock formations, the grottos, the waterfalls, and the ancient pagodas.

I recalled hearing about fictional Francine's escapades during my youth while sitting with Gram on the front porch swing. Now I was reading about them in her journal.

Gram's children had grown up and had kids of their own

by the time she claimed to have done many of those things. There she was, maybe a grandmother already. Did she really run off to far-away places? Did she leave Poppa at home to fend for himself?

For that matter, why was there no mention of Poppa in all of Gram's travels? It appeared that she had gone alone. So, why didn't Poppa go with her? Or one of their three sons? My dad, for instance. The fact that she joined those tour groups by herself cast more doubt on those fantastic stories of hers.

A possible answer came in an entry she wrote in the spring of 1980 during Gram's cross-country hot air balloon ride in New Mexico.

How I wish Alberto could have been there with me. My husband does not share my spirit of adventure, but he is kind enough to wish me well, and he stays home and takes care of things, while I check off more items from my bucket list.

There was my answer. Poppa stayed home, and Gram went running off chasing her dreams. If that were true, then they had a most unusual marriage. Two people with different personalities and goals, living together, loving each other, and supporting their chosen activities. There was no indication of jealousy or mistrust.

I sat back and continued to read her account about the balloon ride.

Three of us climbed into the basket along with Sam, the owner of the balloon. I wasn't prepared for the lift off, the blast of propane, or the eerie silence during our flight. Other balloons lifted off at the same time. We drifted over the terrain, unhampered by the flow of traffic on the highway below. All around us, an entire army of silk balls dotted the clear, blue sky with color. Aside from the occasional

whoosh of hot air filling one of the balloons, we could hear dogs barking and people talking on the ground below us. Music poured from car radios, and children shouted and ran across a field, trying to keep up with our balloons.

In time, the sun dipped lower in the west, but a gentle breeze sent us in the opposite direction to a place where desert and prairie collided. The landscape turned from green to brown, and the ground was flat enough to land safely. Sam adeptly controlled our craft, took us higher, then lower, and finally selected a spot for our landing. We anchored there among a host of other balloons. As the sun dipped beyond the mountains and the sky turned black, they kept the balloons inflated just enough to create a brilliant display of giant colored light bulbs resting on the ground for the night.

The following spring of 1982, she wrote about a trip to Florida when she hit a couple theme parks, then stopped at an alligator attraction, where she convinced one of the handlers that she was a writer working on a story for a magazine. He escorted her into an exhibit, singled out one of the gators named "Sunshine," bound its mouth with electrical tape and let her climb aboard the beast. That, to me, was one of her most unbelievable tales.

In the summer of that same year, Gram claimed she took twenty hours of flying lessons in a Cessna 150.

I loved the thrill of the takeoff and the challenge of landing in a crosswind. I worked hard to find my way back to the airport using the visual guideposts—railroad tracks, drive-in movie theaters, and specific highways. Best of all, I was able to solo on my 60th birthday!

I had neared the end of Gram's journal entries. The last one was dated *May 1989.*

This one I had no trouble believing. Gram said she flew to

Hawaii where she enjoyed a Polynesian luau, a boat ride on the Pacific, and a helicopter excursion over a volcano. Before returning home, she visited Pearl Harbor, a reminiscence that brought tears to my eyes.

I went there to pay tribute to my brother, Carmine, who lost his life at Pearl Harbor on December 7, 1941. I pulled an orchid from the lei around my neck and tossed it into the water, then watched it float lazily off to sea.

"Goodbye, Carmine," I quietly sobbed. "Thank you for your sacrifice. In fact, thank you all."

So, in the midst of all her fantastic tales, Gram had occasionally inserted a little truth. I had no idea how to determine which were made-up stories and which were reality. Perhaps it didn't really matter. Gram had enjoyed telling them to me, and I had enjoyed hearing them as a child. Now, I'd enjoyed them again.

The remaining pages were blank. I closed the book and sat for a long time, just breathing. I didn't move until the sun dipped below the horizon. At that point, I started hitting wall switches.

I stored Gram's journal in the hutch along with the other items I'd found in the trunk. I still had to go through the album and the box that lay on the bottom. They were the last two treasures Gram had left behind.

Early the next morning, I phoned Mom and told her I was coming over for breakfast. I wanted to talk to Dad about the real estate deal I'd signed with Beverly Strong. And we needed to decide what to do about Newman Brothers.

My folks always got up at the break of dawn and had breakfast by 7:30. Instead of driving, I jogged the couple of blocks to their house.

I didn't hit Dad with my concerns the minute I walked in, not before his second cup of coffee. I sipped an orange juice and got to work on the Spanish omelet Mom had whipped up for me. Dad asked how the work was going on the house.

"You guys need to come over and see the finished product," I said, dangling a long-awaited invitation. "I think you'll be pleased. Everything's done."

"How's this afternoon?" Dad suggested.

I nodded and kept eating. Then Gram's journal came to mind. "Say, Dad, I need to know, did Gram *really* do all those things she talked about when I was a kid? You know, those crazy stories she told me about a girl named Francine who traveled the world and had all kinds of wild adventures?"

He snickered and cut into his omelet. "What do *you* think, Frannie?"

"I think she was a very good storyteller."

"I guess you found her journal."

"I did. I've been reading it. I found her entries as unbelievable as the stories she told me when I was a child. I didn't believe them then, and I don't believe them now."

Mom was at the sink. Her shoulders kept shaking, like she was trying to keep from laughing out loud.

A sly smile crept across Dad's lips. He hid behind his cup and drained the rest of his coffee.

Flustered, I set down my fork. "Are you two gonna tell me or not?"

Dad's blue eyes sparkled with mirth. "Have you found the photo album?"

"It's in the trunk. I haven't looked at it yet.

"Then, you'll find out soon enough," he said with finality.

I could see I was getting nowhere. I figured it was time to turn the conversation to the problem with the Newman Brothers.

"Remember that newspaper article, Dad, the one about those contractors coming here from Texas to demolish the old houses?"

Dad's smile disappeared. "Do I remember? Like it's etched on my forehead."

Mom plunged a dish into soapy water. "He tossed and turned that whole night. I hardly got a wink of sleep."

"Why do you bring this up now, Fran?" Dad said, frowning.

I steeled myself for his reaction. "One of their front men came to Gram's house and made me an offer."

Dad straightened. "You didn't take it, did you?"

I shook my head. "No, but I think I did something just as stupid."

Dad froze and gave me his full attention. Mom shut off the water and turned away from the sink. She fixed her eyes on me.

I looked back and forth between their two inquisitive faces.

"I signed an agreement with a real estate agent, and now I have reason to believe she's been hired by Newman Brothers to help acquire the old homes. But," I added in my defense. "I didn't know until later, when her associate came to the house and warned me."

Mom was wiping her hands on a towel, but it looked more like she was wringing them. Dad leaned toward me, his face screwed up in disappointment.

"Look," I said, before either of them could speak. "Ms. Atwater, the other agent, thinks I might be able to get out of the contract."

Mom nodded. "I know Peg. She's a good woman, belongs to my sewing club. But what can *she* do?"

Before I could answer, Dad spoke up. "Exactly what did that contract say?"

I shrugged. "It says the agent has power to go ahead and pursue a buyer, maybe even close the deal." I licked my lower lip. "Listen, you both knew I wanted to fix up the place and sell it. I've been straight about that from the beginning."

They just looked at each other and then back at me.

"Mom, I told you from the start I wasn't gonna stay. I simply wanted to honor Gram's wishes and make the renovations."

I began to crumble and expected a gusher of tears at any moment. Then, Dad did the strangest thing. Instead of reprimanding me, he reached out and placed his hand gently on mine. The frown left his forehead, his eyes glistened, and his entire demeanor softened.

"It's okay, darlin'. You didn't do anything wrong."

Tears came, not from my anxiety of moments ago, but out of a deep love for my father. Mom handed me a tissue, and for a moment I basked in the love and compassion of two people who had taught me more than the basics of life. They'd taught me what it means to love unconditionally, not only in the way they treated me, but also by setting an example in the way they treated each other.

I mopped the moisture from my eyes and gazed at Dad. "Remember what you said about going to the mayor's office and approaching the city council?"

He grunted. "I was spouting off."

"Well, I took you seriously, Dad." A surge of courage rose up inside me. I wanted to make things right. I stared at him with determination in my eyes. "Let's do it. Let's go to Mayor Bosco and ask him what can be done to stop this invasion of our town."

I had said *our* town. Not *your* town or even *his* town, but *our* town. A fire had been kindled inside me, and it was about to build into a raging blaze. I wanted to fight. I wanted to summon the reporter instincts I'd left sitting at my desk at the *New York Dispatch* and conduct my own investigative research right here in Cittadina, *my* hometown.

"Look, Dad. We can take legal steps. We can talk to the mayor, get him on our side, and we can get our issue on the agenda of the next city council meeting. When do they meet?"

"The first and third Tuesdays of each month at 6 PM," Dad said with a nod. "But we can go to the mayor's office right now."

I rose from my chair. "You comin' with us?" I asked Mom.

Her face was aglow, like she'd just seen her first grandchild. "I wouldn't miss this for the world," she said. She untied her apron, flung it on a chair, and went for her purse.

Dad was chuckling. "Come on." He stood to his full height and tossed his napkin on the table. "Let's go see the mayor."

The three of us waited on soft leather chairs in the outer office, while Mayor Don Bosco finished his morning phone calls. His secretary, Miss DiMucci, kept glancing up from her paperwork, smiling, like she was making a silent plea for our patience.

"He'll be a few minutes," she said more than once.

A half hour later, a buzzer on Miss DiMucci's desk sounded. She ushered us into Mayor Bosco's office and shut the door behind us. We settled on three plush chairs across from Bosco's desk. He lolled on the other side, his high-backed, ergonomically correct, executive chair nearly disappearing beneath his bulky frame. Mayor Bosco had to be at least 300 pounds. On his desk stood a thermos of steamy liquid and the remnants of a box of donuts. He blinked like a man who was about to fall asleep.

I hoped hizzoner the mayor would stay awake long enough to hear our plea.

Dad plunged right in. First, he cited the newspaper article, then he mentioned Gram's house as an example of the many homes targeted for demolition by the team from Texas.

"We need to stop them before they go any further," Dad pressed.

"What do you suggest, Nick?"

Dad scowled at the affront. "You're the mayor, *Don*. What do *you* suggest? You're the one who knows the laws, the one who can bring this up before the council. Surely, there's something *you* can do."

"I can support you and anyone else who wants to complain, but my hands are tied. There's an election coming up in November. Why, I might not even be in office to follow this through."

"You will if you stand up for your voters." Dad's words had grown louder and more pronounced. "I'm talking about folks who will sell off their properties and live to regret it. Some have already bought into this deal. The newspaper article said Newman Brothers have managed to have some of the properties condemned and made worthy of demolition. The residential streets of Cittadina are riddled with Newman Brothers signs. Old houses are coming down at a paralyzing rate of speed. In another month, you won't recognize this quaint little town you've faithfully served for the past twelve years."

I beamed with pride at Dad's bold and masterful handling of the issue. We waited in silence while Mayor Bosco cleaned his teeth with his tongue, emitting little popping sounds. He spent the next two minutes pouring coffee into a mug and drinking it.

He's stalling, I figured.

Mom straightened, like she was about to say something. Dad gently pressed his hand against her wrist. Like a typical reporter, I took it all in, scribbled on a notepad and sorted through the usual questions when approaching a civic leader.

But, first, I wanted to see the mayor's reaction to Dad's challenge.

The big man lowered his coffee cup to the desk and pressed a finger to his plump lips, like he was sorting through possible responses.

"Nick," he said at last. "I'm not sure I agree with your concerns.

Those old wooden matchboxes should have come down long ago. You, as well as I, live in the true historic district." He shook his head. "Those old houses have far too many flaws. Ancient electrical wiring, faulty plumbing, roofs that sag and leak. They're an eyesore, my friend. An eyesore."

Dad slid to the edge of his seat. "Not *all* are falling apart, Mayor. I just had an inspection done on my mother's house. It's in top condition, can rival any of the newer homes being built."

"Well, that's one," the mayor said, snickering.

Dad's face turned bright red. I needed to speak up before he launched into a tirade he might regret.

"Mayor Bosco," I began, my tone serious, my eyes glued to his face. "I work as a reporter in New York City. I'm considering writing a follow-up to the story that ran yesterday morning in the Gazette. I'd like to know why you're siding with the builder."

He accepted my question with a nod. "Like the newspaper article said, Walmart has plans to build a huge warehouse and state-of-the-art grocery store outside of town. Other big businesses will be sure to follow, which will enhance the economic structure of Cittadina and put us on an equal playing field with bigger cities. It stands to reason we should also upgrade and modernize our residential sections. In the end, everyone will benefit."

I frowned and shook my head. "What you're proposing, Mayor, is the end of small town America."

"No, I'm proposing progress."

I glanced at my father, expecting him to say something. He didn't. Then he set his eyes on me as though prompting me to keep going. Inside I was smiling. First, my dad had stepped back and had allowed me to handle the house renovations on my own. Now, he was yielding the floor to his reporter daughter. It couldn't get any better than that.

I plunged ahead with confidence. "Mr. Mayor, I know how these big conglomerates work. They slither into town, sweet-talk officials—maybe even pay some of them off." I thought Bosco might have squirmed a little. "They delude the homeowners, one at a time, into believing they're getting a lucrative deal. When someone stands firm and refuses to sell, they get the town leaders to condemn the property. Then they strike. I'm concerned for my grandmother's house and for many others. I came here to talk to you before I interview anyone else. I intend to visit the folks who are being pressured by Newman Brothers, people who still own homes built by their ancestors. Mayor Bosco, I want to know, what do you intend to do about this?"

He cleared his throat, shifted in his chair, then his sharp eyes daring me, he gave me what journalists call, *a safe answer.*

"I will discuss this with the other council members and get back to you in a few days."

"That'll be too late, Mayor. My boyfriend is a New York lawyer. If I need to, I'll get him up here to take a closer look." His smirk didn't dissuade me. "I'll do whatever I can to protect my grandmother's house from going down."

"Isn't that a conflict of interest?" he retorted, a smirk on his round, flushed face.

"Not if it's part of a class action lawsuit."

We had embarked on a tennis match type of argument. Words go back and forth and nobody wins. I had to stop the confusion.

"How do we get our item on the agenda for the next meeting?" I asked him.

"File for it online."

"Thank you, Mayor, we'll see you there."

With that, the three of us stood up and marched out of his office, leaving him slack-jawed and frowning.

CHAPTER TWENTY-FIVE

My folks and I stopped at Mama Mia's Cafe, settled around a little table in a quiet corner, and ordered three coffees and blueberry scones. All three of us wanted to hash over what had happened at the mayor's office. We needed to set a plan in motion, and we had to do it fast, before the next meeting of the council.

"Is that true what you said, that your lawyer boyfriend might come up and help us?" Mom's face lit up like she was planning my wedding.

"I don't know, Mom. He's in California right now at a workshop at UCLA, but he'll be back in the city this coming weekend. If I need him, I'm sure he'll hop on a flight and get here as fast as he can." I added a gentle reminder. "Remember, we're only dating right now. No marriage plans. So let's stick with the issue at hand."

Mom smiled at me through her disappointment, then bit into her scone.

For the next hour, we tossed around ideas. In the end, we agreed that I needed to go home and apply for a spot on the agenda at the next city council meeting. Then, I'd spend time on the computer researching Newman Brothers Company in order to gather information for our presentation at the meeting.

My parents agreed to visit people they knew who lived in the old houses and get their reactions to the newspaper story. They also needed to encourage them to attend the city council meeting. The more support we could get, the better.

We caught up on the phone later that day. My request was accepted into the agenda. My internet search turned up three other exploitations by Newman Brothers. They'd already been to Indiana, Missouri, and Nevada. I printed out newspaper articles about a lawsuit which the people of a small town named Olsen, Indiana, filed against the Newman Brothers. To my disappointment, the court's decision went in favor of the company.

Unless we could rally the residents of Cittadina to join us at the council meeting, we didn't have much of a prayer.

Then I thought, *Maybe that's exactly what we need. Prayer.*

It had been a long time since I'd gotten on my knees and spoken to God about my problems. For the past decade or so my life had gone fairly well. I'd been on a high-speed treadmill, swept along on the rat race with all the other high energy people who knew where they were going and how to get there.

Coming to Cittadina had slowed me down. Even my sense of newspaper work had taken a back seat to my renovations on Gram's house. I'd transferred all my energy to painting and polishing the house and planting a garden. I was a duck out of water. If I were in New York City, I'd have all sorts of resources at my disposal, plus feedback from the other reporters and my editors. But this wasn't the big city. This was small town America, and I'd gotten involved in something that could turn me into a newspaper source instead of the reporter who was writing about it.

Early Tuesday morning, I jogged over to my parents' place with renewed enthusiasm and sat with Dad at the breakfast table. Mom ladled out bowls of steaming oatmeal. I buttered a piece of toast, topped it with a teaspoon of homemade strawberry jam, and laid out my plan.

"We need to stop Newman Brothers before they level another house," I began. "We need to do it legally and fast. Every few days they bring down two more houses. Before long, nothing familiar will be left standing on the streets of Cittadina."

Dad sipped his coffee, then nodded his agreement. "What do you propose, darlin'?"

"We can request that the city stop issuing demo permits to Newman Brothers. We need to go into that meeting with facts. We need to convince at least three of the council members that putting a hold on the demolitions will be the best action for now."

Dad lowered his cup to the table. "What else?"

"You and Mom already talked to a lot of the people who live in those old homes, right?"

Dad nodded. "We did. Most of the residents we talked to already had been approached by George Newman. While they didn't want their homes destroyed, they liked the idea of getting a tidy little sum in their pockets. Most of their homes need a ton of repairs. By moving elsewhere, they can start fresh with a nice down payment. Some homeowners even said they might relocate to Florida or somewhere out west or they might move in with their kids."

A wave of defeat was already sweeping over me. "Were any of them in favor of saving their homes? For sentimental reasons at least? Or, because they simply like living here?"

"A few, but I don't know if they'll be enough to make a difference."

"We need to give them an incentive, maybe talk the council into applying for a state grant to enhance their properties. That way the bulk of the cost won't fall on the homeowners. It will be handled by the grant money." I took a breath and continued. "I'd like you and Mom to revisit those folks and get them to sign a petition. I'll print one up with all the legal jargon and get it to you. We need to work fast to be ready for the meeting."

I paused, then added. "There's something else we can do."

Dad stared at me, his eyebrows raised with interest.

"I know this sounds ludicrous, but we can try to get the Historic Association to declare the homes of Cittadina of historic interest. Now, it's true, Victorian homes like yours and the mayor's are already on the historic registry. Somehow, we need to show the people of Cittadina that their homes have value that goes beyond the almighty dollar. Even if they don't qualify for a historic registry, they can still be deemed of historic interest."

"That sounds simple enough," Mom interjected. "I have friends on the Historical Association board. I can make a few phone calls today."

I nodded with enthusiasm. "Besides the old houses, a historic district also can include a huge section of the downtown business area. The barber shop has stood in the same spot for several decades. It still has the original red-and-white striped pole out front. Then there's the five-and-dime, the movie theater, the library, even the courthouse. No matter what they're used for now, they're part of the city's cultural fabric. We have to give those council members a reason to delay the demolitions."

"Do you have any legal recourse in mind?" Dad said, scraping up the last of his oatmeal.

"A preservation ordinance, complete with bylaws regarding demolitions. At the meeting we can suggest the formation of a preservation review board that will establish those guidelines. The council members can appoint a committee to oversee our local historic district's boundaries and decide what can be done safely and within the law. If they can't get a grant, then maybe tax dollars can be allocated for enhancements, so the burden doesn't fall solely on the homeowners or business people."

"Don't historic districts also have restrictions concerning renovations?" Mom interjected. "I read something about that a while back." She shrugged. "I'm just playing devil's advocate," she said with a smile. "We'll need to be ready for anything that comes up."

I smiled at her, glad to have her participating. "Of course there are restrictions," I agreed. "By discussing those issues now, we'll be more prepared when the council members present them." I paused to regroup, then pressed ahead. "We have a lot more legwork ahead of us before the meeting. We need to get the homeowners to sign the petition, and we also need to get the support of local businessmen, religious ministers, civic leaders, and other elected officials apart from the city councilmen. We'll divide up the work between the three of us and meet back here Friday afternoon. What do you say, Mom? Dad?" I looked back and forth at the two of them and held my breath.

Dad grinned like he'd just won the New York lottery. It appeared he was enjoying this whole thing. Up until now the extent of his community involvement had been filing people's taxes and reading the morning newspaper. It seemed I'd lit a fire under him, and the initial flame was about to turn into a roaring blaze.

I went home. For the next two days I got to work searching the national and state programs on the preservation of historic homes. I printed everything I found. Who else but a newspaper reporter carries a computer and printer along when planning to stay somewhere for weeks at a time? I'd even brought a large box of computer paper with me. Some people might think that was overkill. I thought it was normal.

Within a half-hour, I had created a decent package of information. Satisfied that I'd covered everything we needed, I flipped through the pages.

1966: U.S. approved the National Historical Preservation Act, which then created a National Register of Historic Places.

1980: NY State Legislature passed the State Historic Preservation Act (SHPA), which created a State Register of Historic Places.

April, 1963: NY State Municipal Home Rule Law authorized a county, city, or town to enact local laws to protect and enhance the local environment.

I also listed the qualifications for acceptance in the National Register of Historic Places:

1. *Building must be at least 50 years old.*
2. *Building must be connected to significant, historic events.*
3. *Building must be connected to the lives of significant individuals*
4. *Characteristics or construction techniques must reflect a specific time period.*
5. *Property must have prehistoric or historic significance.*

Some of those requirements fit Gram's house to a T.

I then added the benefits of being listed on historic registers:

1. *Homeowners are eligible for government funds for restoration and upkeep.*

2. *Homeowners may receive 20 percent federal income tax credits for renovations.*

3. *Whether or not properties are listed on national and state registers, local governments have the authority to enact their own zoning and historic preservation laws that offer protection from incompatible alterations and demolition by the home owner.*

This, to me, was crucial for our argument and could convince the council members that a moratorium might be necessary. The next two items held equal significance.

1. *Municipalities may establish Historic Preservation Districts that encompass certain neighborhoods, downtown areas, and other properties of historic significance.*

2. *Historic designation of homes and districts increase property values.*

Next I addressed concerns that might be posed by residents or council members. I wanted to be prepared for anything.

- *Owners of property may be opposed because they believe they will be subject to regulations that control what they can do with their property.*

The truth was, if they had not accepted federal funds for repairs or alterations, the restrictions did not apply to them.

- *They may fear they will need a permit or hearing to decide what changes can be made on their property.*

Similarly, the rules had been formed to *manage* change, not to stop it. While the most significant historic elements needed to be protected, other changes compatible with the historic architecture were allowed, particularly if deterioration had begun.

- *You have to be rich to own a historic home.*

Many modest homeowners proudly lived in homes of cultural heritage. Including Gram.

- *Preservation costs more than demolition and new construction.*

While historic buildings may have needed reinforced foundations, new roofs, electrical and plumbing upgrades, the cost of renovations could be less expensive than rebuilding on the same site. And finally—

- *Old buildings aren't as safe as modern constructions.*

In reality, safety depended more on quality of construction than on age of materials. My great-great-grandfather had proven that. Thanks to Salvatore, Gram's house was as sturdy as anything built today, maybe even stronger.

By Thursday afternoon, I looked over my notes one more time, then I flopped back in my chair and let out a sigh. It was 7 o'clock, the sun was setting, and I hadn't had dinner.

A Caesar salad and a glass of red wine sufficed. I went to bed satisfied with my research and primed for a healthy debate at the courthouse on Tuesday, which left me the weekend to kick back a little.

My plan to leave Cittadina on Monday had changed. I'd gotten involved in a battle, and I wasn't about to leave until it was settled.

CHAPTER TWENTY-SIX

On Friday, I went to my folks' house and spread ten pages of research on their kitchen table. Dad poured over the paperwork with the enthusiasm of a tax collector doing an audit.

"You did all this?" he crowed as he flipped through my notes. He shook his head in wonder. "My daughter, the reporter. You did a fabulous job, honey." He kept flipping. "This is great. Just great."

Of course I beamed. My throat all but closed up with emotion. My dad—the man who'd dreamed of me becoming a school teacher and living in Cittadina forever—had finally acknowledged my career. And he'd done so with pride.

My parents then showed their own spread of paperwork. They'd acquired 253 signatures on the petition I'd given them. Seven pages listing names, addresses, and phone numbers.

Tomorrow was Saturday. With little more to do, I suggested the three of us relax over the weekend and catch our breath. My parents agreed, saying they'd been invited to a friend's house for a barbecue Saturday afternoon. And Sunday, they would go to church and spend the afternoon in prayer and fasting.

It was time for me to visit Gram's trunk again, so I phoned Luigi's and placed a to-go order of fettuccine Alfredo and a house salad, picked up the food, then went home for another session with Gram.

This time, I sat at the table with my dinner in front of me and Gram's big, cloth-covered photo album to one side. I ran my hand over the fabric cover. The floral pattern bore a resemblance to the property's first garden, created by my great-grandparents. During Gram's last year of life, the plants had begun to fizzle along with her own declining health. Now Brian and I had restored most of the garden and even included a little patch of mature vegetable plants.

I opened the album and released a smell akin to old library books. The first few pages contained sepia toned photos. There was a shot of my great-great-grandparents—Salvatore, standing thin and tall, attired in a dark suit with a white bowtie, Rosanna beside him, swathed in white lace, her hair piled high with ribbons and a sheer veil trailing past her waist. Neither smiled, but that seemed to be the demeanor of people who posed for photos back then. Stone-faced and serious, not the hint of a smile, nor a hair out of place.

I gazed at their photo for a long time. This was the man who meticulously designed and constructed the house I'd been renovating, and this was the woman he built it for. I'd read Salvatore's ledger, knew the placement of every board, the location of every wooden nail. I pictured the four bedrooms they wanted to fill with children, the now non-existent outhouse out back, the kitchen and the most simple cooking implements—a metal sink with a hand pump, a wood-burning stove, a handmade table and chairs, crafted by my great-great-grandfather, and little feminine touches added by Rosanna.

Now, 132 years later, the house was still standing, and I was trying to save its life. The threat of demolition had awakened a fighting spirit inside me. I had already taken the first steps toward what threatened to become a major battle. Dad had joined the fight, and I was depending on his notable standing in the community and his ability to rally friends and business acquaintances. After all, he'd been born and raised in this house, and he'd spent his life working in this town and contributing to its betterment.

The next page had a photo of the house, an A-frame structure standing alone on a desolate piece of property. No flowers yet, and no trees, merely patches of scrub grass amidst dismal stretches of dirt and stone.

A family photo on the next page had Salvatore and Rosanna seated with the twin sons, Franco and Giovanni, standing on either side of them, Armando resting his head against Rosanna's arm, and, on Salvatore's lap, baby Enzo, my great-grandfather. More photos showed the kids playing stickball on the hard-packed dirt path in front of their house. Then, a picture of Enzo pulling a wooden wagon filled with homemade toys.

On the next few pages the photos turned to black-and-white. One showed a smiling Catherine surrounded by rose bushes in the backyard. Several photos had one or the other picking vegetables from the garden or tending to the array of flowers surrounding the property. In one rather special photo, Enzo was handing Catherine a bouquet of fresh-cut flowers, his face aglow with a message of love. Then, there was one of Enzo posing straight and tall in his World War I uniform, an American flag waving on the pole behind him. Finally, one showed Catherine holding baby Alberto, my grandfather, while Enzo hovered close beside her. *Home from the war,* I mused, *and starting their family.*

I kept flipping pages. A progression of photos showed the changes my ancestors made on the house and property, both outdoors and inside the house. The updates in the kitchen. A new sink with real faucets, a gas range to replace the wood-burning stove, the addition of a downstairs two-piece bathroom and laundry, the former wash tub and galvanized washboard replaced by an electric washer and dryer. The outhouse gone and in its place a shed for Gram's gardening tools. The changes didn't take away from the house's character, they enhanced it.

I tried to imagine how Catherine and Gram might have reacted to every change that took place, their thrill over updated appliances that made their homemaking far easier, and most of all, the transitions in the garden, with new flowers and shrubs blending with the mature plants and trees, plus a flourishing vegetable garden.

The photos brought to life the descriptions in Salvatore's ledger and my great-grandparents' letters. They put faces on my age-old relatives. I could see why Salvatore raved about the beautiful Rosanna. She was a gorgeous woman. I hoped I had gotten some of her genes. Perhaps my long, dark hair.

Photos then changed from the black-and-white images to full color photos of Catherine's gardens after Gram got a hold of them. I was lost within a rainbow of color surrounding the house on Maple Street. Over the years, the maple trees changed from thin saplings into full-grown, towering umbrellas of red and gold. My great-granddad planted three of them—one in the front yard and two out back, and somehow they'd survived while the rest of the garden had withered and died.

From there, the photos transitioned through each generation. Images showed Gram and Poppa with their brood of children and grandchildren. There were graduation photos of my dad and his brother, big, broad Uncle Giuseppe, and a picture of Paulo standing proudly in his Army uniform.

One photo jumped out at me and caused me to catch my breath. It was of a young, dark-haired girl in a blue graduation cap and gown. It was like looking in a mirror. Beneath the photo was written, *Viviana, high school graduation, June, 1986.*

I frowned in puzzlement. The photo was taken a few years before I was born. Yet, I'd never met anyone named Viviana. Perhaps she was an aunt or a long-lost cousin. If she were a relative, what had become of her? And, why had no one ever mentioned her to me?

Though perplexed, I forced my attention back to the album and turned another page. More family photos followed.

I couldn't help but notice that I was in a ton of photos, more than any of my cousins. Me as a baby in Gram's arms. Me in my confirmation dress. Me graduating from high school. And multiple photos of my cousins and me celebrating parties and holidays and milestones. But always, I was in the spotlight. If I'd had any doubts, I now accepted the fact that I was Gram's favorite.

When I got to the middle of the album, my hand froze on the page and I stared in astonishment. Suddenly, all of the photos were of Gram—perched high on a camel, the Judean wilderness stretching in the distance and a square-topped Mount Sinai looming behind her. Gram on the deck of a large fishing boat, her arm extended high above her head and a five-foot shark dangling from the line in her hand. Gram, her eyes big and round but with a smile on her lips, as she straddled the back of an alligator with a death-grip on his taped snout.

I turned page after page. An array of photos, all in color, confirmed the stories Gram had written in her journal, the same ones she'd told me when I was a little girl sitting beside her in the living room or on the front porch swing, stories about a make-believe adventuress who shared our name. And all the while I had assumed they'd come from the imagination of an old woman who could tell a good story.

Now I had to admit, they were all true. Gram had experienced every one of those adventures and maybe more. While I preferred to remember her in a flour-dusted apron in her kitchen or carrying a big platter of homemade spaghetti to the table, she'd once worn a life vest and went bouncing over rapids in a raft with a bunch of other laughing and screaming people. She'd ridden a motorbike around a small island in the Pacific. She'd skied the trails of Salt Lake City, dared to ride a zip line in Indiana, had gone deep sea fishing in the Atlantic, and had climbed a 10,000-foot mountain in the Alps.

Gram *hadn't* lied to me. They *weren't* made up stories. She really *did* ride the Bullet Train when she visited the world's fair in Japan. She'd slept on a hard cot in St. Catherine's Monastery, and she'd climbed Mount Sinai on a camel. She'd walked the streets of Jerusalem, traveled up Mitla Pass, and visited Calvary.

The next page showed Gram inside the basket of a hot air balloon, and another standing in front of a Cessna 150, in her hands, the torn bottom of her T-shirt with the date of her solo flight printed in large black letters. She'd done it all, and she'd lived to talk about those adventures to a wide-eyed, precocious little girl who'd adored her grandmother enough not to call her a liar.

Stunned, I continued through the album of evidence.

The last page held a photo of a teary-eyed Gram with a lei of orchids around her neck and the Arizona memorial behind her. I stared at that photo for a long time. It spoke to me about family. About loving someone so much you can't let them go even after they leave forever. Decades had passed since the Japanese bombed Pearl Harbor. Yet, she hadn't forgotten her big brother or the sacrifice he'd made for his country. And she hadn't forgotten her promise to go there and honor him. There she was, many years later, still weeping over the loss.

I had to admit, that kind of loyalty prevailed amongst my relatives. They'd come from all over the country for Gram's funeral. Aunts and uncles and cousins I hardly recognized. They dropped everything—jobs, appointments, responsibilities—and flowed in to pay tribute to our last living matriarch.

And what had I done? I'd hurriedly left home nearly fifteen years ago with no intention of ever coming back for more than a brief visit or an occasional phone call. They had become mere characters who'd played a small part in the first eighteen years of my life. Poppa's funeral ten years ago had drawn me back for only one day. Then I took off again with no plans to return for a long time.

Then Gram died. The blow of losing her hit hard. But even then I was able to move on. Until they read her will.

I wanted to reject the inheritance. I didn't want to leave the life I'd learned to love for the one I'd been trying to forget.

I closed the album. Tears slid from my eyes and dropped onto the floral fabric cover. How much more could I have learned from that wise, old sage if I had stayed around a few more years? I flipped back through those last few pages of her album, the ones that showed my grandmother as a younger woman fulfilling her bucket list. Perhaps when I became old enough to join her, she might have taken me on some of those adventures.

Never before had I acknowledged the mistake I may have made when I turned my back on my heritage and left town. All this time I'd been blaming Jeff. The truth was, I didn't run away from a broken romance. I ran away from myself. Now, Gram and this house and everything in the trunk was bringing me back to my roots.

There remained one more item in the trunk. I went to the attic, removed the box from the bottom and carried it downstairs to the kitchen. I placed it on the table, opened the top, then stared in awe. Inside were several more confirmations of Gram's wild adventures.

There was a bowling trophy with *Francine Rossi* engraved along with the accolade, *Best Player, 1940 County Tournament.* The next items had me gasping. A blue metal carabiner from her climb up Via Ferrante, a small yellow rock tagged with the words, *Mount Sinai, March, 1971,* the bottom of a T-shirt inked with the words, *Solo Flight* and the date, *June 8, 1982,* and finally, a tiny New Testament with a purple orchid pressed within its pages next to a highlighted Psalm 116:15, *Precious in the sight of the LORD is the death of His saints.*

I shook my head.

"I never knew," I said aloud. "I never knew."

Tears spilled from my eyes, and I realized I hadn't cried this much in years.

"Please, God, tell Gram I'm sorry. Sorry I didn't fully believe her. Sorry I left too soon."

In one month's time, I'd gone from a diehard newspaper reporter in the big city—a liberated woman with her own apartment doing whatever she wanted—to a ten-year-old girl who hadn't yet made up her mind about her future.

The commitments I'd made so firmly now seemed trivial. I had come back to square one. Without expecting it, I was starting over. I'd been given the chance to change my future. Such an opportunity both excited and frightened me.

CHAPTER TWENTY-SEVEN

With the city council meeting looming, I still had Monday and Tuesday free to do whatever I wanted. It was time to share with my folks all the things I'd found in the attic. Plus, I wanted them to see what I'd done to the house. I invited them for breakfast.

Before they arrived, I mixed a batter for pancakes, fried some bacon, poured three glasses of orange juice, and brewed a pot of coffee. Then I set the dining room table with three settings, a bottle of Vermont maple syrup, and a tub of whipped butter. I placed a bowl of peaches and pears in the center.

They walked into the house, turning their heads from one side to the other, taking in all I had accomplished. It was one of the best show-and-tell events of my life.

"How wonderful," Mom said, her eyes sweeping over the new appliances. "Everything looks so fresh and modern."

"Good job," Dad said, nodding.

I guided them through the rest of the house, the living room, the three bedrooms, and the bathroom. Mom paused in the doorway and nearly swooned over the spa-like decor. Candles lined up on the window ledge, two brand new sinks, and the large walk-in shower with bottles of shampoo and conditioner grouped on a shelf.

We returned to the kitchen, where I began ladling pancake batter on the hot griddle. I took a plate of them to the dining room where Dad already had taken a seat at the table. He lifted his fork and grinned. "I smell pancakes and bacon," he said.

As soon as Mom and I were seated, Dad launched into a prayer of thanks, including a word about how I had turned the house into a showplace. Then he reached for the mound of pancakes and slid three of them onto his plate.

I didn't waste any time letting them know why I'd invited them for breakfast.

"Mom? Dad?" I said. "I need to ask you guys something, and then I need to tell you something."

Dad nodded his approval but kept shoveling pancakes into his mouth.

I eyed him with pleasure, thrilled that he was enjoying the breakfast I'd prepared.

"Dad?" I repeated. "What was it like growing up in this house? What kind of memories do you have?"

He chuckled. "Other than the scraps my brothers and I got into, I'd say most of my memories are fond ones. We were like any other typical Italian-American family. We held to tradition, honored the old folks, and made sure we had plenty of good food in the house."

" What about traveling, Dad? Did you ever go anywhere with Gram?"

He stopped eating and looked at me. "So, you found the photo album."

"I sure did." I released a sigh. "Did you and your brothers know your mom was traipsing all over the world having one adventure after another, while you stayed home with Poppa?"

He nodded and reached for a piece of bacon. "That's right, but Pop asked us to keep quiet about it. He didn't want people talking about his wife like she was an unfit mother or that she'd lost her good sense. So, we waved goodbye to her and went about our own business."

He finished off the piece of bacon, then he eyed me with concern. "You have to understand, Frannie, things were different back then. A woman didn't just run off and do whatever she wanted to, not while she had young children at home. The truth was, when your Gram was home, she was completely ours. She did most of her wandering before she got married. When she married your Poppa, she settled down. After she had us kids, she put her adventures on hold and didn't start them up again until we were old enough to help our father."

I poured his coffee and waited for him to tell me more.

He took a sip, then coddled the cup in his two hands. His blue eyes began to shimmer, like he was remembering.

"My mother made the holidays something special, even those we thought of as insignificant. On Arbor Day, she went and planted a pine tree at the far right corner of the property. She said she did it in honor of her brother Carmine who was killed at Pearl Harbor. Then, years later, she planted another one on the opposite corner for my brother Paulo, who died in Afghanistan.

I blinked hard against a sudden sting in my eyes. "I remember Uncle Paulo," I said. "He was such a serious guy." I savored the memory of him for a few seconds more. "Did he ever marry?"

"Almost," my father said. "When it didn't work out, he re-enlisted and married the Army instead. The rest of us stuck around and kept celebrating holidays together. Family was important to your grandparents. They didn't let a single holiday go by without hosting some kind of party. Remember, your great-great-grandpa came here from the old country, so those family memories started with him, particularly anything to do with America, like the Fourth of July and Thanksgiving Day. Salvatore was a true patriot, as was my grandfather, Enzo, who served in World War I. They passed their patriotism down from one generation to the next."

"Which brings me to what I wanted to tell you two. In between working on the house and spending time with you guys, and now the city council business, I've been going through all that stuff in Gram's trunk. Did you ever get a chance to go through it?"

Mom smiled at me and shook her head. "I'm afraid not. Your grandmother gave strict orders that it was meant for no one but you. Neither your dad nor I ever received permission to look inside that battered old trunk. Oh, we had already seen the photo album, and once I caught a glimpse of Gram's journal, but she was firm. She told us the trunk was part of your inheritance and everything in it was for your eyes alone."

"I don't suppose Gram will mind if I shared everything with you now."

Dad's eyebrows went up. "Do you want to?"

"Of course, Dad. You need to see what I found. Journals, photos, letters—there's a whole treasure trove of memorabilia. I've gotten to know my ancestors, and I have to say, this whole experience has changed my life to some degree."

Mom rose from the table. "There's one more thing. I've also been holding something for you—again at your Gram's request. It's in the car. I put it in there when you invited us for breakfast, thinking you might be ready to see it."

Without another word, Mom headed out the door. Minutes later, she came back carrying a large family Bible, the cumbersome kind people place on their coffee table but never carry to church. Inside there was a place to write the family tree and any other notations a relative might want to add.

"Your Gram passed this to me years ago," she said, lowering the huge book to a clear spot on the table, between my father and me. "She told me to add whatever I wanted and then pass it on to you after you finished going through her trunk. So, here it is."

She smiled with satisfaction as I ran my hand over the burgundy cover and the raised words, *The Holy Scriptures,* etched in gold lettering. All the pages were edged in gold. The book must have been four inches thick, about twice the size as Tolstoy's *War and Peace,* and much larger in dimensions.

"This is a family treasure," Dad murmured, sounding like his throat had tightened up. "After your grandmother gave this to us, your mom and I signed up with a genealogical group to gather information on our family's history. We traced our roots back to Italy, before Salvatore came and settled here. We filled the blank pages at the front with the things we discovered. In fact, there was so much information, we had to slip a few extra sheets of paper inside."

He placed a hand on the cover. "Don't look at it now," he said. "Wait until we leave. There's a wealth of information in here." His eyes crinkled at the corners. "You're gonna find your roots, darlin'. You're gonna travel another adventure into the past that will likely change the way you think about yourself. And about us."

He and Mom exchanged glances, leaving me wondering what he must have meant. He slid his hand away then and sat back. I looked back and forth at my folks. They were smiling, but I detected a hint of sadness in their eyes.

"Has Tom seen this?" I wanted to know.

Mom shook her head. "Not yet. It'll be up to you to share it."

"He's older," I reminded them. "He should have seen it first."

Another shake of Mom's head. "This was your Gram's wish."

I ran a hand through my hair. I gazed at Dad, my eyes questioning. "I don't know if I deserve to be the first."

He nodded at me and smiled. "Like your mom said, it was Gram's wish."

"I'll need a wheelbarrow to move it around."

"Dad laughed then stood. "We're gonna leave you alone with it. Read it at will."

I eyed my folks with suspicion. I figured they hoped that by tracing my roots all the way back to Italy, I might be convinced to stay in Cittadina until the day I die.

Internally, I was screaming, "No!"

After they departed, I moved the Bible to the side table in the living room. I suppose I should have been curious, but couldn't handle one more journey into the past. Now that I had finished with the items in the trunk, I wanted to start looking ahead, wanted to set my mind on returning to New York.

The city council meeting was Tuesday evening. Once my parents and I made our plea to stop Newman Brothers from tearing down more homes, I could start packing. Before leaving for New York, I could open the Bible, read through the notations with an open mind, and then I could pass it, along with everything I found in Gram's trunk, to my brother.

The renovations were done. I'd signed with a real estate agent. It didn't matter to me if Beverly Strong worked the deal or if she relinquished it to Peg Atwater. I wanted the place sold, with one stipulation. Newman Brothers could not get their hands on it. I trusted plenty of other potential buyers would come to the open house.

My ancestors had made a life for themselves in Cittadina. I could have done that too, but I chose New York City. I had a job waiting for me, and a man who hopefully hadn't given up on me. My renter's one-month lease had already expired. I needed to call the girl and tell her I was coming back. Didn't she say she needed the apartment for only a few weeks until the condo she was buying was ready? Something about closing dates or whatever.

I tried to ignore the flickers of doubt that hampered my decision to leave. Even from the grave, it seemed my grandparents were pressuring me to stay. Somehow, I had to silence them. This was supposed to have been for one month, not for the rest of my life.

Tears of frustration spilled from my eyes. I was in a battle far more threatening than hand-to-hand combat. This war was being waged in my mind. And in my heart. If I didn't stand strong in my decision to go back to New York, I was bound to lose.

But I realized the truth. I wasn't fighting anyone except myself.

I thought about the people I could affect with my decision— people I had placed behind my own needs and wants. If I stayed in Cittadina, my parents would be thrilled, but Val might question my sanity. So would Jane Dawson, my editor, and everyone else in the newsroom. And Brian? He'd be disappointed—maybe even tell me goodbye for good.

Why does life have to be so hard? Why couldn't I have remained where I was, never to have known the pressure of owning a house? Now it was too late. I stood in the middle of the living room, eyed the freshly painted walls, the polished floors, and the decorative touches, and a mix of pride and pleasure swept over me.

Then my gaze fell on Gram's rocker, and I began to cry. Again. Crying at the drop of a hat seemed to be my lifestyle anymore.

CHAPTER TWENTY-EIGHT

On Tuesday, my angst was forgotten for the moment. I ambled over to my folks' place a little before 4 PM. From the aroma of tomato sauce wafting through the open window, I expected we'd be dining on Mom's famous baked ziti again. I joined my parents in the kitchen where, along with the main course, a tossed salad and a basket of garlic bread sat on the table. Dad was standing by his chair, twisting a corkscrew over the top of a bottle of red wine. I had nothing to do but sit at the table and wait for him to say the blessing.

Like always, Mom's sauce tasted tangy and sweet. Years ago, she'd gotten Gram to give out her secret recipe. I had yet to ask for it, living in the city and rarely having time to cook, although I *could* put together a decent meal—perhaps one of Brian's favorites—steak and potatoes or a chicken and rice stir-fry.

After dinner, we recounted the signatures. In addition to the 253 residents who had signed the petition, there were fifteen business owners, and eight government personnel—mostly staff and a couple of minor officials including the town clerk and the head librarian.

"We have enough to impress the city council members," I said.

Dad shrugged. "It's gonna take more than names, Frannie. We need these folks to show up at the meeting."

"I encouraged my friends to come," Mom offered. "Quite a few said they'd try to make it."

I turned to my father. "I think it's best if *you* make the presentation. Those councilmen will be more open to a request made by a respected member of the community. And they all know you."

He frowned for a moment, like he was considering. Then, he nodded.

"You may be right, Frannie. I've done business here for forty years. I know how to talk to these folks. Last year, I convinced them to turn the old, abandoned grade school into a social hall for seniors. Since then, that place has been used for everything from arts and crafts to bingo."

I chuckled. "I'll be right behind you if you need me."

At quarter to six, the three of us strode into the courthouse, Dad in a navy blue suit and tie, and us women in business attire. I'd packed all my notes and the petitions in my brief-case. We grabbed three seats in the front row next to a heavy set woman in a gray dress and jacket. The camera by her side and the pad and pen in her hand screamed, *reporter from the Cittadina Gazette*. She was fiddling with a tape recorder, getting it ready for the meeting. I could relate. I often backed up my notes with tape recordings. It was a good way to make sure the quotes were accurate.

A buzz of voices and rustle of footsteps got me turning around. I was elated to see the hall filling up with residents Mom had contacted. She nodded and smiled at several people as they took their seats.

Glancing toward the entrance, I fell into shock. Jeff Petrino had come through the door wearing a blue denim jacket and black jeans and T-shirt, which set off his dark hair. Jeff grinned at me. I scowled at him. He took a seat in the back of the hall, smugly placed one ankle over the opposite knee, and crossed his arms. He'd kept his eyes on me the whole time. I started to turn away when I spotted George Newman. The tall man ambled into the hall like he owned the place. Then he slid onto the seat next to Jeff. Fuming, I turned my back on both of them.

At that moment, the city council members filed onto the stage and took their places at a ten-foot long table behind their individual nameplates. Mayor Bosco sat in the middle seat. On either side of him sat Councilman Anthony Bartolucci on his right, and Councilman Peter Mancuso on his left. Both of those men looked like they could use some serious dieting. They had a hard time squeezing into the flimsy office chairs the city had provided.

Seated on each end were Councilman Rico Cosco on the far right, and to my delight, Councilwoman Peg Atwater on the far left—the only woman on the panel and not even Italian. I gaped at her, tried to make eye contact, but with no success. She was looking over the agenda and may have been avoiding my gaze.

I walked over to the front table and picked up a copy of the agenda, satisfied to see the third and last item on the list was, *Petition to restrict demolition of old houses.*

The meeting was soon called to order. Everyone stood for the recitation of the Pledge of Allegiance. The town clerk went over some preliminary particulars. Then she recognized Mr. Bruno Sabotini and the first item on the agenda, a permit to dig a second well on his property at the edge of town.

"I need more water flow so to mist my melon plants," Mr. Sabotini pleaded, his broken English muddling his request. "I pay all cost to dig. No charge for city."

He pulled a handkerchief from his pants pocket. He mopped his forehead, then tucked the hanky away again.

After asking him a few questions, to which he answered with indiscernible mumbling, the five held a brief discussion and approved the permit. The clerk called the next petitioner, a group of grade school children who sought permission to hold an art fair at the city park on the second Saturday in December. They assured the council members their project would not interfere with the city's annual "Lights of Cittadina" Christmas display. Their petition also was granted.

Then it was our turn. When his name was called, Dad stood up, grabbed the pile of petitions, and stepped up to the microphone. He handled the request like a pro, presented our facts and figures, and explained the need to keep the old homes intact. I couldn't help but wonder if he'd addressed many other issues before the council in the years since I'd left town. He sure seemed to be able to handle himself with those officials.

The mayor didn't hide his personal feelings. He went on full attack, brought up an equal number of facts and figures and ended by detailing the economic advantages to wiping out the old and installing the new. He praised Newman Brothers for their adept handling of similar transactions in other towns across the nation, even gave examples, then talked in a honey-coated voice about the aesthetic advantages of giving a facelift to those old, rundown sections of town.

"Newman's fine quality homes will draw folks from other places," he blustered. "They'll bring money. More business. New and improved methods of doing things. We'll be able to add many of the amenities we've been putting off for years. Maybe another school. A bigger police department and more fire stations. With the arrival of Walmart's warehouse, other businesses will move in. No longer will Cittadina be a forgotten little village in the backwoods of New York. Cittadina will at last be the kind of town we can be proud of." He stared at my father. "It's called progress, Mr. Capellini. Ever hear of it?"

Dad didn't back down. "We don't have to bring in a wrecking ball to make progress," he said. "We can enhance what we already have. Many of those old houses simply need a facelift, maybe some aesthetic landscaping. People still like historic settings, Mr. Mayor. You want to draw money here? Then turn this town into a historic landmark. People will flood in." He lifted the petitions in the air. "In less than two days, my wife and my daughter and I acquired 253 individual signatures, plus the support of local businesses, petitioning this council to hold off on the demolitions until further study can be done. The people who signed want to stay in their homes, and they don't want the house next door torn down either. They want to maintain the historic integrity of their neighborhoods."

He paused briefly but didn't lose his stride. "I'm requesting a moratorium—a temporary postponement of Newman Brothers' activities."

A snicker came from the back of the room. I ignored it, but lots of people turned around.

Dad continued. "As the ruling body of our village, you councilmen have the authority to stop the demolitions. The homes I'm talking about date back more than a hundred years. I only want a little time to show what those properties looked like in the beginning, what renovations need to be made, and what will be the financial and aesthetic losses if you allow Newman Brothers to continue."

Dad's comments nearly brought Mayor Bosco out of his chair. His face turned red, and it appeared he was struggling to control his temper. "What makes you think those houses qualify as historic?" he challenged. "They're a bunch of dilapidated litter boxes. They're unsafe, unattractive, and they hurt our local economy."

Someone clapped in the back. Again, I ignored the interruption.

Dad shook his head. "You're missing the point, Mayor Bosco. Think about what makes a home worthy of preservation. It goes beyond their outward appearance. There's history in those homes. People's ancestors built them. Others bought them because the historic nature of the construction appealed to them. Those houses and neighborhoods may not have belonged to famous people or anything else that makes them historic. They're simply old. But, just like old cars that have become classics, they were well built by artisans, and they mean something special to the families who live in them. You're right when you say they'll never make it onto a historic registry. But that doesn't mean they don't have historical significance. Each old house is more than a collection of boards and mortar. Each one is part of someone's roots."

The packed hall erupted in cheers and applause. My heart pounded with pride for my father. To the folks who came to the meeting to support us, Dad was a hero. I smiled at him through blurred vision. My sense of family pride had escaped me over the years, but now it was back in full force.

By now, the mayor was banging his gavel and calling for quiet. The room settled into an electrified hush. Then a discussion ensued between council members, with the mayor quite vocal in his effort to deny the moratorium. Ideas flew back and forth, some way over my head, but Dad seemed to understand everything that was being said, for he was alternately nodding and shaking his head.

At one point, the arguments became heated. Peg Atwater butted heads with Mayor Bosco. My favorite Realtor took a firm stance. She vocally approved of the moratorium and also recommended that a review committee be formed.

In the end, a 4-to-1 vote approved a three-month moratorium stopping the demolitions to give a review committee time to do its homework, thanks to Peg Atwater's recommendation.

"Nicholas Capellini will chair the committee," said Mayor Bosco, sneering at Dad. It appeared the big man thought my father might fall flat on his face. "Have an initial report ready at the next meeting in two weeks," the major commanded, his eyes still on my father. Then he pounded his gavel, ending the meeting.

My dad, red-faced and scrunching his lips, settled back in the seat beside me.

"I really stuck my foot in it now, haven't I?" Dad mumbled.

"You can do it, Dad. And I'll help."

He nodded, but I could tell his heart wasn't in it. "I'm supposed to be retiring soon," he protested. "Your mom and I wanted to go on another cruise." He stared at me. "Anyway, you're leaving soon, aren't you?" A tinge of hope laced his tone.

"All the more reason why you need to get started tomorrow," I told him as I rose to leave.

I ventured a quick look at the last row of seats. Jeff and George Newman were heading for the door. Together.

Because of them, I left the meeting with mixed emotions

flying around in my head. Anger, of course, laced with a certain amount of suspicion. I couldn't help but wonder what Jeff was doing with George Newman.

At the same time, I was elated that Dad was going to head up the committee. But where should he begin? I looked at him and my feeling of pride intensified. Not only was he handsome, he also possessed a calm demeanor that made him the ideal choice for heading that committee. Being tall and somewhat imposing, he could easily convince people to follow his lead. He'd proven himself time and time again in business. He wouldn't fall flat on his face. He'd win.

I shifted my gaze to Mom. She was still limping from all the walking they'd done around town. But the frown on her face told me it wasn't only about the pain in her foot.

"It looks like I won't be seeing much of your dad for a while," she whimpered.

I smiled with sympathy. "Sorry—" I began.

"Stop it, Roberta," Dad cut in. "You'll see me every hour of every day, because I'm not doing this alone. You two will both be on the committee with me." He stared bullets at me, silently forbidding me to leave Cittadina until this job was done.

"And," he said, his tone softening. "We'll get a couple more crazy people to join us. Got any ideas?" He looked at me again and raised his eyebrows.

"I don't know, Dad. I would say, ask my friend Penny, but she's not talking to me right now." I thought for a second. "We could get with Peg Atwater. If she can't join the committee because of her position on the city council, perhaps she'll recommend someone. And don't forget the people who signed the petition. Many of them attended the meeting."

Dad nodded. "Yes, of course. Your mom and I will approach them. And, Frannie, you talk to Peg."

With a beginning plan in place, we parted outside on the sidewalk. On my way home, my mind was on the little conspiracy I'd witnessed between Newman and Jeff. They were both frowning when they left. The man from Texas must have been put out over the delay.

If Dad could work out a good plan of attack, Newman's work might be brought to a complete and unsalvageable halt.

Alone at home, I dialed Penny's cell number. I figured she might not answer, but I had to at least try to talk to the girl. It was time I found out exactly what Jeff Petrino was up to.

CHAPTER TWENTY-NINE

Penny picked up on the second ring, but she didn't say anything.

"You already know it's me, Penny," I remarked. "Tell you what, I'll get right to the point. I need to know where Jeff lives."

She snorted. "Why? So you can make another pass at him?"

"You know that's not true. He's the one who made a pass. He's the one who can't be trusted."

"Then why do you want his address?"

"I want to find out about his connection with Newman Brothers. He's joined their side, and I want to know why."

"Right." Her tone was noticeably sarcastic.

"It's true, Penny. He's helping them tear down the old houses, and Gram's house is on their list. I'm sure of it."

"Oh, Fran, you've gone off the deep end. Why on earth would Jeff want to tear down a house he helped to restore?"

"I don't know. Maybe he was casing the place. Maybe he was looking for the flaws. If they can get Gram's house condemned, we won't be able to stop the demolition. I'm almost certain he's a spy for George Newman."

"You know what I think?" A sharp edge had taken over Penny's voice. "I think you're still carrying a torch for Jeff. You're sorry you walked away, and now you want him back."

"Penny, I *have* a boyfriend."

"Yeah? And where is he?"

"He's working in the city, taking classes, even went out to California for a couple of weeks." I sighed in frustration. "I can see we're going nowhere, Penny. We've been friends for twenty years. I don't want to hurt you, but you need to know about Jeff. He has *not* changed. He's the same con man he was in high school, and he can't be trusted."

She didn't respond. The silence was like a knife cutting into our phone call.

"Look, Penny, I need to ask him about his relationship with George Newman. I just want his address, and then I'll leave you alone."

"Why don't you call him? You have his business card. You've got his number."

"I want to confront him face-to-face. I want to look in his eyes, so I'll know if he's lying to me. That's why I need his address."

"Well, I'm not gonna give it to you, Fran. You're the smart newspaper reporter. Why don't you use your investigative skills and find it for yourself?" Her words cut into my heart, but not as much as the next thing she said. "You're a bitter, lonely woman, Fran, and you're still pining over the one who got away. Get over him, girl. Finish the work on your grandmother's house and go back to New York where you belong. Believe me, you won't be missed."

The line went dead.

I was chewing my lip so hard I drew blood. Tears rushed to my eyes. It took several minutes for me to calm down enough to figure out a plan. Dad had suggested I talk to Peg Atwater about filling our committee with dependable souls. With all the records real estate offices maintained, she also might be able to find out where Jeff was living these days. I decided to call her in the morning and ask her to meet me somewhere. We couldn't talk at her office with Beverly sitting right there at the next desk. It seemed Newman had spies everywhere, including the man who sat in the mayor's office. For that matter, how many other *loyal* citizens had gone over to the other side?

Choked up over a failed friendship and a mounting anger caused by Penny's accusations, I made my next call to Brian.

As always, he knew what to say to calm me down. I explained everything that happened at the meeting. He listened without interrupting, a true lawyer in action. *Get all the information, then figure out a solution.* That was Brian.

"I'm certain Jeff is behind all this," I told him.

"I'll be finishing up classes in a few days. Want me to come straight to Cittadina when I get done? I can track him down and rough him up a little."

I laughed for the first time. "Sure, Brian. He's 6-foot, 2-inches, lifts weights, and played football in high school. That guy carried my new sinks upstairs like they were made out of papier mache. You want to beat him up? He's Arnold Schwarzenegger, and you're Tom Hanks."

I heard Brian huff at the other end. "Really?" he said, like he couldn't believe me.

"Yes, Brian, that man is all brawn and no brains. And somehow he's gotten himself involved with the contractor. I don't like it one bit."

"And you used to date this guy?"

"Sadly."

"Any chance he might want you back?"

"Well, he did make a play for me, but I shot him down right away. He's dating Penny now and still cheating—on her this time. The guy will never learn."

"Be careful, honey."

"Don't worry. I told him off good. I doubt he'll come around *here* again."

"Still, I'd feel better if I came there and stayed until you're ready to come back to New York."

"That may not be a bad idea, at least for a few days. I was thinking if you could come up you might be able to help us with the legal particulars. Chances are, we may end up in court at some point."

"Well, my field right now *is* real estate law. I'm not sure how much help I can be, but I can give some guidance. Most of all I can make sure that jerk doesn't come within ten yards of my girlfriend."

As always, Brian left me assured about how much he cared for me. We said our usual loving goodbyes and ended the call.

Still, the pressure of what Dad and I now faced returned with full force. Even after a cup of chamomile tea and a couple of Mom's macaroons, I didn't fare well that night. When I awoke at 6 AM, my pillow looked like someone had squeezed the stuffing out of it. My comforter lay in a crumpled pile on the floor. I ran my fingers through my hair. It was a tangled mess of tight, damp curls.

When my head finally cleared, I slipped aimlessly into a pair of shorts, a T-shirt, and my running shoes and left for a jog through the neighborhood. Outside, I took a deep breath of fresh air. There was something exhilarating about being the first one out on the streets in the wee hours of the morning. I trotted past the sleeping houses—the blinds drawn, the shades down, and cars still sitting in the driveways. The only sound was the swish, swish of my rubber-soled shoes flying over the pavement.

I passed several houses with Newman Brothers signs on their front lawns. The crisp morning air cleared more than my lungs, it awakened my brain to fresh determination. I needed to call Peg and meet with her at the time and place of her choice. I needed to ask her to help me find Jeff's address so I could corner him, demand the truth, and make him confess his role in that whole evil plot. I also needed to ask her to help fill Dad's committee with the right people. In her dual role as real estate agent and city councilwoman, she knew a lot of residents.

I returned home a little after eight, took a shower and washed my hair, then donned a blue-and-white dress with a matching jacket and a pair of comfortable slip-on shoes. While my hair air-dried, I ate a breakfast of scrambled eggs and toast, finished off two cups of coffee, then checked the rooster clock. It was almost 10 AM. The real estate office was now open. I dialed the number. As luck would have it, Peg Atwater picked up.

We made plans to meet for lunch at 12:30 at Marco's Seafood House at the edge of town. I arrived ahead of Peg. After we were seated, I ordered parmesan crusted tilapia. She chose the house special of the day, seafood chowder and tossed salad. At first, we sipped iced tea in silence. We made eye contact now and then and let a message of desperation pass between us.

"One of us has to start this conversation," Peg said at last.

I flushed a little. "I had everything all planned out in my head, and now I'm not sure I want to involve you, Peg. Things could get sticky—you know—with you being on the council and all."

She ate a little soup and eyed me with confidence. "Not a worry, Francine. I can't be on the committee, but nothing's stopping me from giving you a little guidance and information."

I nodded. "You were the most vocal, at least as far as our side goes. But the mayor troubles me. He's totally sold out to the other side, and he's not hiding it."

Peg chuckled. "You don't have to be afraid of that blowhard. I've had run-ins with Mayor Bosco before. His bark is worse than his bite, mostly because he rarely knows what he's talking about." She released a long sigh. "It saddens me that he doesn't side with the citizens of Cittadina more often. Big business. That's his forte. He assumes that by letting people like George Newman weasel their way in, it will help our economic system. He's wrong. They'll destroy our town. The people don't like the way Bosco's misused his office. Come November, he'll be out and someone else will be in. Maybe it'll be me."

"You're running for office?"

"Threw my hat in the ring last March."

I savored the moment, enjoyed the outer crunch of the fish and the tender meat inside. "So, you're in?" I said, pausing between bites.

Peg finished off her soup and switched to her salad. She looked me in the eye and nodded. "You bet I'm in. For more reasons than one."

"Really?"

More nodding as she dug into her salad. "First of all, I don't want to see those old houses torn down. I've worked in real estate long enough to appreciate the historic nature of those relics. They're well-built, constructed by craftsmen from the old country, and they've withstood all kinds of weather over the years, far better than some of the makeshift buildings they slap up nowadays."

I giggled over her last statement, then reality sank in. Gram's house was more than an old relic. It was a monument to the immigrants who'd settled that town more than a hundred years before. And it was still standing.

I had come to appreciate the old house, and I'd also begun to love it. Every board, every nail was put in place by my great-great-grandfather. Every change and renovation over the years had been implemented by more of my ancestors. My own father had grown up in that house, and I had spent many a weekday afternoon helping Gram in her kitchen and gobbling up most of the sweet pastries we'd made. I'd eaten Sunday dinners in that house, and I'd seen other relatives come and go. I hadn't made much of an effort to get to know them. Ironically, over the past few weeks, I'd come to know my great-great-grandparents—whom I'd *never* met—better than any of my contemporary relatives.

I gazed into Peg's dark eyes. "I don't want my grandmother's house demolished. I don't want any of the old homes destroyed. Neither do the people who live in them, now that they know what George Newman plans to do with them. Those homes symbolize the history of this town and the people in it."

Was that moisture in her eyes, or a reflection from the overhead light? Her brow wrinkled with compassion and she leaned toward me.

"Then we have to stop Newman Brothers from going any further. Tell me how I can help."

"First, I need to find out where Jeff Petrino lives. He's connected with Newman Brothers in some way. He's the town's favorite handyman. I think he uses his trade as a guise to snoop around and help George Newman acquire homes."

Peg nodded. "That's an easy one. His parents moved to Florida. I handled the sale of their house and have their contact information. I can ask them where Jeff moved to. But first, I'll look in my file. I may have made a notation there." The lines on her face deepened, and her eyes seemed to grow darker. She shook her head. "I wouldn't approach him, if I were you. Not alone, anyway."

"I don't understand."

"You already know you can't trust him. I've heard things too. Word is, he's gotten mixed up in some messy business. He barely ekes out a living with his construction work, yet he's spending money like he won the New York lottery."

I frowned in puzzlement. "How do you know that?"

"My friend Martha works at the bank. She let it slip out that Jeff's account has flourished since Newman Brothers came to town."

"No surprise," I agreed. "I've suspected something's been going on between him and George Newman. Perhaps Jeff is a small pebble in a large pond, but he's doing something bad to this town, and we need to stop him." I paused to consider what she'd said. "Maybe we should forget about Jeff Petrino for the time being. We need to concentrate on getting Newman Brothers out of here. Once they're gone, Jeff won't have that extra income."

"Right." Peg nodded. "I'll see what I can find out about their activities without Beverly suspecting. It's obvious she's part of the team they sent in. I won't be able to join the committee, but I can do far more research as an outsider right now."

"Should I cancel the listing agreement I signed with her?"

"Not yet. I know it has that indelible clause. But if you cancel with her and sign with me, I could be accused of unethical practices. Give it a little time. Once Newman Brothers leave, I guarantee, Beverly Strong will also disappear."

At that moment, my phone buzzed. It was Mom.

I hesitated, then answered her call. Her voice was garbled, like she was crying, or worse, near hysterics.

"Mom. Mom. I can't understand you. Please, slow down and tell me what happened."

"It's your father, Frannie. He—He was hit by a car. A few minutes ago. He just left the house. Was going for a walk."

I straightened. "How is he? Did you call 911?"

"Yes, yes. The police came. And an ambulance. They've taken him to Rochester General."

"What are his injuries?"

"I–I don't know. There was a lot of blood. He looked mangled, Frannie, terribly mangled."

"Where are you?"

"I'm still home. Uncle Giuseppe said he'd drive me to the hospital. Please, darling, please meet us there."

Peg stared at me, a wrinkle of concern crossing her forehead.

"It's my father," I said as I hung up. "He's been in an accident."

She shooed me off with a wave of her hand. "Go, dear. Go. I'll take care of the check." She shrugged and managed a sympathetic smile. "Business expense."

I left my unfinished meal on the table and sprinted toward the door.

CHAPTER THIRTY

Rochester General was almost an hour away. I pressed the accelerator to the floor, wove in and out of two lanes of traffic, and kept checking my rearview mirror for red and blue lights. Somehow I made it to the hospital without one sign of Smokey.

I found Mom in the waiting room adjacent to the emergency department. Like every other trauma patient, Dad was somewhere behind those double doors. The moment Mom spotted me, she lunged off the plastic chair and flung herself into my arms. We held each other for a long time, weeping and trembling.

Mom was sobbing so hard she couldn't speak. She grew weak and started to sink to the ground. Next thing, my Uncle Giuseppe was at our side. He helped me settle our mother into a chair, then he turned to face me.

"He's not good," my uncle said, his gravelly voice tensing up. He swallowed and blinked a stream of tears from his eyes. For all of Giuseppe's gruffness and size, he was a sensitive man, full of emotional tenderness.

"All they told us so far is he's in critical condition," my uncle managed to say. Then he sagged into the chair next to my mother.

I took the seat on the other side of her and reached for her hand. "How did this happen, Mom?"

She mopped tears from red and blotchy cheeks. "He said he was going for a walk," she said. "He no sooner stepped out the door when I heard the screech of tires, followed by a thud. I knew something had happened. I ran to the front door and there he was, lying in the street like a dead man."

"Did you happen to see the car that hit him?"

She shook her head. "Whoever did it squealed around the next corner and peeled out of there. He was long gone."

"Were any neighbors outside? I mean, did anyone see it happen? Were there any witnesses?" In the midst of my grief, my reporter instincts had crept in, and I asked the typical questions.

More mopping of Mom's face, then she shrugged. "Only Mrs. Juno. But I'm not sure what she saw, if anything." She bowed her head. "We need to pray, Frannie." She looked at my uncle. "Giuseppe, will you?"

He bobbed his head and in a soft voice I could barely hear, he mumbled a heartfelt plea for Dad's recovery. Then his voice grew louder, filled with anger. "And, help the police catch the *malvagio* who did this."

I looked at Mom. "Malvagio?"

"Evil one," she translated. "Your uncle could have said something worse, but he wouldn't in the middle of a prayer. He will later though. You can count on it."

All three of us fell silent, as though each of us had entered a confessional of sorts where we could communicate in private with God. I stumbled through a mental prayer of my own, simple words I dragged up from my childhood.

It occurred to me that perhaps the trouble surrounding Gram's house and the preservation of it might be something else I could give to God. I didn't have to take the entire burden on my shoulders. Nor did I need to place it on my father's back. I once read a statement by John Wesley about the difference between bearing one's burden as compared to taking up one's cross. *When we bear a burden,* Wesley wrote, *we submit to the troubles that have come upon us. When we take up one's cross, we purposely choose to suffer pain in order to do something good.* Regarding Gram's house, I'd sort of experienced both. Through my inheritance, I'd received the burden of fixing up the house and selling it, and by hanging around to help save the property, I'd taken up a cross of sorts.

Along with that responsibility had come voices of the past

turning my efforts into a labor of love. The items I'd found in the trunk had drawn me closer to my ancestors. And in recent days I'd begun to feel more comfortable living in Gram's house and getting familiar with my hometown. Instead of loathing the differences between Cittadina and New York City, I had begun to embrace them.

I continued mulling over such thoughts as the minutes crept by. I went for coffee for the three of us. Upon returning, I wrapped an arm around Mom and fell into small talk with Uncle Giuseppe.

Two more hours passed. Then a doctor came through the double doors and stood before us, his face grim.

"Mrs. Capellini?" He kept his eyes on Mom.

She could only nod.

"I'm Dr. Bishop." He ran a hand through his salt-and-pepper hair, a sign of exhaustion confirmed by the dark circles under his eyes.

Giuseppe and I stood to face him.

"I take it you're the brother and the daughter?" the doctor said.

"Yes, we are," Giuseppe answered. "How's Nick?"

"Well, he's alive." Dr. Bishop's grave tone troubled me. "He has a fractured tibia on his right leg, multiple breaks in his forearm, three broken ribs, and he suffered a concussion. He's not conscious right now. We had to sedate him for all the repairs we made. We're checking for blood clots and watching for signs of pneumonia. I can't let you see him yet. I suggest you go home, rest up, and come back tomorrow morning."

Mom looked at me, then at Giuseppe, her watery eyes questioning. My uncle drew close to her. "It's okay, Roberta. We can't do anything right now. Let's all three of us go to your place." He turned to me. "Francine, can you stay the night with her?"

I nodded. "I'll stop at Gram's and pack an overnight bag."

Like a phantom, the doctor had already disappeared behind the double doors. We gathered up our things and started for the exit when a policeman came in and blocked our path.

"Are you the Capellini family?

"Yes, we are." Giuseppe stepped up.

"I'm Officer Frank Marcello, Cittadina PD."

"You have any news about the accident?" my uncle pressed.

Marcello nodded. "We found a witness. A Mrs. Juno. She said she'd gone outside to pick up the newspaper, and bam! She insists it was no accident, that the driver headed straight for Mr. Capellini."

"Did she get the license number?" I asked.

"No, everything happened too fast. But she described the vehicle. It was a green-and-black Jeep."

A cold chill ran through me, and I gasped loud enough to draw the attention of everyone in the waiting room.

"She was quite certain about the model," the cop said. "She claimed her son has one exactly like it, except his is red-and-black."

I was ready to burst. "I know who owns that car. His name's Jeff Petrino, and he lives in Cittadina. He's a contractor, or so he claims."

Marcello tilted his head and narrowed his eyes. "Why would he want to target your father?"

"Why? Because my Dad is in charge of a project that could stop the shady deal Jeff's working on. That creep may be involved with an out-of-state group that wants to demolish all the old homes in Cittadina. And my father stepped up to stop them."

The policeman nodded. "I heard something about it. So you're the folks I read about in this morning's paper? The ones who are trying to save Cittadina's history?"

I realized our petition had caught the attention of the reporter I'd seen at the meeting. "Yes, we are," I told the officer.

"Mr. Capellini's photo was on the front of the B-section," he said, raising his eyebrows. "I have to say, I wish I'd been at that meeting. The article called him a town hero."

I stood in amazement. From my own work in New York, I knew how much clout newspaper coverage can have. And from what the cop had said, the story sounded favorable.

Marcello didn't comment further, merely jotted a few notes on a small pad, asked for our contact information, then nodded his head and pocketed the notebook. "I'll look into the hit-and-run and get back to you," he promised, then added, "I'm sorry about what you folks are going through. I hope you win the case."

Then he was gone.

Giuseppe took Mom home. I went to Gram's and stuffed some items in an overnight bag. Before going to Mom's house, I stopped at Luigi's Restaurant for a take-out dinner of lasagna, salad, and a box of cannoli for the two of us.

When I arrived, Mom was sitting in the living room, staring off into space. She'd be worthless until Dad was out of the woods. Giuseppe said goodbye and left for his own home, and I hurried into the kitchen to set the table.

At first, we ate in silence, but after a few bites of the lasagna, Mom began to relax. She talked about the early days when she and Dad first started to date, their beautiful church wedding, and the thrill of having two wonderful children, a boy and then a girl. A wistful smile tugged at her lips.

"The good old days," she called them, "when everybody was healthy and safe." Then she set down her fork and stared into my eyes, her own brown irises shimmering within a fresh flood of tears.

"Have you looked inside yet?" she said, a childlike tone in her voice.

"Huh? Inside what?"

"The Bible I gave you."

The last remnant of our legacy was still sitting right where I'd left it, on the end table next to Gram's rocker.

"I'm sorry, Mom. I haven't had time yet. But I will."

She nodded her acceptance. The wistful smile disappeared, and she began to eat again, but she'd taken on the look of a tired, old woman. It saddened me to see her suffer as she was. At any moment, more news could come from the hospital, and it could go either way. Mom could lose her one true love, and a huge piece of herself would be gone. Or Dad might be on the way to a full recovery.

I reached out and gently squeezed her free hand. "He's gonna be all right," I said softly and with confidence. "He's a fighter, Mom. He's strong. He never gives up. And neither should you."

Her simple nod worried me. I'd never seen my mother so down. What had become of the vibrant, confident woman who, two days ago, had trudged the streets of Cittadina on a mission with my father? Then the truth struck me. The key lay within the words—"with my father."

They were a team, and always had been. Like Salvatore and Rosanna, Enzo and Catherine, Alberto and Francine, my parents—Nicholas and Roberta—had been partners in life. When one hurt, so did the other. When one succeeded, the other also rejoiced. They laughed together, and they wept together. They lived within a bond that went beyond the matrimonial altar, it began and ended with two hearts that had become one.

At that moment, I thought about the Bible sitting on the end table at Gram's house. I had to open that book and find out what was written inside. I had to do it for my mother.

"I'll go and get it," I told her. "Right now." I rose from the table. "You finish eating. When I come back, I'll clean up our dishes. Then you and I will sit here, and we'll open that old Bible. We'll focus on the notations written on the family history pages. We'll read them together, Mom. We'll let our ancestors speak to us, and maybe we'll find comfort through their words."

CHAPTER THIRTY-ONE

That old Bible had to weigh at least four pounds. I picked it up and placed it inside a cloth tote, then lugged it out to the car and laid it gently on the front seat. Then I drove back to Mom's house, eager to start reading those entries together with her.

Perhaps this little project of ours would keep Mom from worrying about Dad, although I doubted anything could soothe her mounting anxiety. It seemed that when two people have joined together like Mom and Dad had, a part of them always stayed with the other person. Although Mom was sitting at home waiting for my return, I was certain a piece of her was lying on that hospital bed, hurting along with the man she'd loved for more than forty years.

I hurried over the few blocks that separated my folks' house from Gram's. Upon entering the kitchen, I found Mom had cleaned up our dinner dishes and was back at the table with two steamy cups of herbal tea. The minty steam was still wafting out of the cups.

I pulled up a chair beside hers, lifted the Bible from my tote, and slid it in front of her.

"Go ahead," I encouraged Mom. "You turn the first page."

She looked at me and grinned. Her soft brown eyes crinkled at the corners.

"Frannie, dear, I already know what's in there. Gram and I researched our family's genealogy, and the two of us wrote most of the notations. This is for you, dear. Not for me."

She moved the Bible in front of me.

"Okay, Mom," I said with a sigh. "But let's do it together. I might have questions."

Mom's smile grew wider. Perhaps digging into this old Bible was going to act like medicine to my mother. If nothing else, it served as a temporary distraction.

I ran my hand over the worn leather cover. It was smooth, but in some places it had faded, and a long crack ran down the spine. I opened it to the first page. The threads on the spine had come loose, leaving the cover hanging to one side. The first two pages were blank. Then came the title page, and the words, *Edited by the Reverend Andrew P. McCarthy, PhD.* and the publisher, *St. Augustus Press, Boston, Mass., January 10, 1952.*

In addition to both the Old and New Testaments, the first third of the book was dedicated to photos of various Roman Catholic cathedrals, pictures of places in Israel where Jesus went, and loads of text about the life of Christ, the growth of the church, and applications of scripture for daily living.

Then came several pages that contained our family's genealogy, accompanied by notations written by Gram and Mom. This section captured my full attention.

Gram had created a family tree starting with Salvatore's father, *Bruno Capellini, born Jan. 14, 1826, on the outskirts of Albi, province of Catanzaro, region of Calabria, Italy.*

A lengthy account followed in the same handwriting. I read it aloud so Mom could hear, though she must have read the passage multiple times herself.

Bruno Capellini and Justine Gambolini, daughter of Francesco Gambolini and Rosa Campagno, married on Sept. 29, 1849, in the St. Jerome Chapel, Albi, Italy. They had seven children; four sons: Bruno II, Mikael, Joseppe, and Salvatore; and three daughters: Nadia, Christina, and Patricia. All of the sons followed Bruno into farming, except for Mikael who entered the ministry and, in time, rose from the priesthood to the position of bishop in the district of Rome.

Salvatore, the youngest, sailed to America in 1887. Several of his siblings followed years later and settled in various parts of New York State. They left behind their mud brick home in an area of Italy that was plagued by earthquakes and soil erosion. Salvatore and his siblings had joined a growing wave of Italian immigrants seeking a fresh start in America.

Then Gram's account turned personal. I read it with fascination.

Alberto and I visited the remaining members of the family in 1954. We were newly married and enjoying a honeymoon trip to Italy. It was one of the few times I could get my husband to travel with me. By this time, Bruno and Justine had passed away. We visited their gravesites in a rundown little cemetery in the valley.

We also spent time with my husband's distant cousins. Their lifestyle was quite different from what we enjoy in America. Their houses were simple structures, but spotlessly clean. They lived off of home-grown vegetables or whatever they purchased from other farmers. Grape vines grew everywhere, on walls, makeshift trellises, and poles. Chickens and pigs ran free throughout the village. Most everyone is a laborer. Brick masons, carpenters, farmers. They can barely fulfill the needs of their large families.

By the time Alberto and I left, some of my clothing and several pieces of jewelry had disappeared from my luggage. I chose not to accuse anyone, for by this time my heart was breaking for them. Suddenly, my possessions did not matter as much as family did. I knew I could replace everything within days of returning home. But family you cannot replace.

I considered this. More lessons in life from my Gram. More conviction about my own failure to appreciate family.

Her writing went on.

Such was the legacy of Bruno and Justine. They had lived and died right there in that tiny village near Albi. Unlike several of their children, they had never ventured outside their village, never knew what it was like to have indoor plumbing or comfortable beds or a pantry abundantly stocked with food for tomorrow. They lived hand-to-mouth, and for relaxation, they sat on handmade wooden chairs on the front stoop of their little house, nodding to neighbors during the day and counting the stars at night.

I stopped reading for a moment and tried to get my bearings. Somewhere along the way I had lost the current time and place and had segued back to the late 1800s in Albi, Italy. I imagined the tiny, rustic dwellings where my ancestors lived. I thought about Bruno and Justine raising seven children in a tiny three-room house, a humble farmer and his wife, struggling to survive. This was the legacy I had come from.

For a moment, I mentally stepped away from the modern conveniences I enjoyed, and I was sitting with Bruno and Justine in a wooden chair outside their home. The thought struck me that if Salvatore had not migrated to the United States, I could have been born in that place, unaware of the outside world, and perhaps, like Bruno and Justine, content with the life I'd been handed.

"Are you going to read on?" Mom prodded.

Her expression changed from puzzlement to concern.

"What's wrong, darling?" she said, her voice soft.

"Mom, did you ever wonder what your life would be like if you hadn't been born in America?"

She tilted her head, and a whimsical smile tugged at her lips. "No, I don't think I ever did, Frannie."

"Reading these notes, I can't help but wonder how different my life might be if I'd been born in that little village near Albi.

If I'd been poor instead of well-off. If I'd gone right from child-hood into a life of drudgery with seven children to feed. No high school education. No college. No chance to better myself in a career of my choice."

"Not all of your grandfather's relatives had that kind of life," she noted. "Several moved to Rome and took office jobs. I know of at least two who went to college and became professionals." She grew pensive and raised a finger to her cheek. "Let's see, I think one became an orthopedic surgeon, and another is a pro-fessor at the university in Rome. They're not all farmers, honey. And don't forget, after Salvatore moved to the United States, several of his siblings followed. His children did well, and so did their grandchildren. Many of Bruno's descendants now hold good jobs throughout New York State. If we ever have a really big reunion, we'll track down those distant cousins, and you'll get a chance to meet them."

Again she was assuming I would be living in Cittadina. I didn't say anything to dampen her spirits. Instead, I simply smiled at her and turned my attention back to Gram's notations, my curiosity piqued as I continued reading.

Salvatore was born on June 4, 1861 near Albi. Like his brothers and sisters, he attended school until he was 12. Then he went to work with his father in the field behind their house. Salvatore was more restless than his siblings. Mikael had gone into the priesthood, but Salvatore insisted the ministry was not for him. His older brothers and sisters got married, but, as years passed, he hadn't met anyone who could get him to the altar.

Salvatore was a dreamer. He kept looking beyond his humble existence in Catanzaro, kept imagining a life other than what he could see. So, it was no surprise to the family when, with a few lire in his pocket, he kissed them all goodbye and left for America.

Salvatore arrived in New York City on August 15, 1887. He was 26 years old when he hired on with a work crew building houses in the suburbs of New York. He developed his skills as a carpenter, learned English, and applied for citizenship.

Then, he met and fell in love with Rosanna Destino, an immigrant from Rome, Italy. They married on April 13, 1889. The following year, Rosanna moved back home with her family while Salvatore went to Upstate New York to a small village populated by Italian immigrants. He purchased a plot of land there, and he used his skills as a carpenter to build a two-story house where he and Rosanna would spend the rest of their lives.

In addition to finding work as a carpenter, Salvatore also farmed a small plot of land behind his house. Ironically, he had followed the same path as his father, Bruno. But, instead of settling down in Italy, he was doing the same type of work in America. The only thing that had changed was the location. Salvatore lived and died in Cittadina, never to venture beyond the little town he had come to know and love.

I stopped reading again and turned to face Mom. "I read his daybook," I told her. "He wrote, in detail, every step he took to build the house. I know about every board and nail that went in. He chose a sturdy, long-lasting design, a floor plan that protected the upper floors from danger if a fire started in the kitchen below. He described how he and the neighbors dug a well, how they helped him clear the land and lay the foundation. Then he helped other people build *their* houses. It's likely he had a hand in building many of the other homes in this neighborhood, homes that Newman Brothers will take down if we don't stop them."

Mom eyed me with sympathy in her dark brown eyes. "We don't have to worry about that right now, dear. Remember, the city council put a hold on their activities for three months."

I nodded and got back to the book. "I'm so impressed with Salvatore, Mom. Maybe he didn't go to college or become a millionaire, but he knew his craft, and he used it to help others."

She smiled sweetly. "It's no different with you, Frannie. You studied to be a reporter, and you're doing a great job. You help people with every story you write. I know the kind of work you do. I go online every day and read the *New York Dispatch*, so proud to see my daughter's byline and the fascinating stories she writes."

I beamed with surprise. "I didn't know you read the *Dispatch*."

"Of course, dear. So does your dad. Why wouldn't we? The thing is, Salvatore chose his career, and so did you. Everyone has that opportunity. For your dad it was accounting. He always *did* like working with numbers, actually won a math competition in college."

I smiled. My dad hadn't missed out on the bigger things in life, like I'd thought. He was doing what he loved, and people depended on him. Come to think of it, I'd never heard him complain about his work, not once. And my mom? She'd always seemed content with being a housewife, raising children, volunteering for local charities, happy with a visit to the hair salon for another dye job or a chance to babysit Tom's son when he and Betsy came to town. She'd lived vicariously through Tom and me and often boasted about our successes. She displayed our trophies and academic awards for all to see. Meanwhile, she'd never expressed any regrets about her own life, never said she wished she had done this or that.

Gram was another story. She pursued her bucket list, then she wrote about her adventures. In fact, the woman had enjoyed the best of two worlds. Life as a stay-at-home mom and an occasional journey into the unknown. I chuckled. Gram went from wearing an apron to donning a helmet and boots. Even in her day, she showed people that a woman can do anything she sets her mind to.

I thought about my own life, working every day and some weekends at the newspaper. Signing up for classes to get ahead in my career. I couldn't imagine doing all that and still finding time to raise a family and then maybe running off to Tibet to climb a mountain.

I tilted my head and gazed into Mom's eyes. "You know, I've

been on a high-speed treadmill for the past ten or fifteen years. I'd forgotten what makes life worth living. While prizes and accolades and high pay make a nice bonus, we all need to take time to kick back. I'm afraid that's what's been missing from my life. Until now."

A wrinkle of concern returned to Mom's forehead. "Why is that, dear?"

I shrugged. "I never thought I was missing anything before." I shook my head and sighed. "If I hadn't come home and experienced all of these journeys into the past, I might have gone on in ignorance for years."

"Why don't you read on, dear? There's so much more for you to learn. You've heard of the wisdom of the elderly? Well, that's what you're going to find in these pages. Let your ancestors teach you things you won't learn in a college classroom. Things you won't experience on your reporter job."

I was about to turn the page when Mom's cell phone rang. She reached for it.

"Oh, my." Her voice was taut with anxiety. "It's the hospital."

CHAPTER THIRTY-TWO

Mom put her phone on speaker so I could hear. The doctor's voice came over loud and clear. "Your husband woke up. Do you want to come and visit him?"

Mom broke down weeping. I leaned closer to the phone. "How is he?"

"He's in a lot of pain, but he's conscious," the doctor said. "We'll keep him here for another couple of days and then set him up for rehab, either at a facility or with home sessions. We're checking out clinics close to where you live."

"There's one downtown in Cittadina," Mom managed between sobs. "A friend of mine went there."

"For now, we'll keep an eye on him, and you can visit him here at the hospital. If you want to stay overnight, we can arrange to have a cot placed in his room."

"Yes, yes. I'll be there in an hour." Mom came out of her chair.

"Drive safely," the doctor said, his tone mellowing. "Your husband isn't going anywhere."

Mom hung up, then flew about the house filling an overnight bag with her essentials. She dashed in and out of the kitchen and living room, grabbing snacks, bottled water, her knitting, and a novel she'd been reading.

I watched her with amusement. This was life, according to my mother, my grandmother, and all of my *grands* before them. The simple life with its own special challenges and blessings. And all the while I had worn myself out chasing an elusive future, when life had been staring me in the face right here in my hometown.

There was nothing wrong with following a dream and making life better. Salvatore had proven that. But at what expense had *I* done so? By running away from my past, I had stilted my future. I hadn't been a whole person. It's no wonder I couldn't commit to Brian or any other man. A big part of me was missing. It was as if I'd been drawn back to Cittadina to reclaim it. This meant I had to face the traumas, shed the embarrassment, and embrace the person I really was.

What Jeff did wasn't my fault. He's the one who cheated. Yet, I'd been blaming myself, convinced my naiveté had chased him into someone else's arms. And Denise? He'd used her, like every other guy who came knocking on her door. Instead of holding a grudge, I should have felt sorry for both of them. They probably would never know the joy my great-great-grandfather experienced when he met and married Rosanna. Or the longing Enzo and Catherine felt when he was away. Or the trust Gram and Poppa shared as he accepted her independent lifestyle, content to stay home while she went off on so many adventures. My ancestors certainly were a unique bunch of people.

Then there was the commitment in my own parents' marriage. There it was, in front of me for the first half of my life, and I'd never grasped it until now.

Jeff and Denise—and maybe even Penny—might never know the thrill of a committed relationship like my relatives had. But it wasn't too late for me. I could still have it all with Brian. I had to let go of my bitterness, embrace my family history, and take a step of faith.

Those thoughts kept rolling around in my head as I drove Mom to the hospital. While I struggled to stay close to the speed limit, Mom gazed out the side window at the passing landscape, her hands folded around a handkerchief she sometimes lifted to her eyes.

When we entered Dad's hospital room, he was sitting halfway up, his eyes on the TV on the opposite wall. A news reporter was talking about the hit-and-run that had landed Dad in the hospital. The police were looking for Jeff Petrino and had issued a warrant for his arrest. "The penalty for leaving the scene of an accident that incurs injuries could result in revocation of the young man's driver's license for one year," the reporter stated.

"One year?!" I blurted out. "And he might only lose his license? That was attempted murder. He should be put away for *life*."

Dad cleared his throat and got my attention. "Calm down, honey. Those news people don't have all the facts yet."

I slunk over to his bed and planted a kiss on his cheek. "Sorry, Dad. After what that reporter said, I lost it."

He managed a painful smile and gazed into my eyes. "An officer was here a few minutes ago. Because of Mrs. Juno's testimony, they're considering charging Jeff with attempt to do bodily harm. That could result in two years in jail."

I pressed my lips together and firmly shook my head. "That's still not enough, Dad. He tried to *kill* you. Jeff is involved with George Newman. The guy must have gotten him to do this."

Dad reached out with his good arm and pressed his hand against mine. "Let's relax and let the courts do their thing. And trust God, Frannie. He's in control."

"Trust God? Are you serious? Why did He let this happen?"

Dad shook his head. "I don't know why. But I do know He can turn this into something good. Like the Bible says, watch and wait. This isn't over yet."

"I know why you were attacked, Dad. It's because you're in charge of that committee. Jeff did this on purpose to stop you from working against the demolitions. We should never have gotten involved in this mess. Let them tear down the whole town. I don't care anymore. I just want you well and safe." I stomped over to a chair and plunked down in it. "I'm going back to New York, and I'm gonna forget about Gram's house and the demolitions and everything else."

Mom stepped close and rested a comforting hand on my shoulder.

"Calm down, Honey."

Dad shut his eyes for a moment, like he was thinking. When he opened them, a spark of energy lit up the blue of his eyes.

"Listen, Frannie," he said softly. "I don't feel like you do. I want to continue the fight. Especially now. This town means a lot to me, especially the old houses like Gram's. If we let this minor setback stop us, then we're not very good fighters, are we?"

"Minor setback," I flared. "You could be dead right now."

He shook his head. "But I'm not dead. I say, let's keep going. I may not be able to do much from a hospital bed, but I'll be released in a couple of days. I still want to form that committee, and by golly, they can meet at my bedside at home if necessary."

I leaned back in the chair and stared in awe at my father. The accident hadn't destroyed his fire. If anything, it had stoked it with more fuel. My dad possessed the kind of spunk I should have had but somehow had lost. He was his mother's son, for sure. If I'd had their fortitude, I might have changed from a brokenhearted female into a headstrong career woman. But, I didn't. Instead, I'd taken the brokenhearted female with me wherever I went, and she was still controlling my life.

I released a long sigh, slumped over, and put my head in my hands. I knew my father was right. Maybe God *could* turn this into something good. Maybe it was time I slowed down and got off the high-speed merry-go-round I'd been riding for too long.

"Okay, Dad," I said, raising my head. "You're still in charge of the committee. What do you propose we do next?"

He shifted his upper body toward me. His blue eyes sparkled. "We choose our committee members and move forward. Peg Atwater will be a big help. She spoke up in our favor at the council meeting. With her experience in real estate transactions, she'll have much to contribute." He paused and raised his eyebrows. "By the way, did you know she's running for mayor against Bosco?"

I nodded. "She told me while we were having lunch."

"I think she's got a chance. When November rolls around, I'm guessing things may change for the better in Cittadina."

I breathed deeply of Dad's enthusiasm. My own motivation had returned, even stronger than before. I wanted to save Gram's house and any others on Newman's death list. I had almost given up, but, even in his broken condition, Dad had restored my will to fight.

"I'm with you, Dad," was all I could say.

As it turned out, Dad did come home two days later and was comfortably settled on his recliner in their living room, with Mom bearing trays of food to him, rubbing his shoulders, and bringing him the daily newspaper. A rehabilitation therapist had been set up to come to the house twice a week.

I was visiting my father the day he came home. A TV news report told about Jeff's capture. Apparently, the state police had found him holed up in a relative's cabin in a remote area outside Albany. It's amazing what authorities can do simply by tracking a person's cell phone.

The report also said he'd been returned to Cittadina for adjudication and pretrial detention. No bail, no temporary release, no chance to skip town again. Almost immediately, Jeff agreed to a plea bargain and implicated George Newman, saying he paid him to go after my dad.

I straightened and pounded my fist in my other palm. "I knew it," I shouted. "I hope they drag George Newman into court too."

"Too late," Dad said with an air of disgust. "Peg called this morning. It seems, George Newman has disappeared from Cittadina. All his demolition signs have come down, and Beverly Strong has vacated her desk at the real estate office. She's also vanished along with every scrap of paper having to do with Newman Brothers' transactions."

"So, no more demolitions?"

"For now," Dad acknowledged. "I still want to organize a committee to work on designating the old sections of town as having historic interest. We can give Cittadina the historic ambiance it deserves, make it a place people will want to visit or even move here."

I flopped back in my chair. "I guess that means my contract also is null and void," I said, a ray of hope entering.

"Most likely," Dad agreed. "You should check with Peg Atwater to make sure. But it looks to me like Gram's house is no longer for sale." He had a sly grin that troubled me.

I knew I had a decision to make. Do I get Peg to put another sign out front? Or do I scrap the idea of selling Gram's house entirely?

Without another word, I planted a kiss on Dad's forehead and headed for the door. When I arrived at the house on Maple Street, I sat on the front porch swing and thought about how my life had changed in only a matter of weeks. It had taken me years to build up what I had accomplished. Now, depending on what I decided, I could tear it all down in one day.

What if I stayed in Cittadina and made Gram's house my home? What if, like Dad had suggested, I gave up my job in New York and applied with the *Cittadina Gazette*? I'd still be doing what I loved, though for a lot less money. But then I wouldn't have to pay the exorbitant rent for that apartment. Nor would I spend a lot of money on theater tickets, concerts, and eating out in expensive restaurants.

But what about Brian? I was now ready to make a commitment, ready to settle down as a wife and maybe one day, a mother. My mom's life didn't look quite so boring anymore. Few people smiled as much as she did. Few people rose from bed in the morning with a full day of activities planned, many of them for the purpose of helping someone else.

But Brian had a lucrative career, and it was in New York City. I'd heard that long-distant relationships don't work.

I went into the kitchen and brewed a cup of herbal tea. Then I sat at the table with the big Bible I'd hauled back and forth between Gram's house and my folks' place. I opened it to the page where Mom and I left off when we were called to the hospital to visit with Dad.

The text was still in Gram's handwriting.

Salvatore and Rosanna had four sons: twins, Franco and Giovanni, born on September 15, 1893; Armando, born on December 2, 1895; and Enzo, born on January 5, 1898.

There he was again. My great-grandfather.

Enzo married Catherine Tomasso on June 8, 1918. They had one child, Alberto, born on October 10, 1925.

Alberto. My Poppa. Gram's husband. Gram's next notation was even more personal.

I, Francine Maria Rossi, was born on February 9, 1927, in Palermo, Sicily. I immigrated to the United States when I was fourteen years old, with my parents, one brother, Carmine, and two sisters, Angelina and Gabrielle. We came through Ellis Island on August 5, 1941. I lived in Rochester, New York, and worked as a seamstress in a clothing factory until I married Alberto Capellini on July 10, 1954. For our honeymoon we traveled to Italy, toured several cities, including Rome, Florence, and Venice, and made a side trip to visit Alberto's relatives in a village outside of Albi.

Alberto and I settled in the house built by his grandfather, Salvatore Capellini. I never went back to my own hometown in Palermo, but I traveled all over the world and had many thrilling experiences meeting people of other countries and participating in lots of daring activities. I have lived a life I do not regret.

Alberto and I had three sons: Giuseppe, who was born on Thanksgiving Day, November 22, 1956; Nicolas, born on March 3, 1958; and Paulo, born on January 18, 1962.

We also had one daughter, Viviana, born on June 5, 1968.

So that was who Viviana was. My aunt. But where was she now? I read on, hoping to find an answer.

Giuseppe went to college and became a court reporter in Albany, until he retired and moved back to Cittadina. Nicolas also went to college and became an accountant, setting up his practice right here in our little village; and Paulo entered the military as a career soldier. He perished in battle in Afghanistan in 2001. He was 38 years old. Nicolas remained at home until May 7, 1988, when he married Roberta Cigliano, daughter of Angelo and Carlina Cigliano of Albany, New York. They purchased a Victorian home on Almond Lane.

I looked to see if Gram had written anything more about Viviana, but there was nothing. Her next notation ended Gram's contribution to our family tree.

I will now turn the records over to my daughter-in-law, Roberta Capellini.

The handwriting changed at that point and I recognized my mother's script. She'd taken calligraphy classes several years ago so she could write flowery note cards to friends and family members. Mom always went the extra mile in everything she did. Like the Harvest Festival. She couldn't make only one apple pie. She made a dozen, knowing the money was going to the Children's Hospital in Syracuse.

Mom's script picked up the text where Gram had left off. Except for the change in handwriting, the genealogy and notations were almost seamless. But I wasn't prepared for what she had to say next.

Nick and I were blessed with our first child, a son we named Thomas Albert Capellini, born on March 11, 1989. I suffered terrible complications, including painful endometriosis for months after. I had to have a hysterectomy.

My mouth dropped open. What had she said? A hysterectomy? That meant she couldn't have more children. But wait—I searched the page. She'd said nothing about me. No mention of my birth. Then I looked ahead, my heart pounding.

Nick's sister gave birth to a beautiful baby girl on June 5, 1992. Viviana died in childbirth.

What? June 5, 1992? That was my birthday. I was finding it hard to breathe. Mom answered the question that surfaced in her next notation.

Nick and I agreed to adopt her child. Francine Maria has been the greatest blessing of our lives.

My face had gone ice cold. Instinctively, I pressed my hands to my cheeks.

"I–I'm adopted? Viviana was my mother?"

The entire room began to swirl around me. I lowered my head, tried to get the blood flowing. I took shallow breaths, then deeper ones. Tears came and I started to sob.

Why on earth did I have to learn the truth this way? Why hadn't my mother told me before? Why hadn't she at least been here to read it with me? Instead, I had to find out alone, in that old house, with nothing but antiques around me, and no one to answer my questions.

Then, everything became clear, and I knew why Gram had singled me out among all my cousins. Why she'd always treated me like I was special. Why she'd chosen *me* to receive the house and the trunk and everything in it. Yes, I was her granddaughter, but now I knew I was much more than that. I was birthed by her only daughter, Viviana. No wonder I looked so much like the picture in the album.

Instead of lavishing me with love, Gram should have resented me. It was because of me that she lost her only daughter, because of me that Viviana died in childbirth. How that must have pained my grandmother to lose her only daughter and at such a young age. Yet, it was obvious, Gram had loved me.

I bowed my head and began to pray from the depths of my heart.

Dear God, I sobbed. *I need you. Please, rescue me from this horrible truth. I killed my mother. I was a baby, but as sure as anything, I ended her life. Please, forgive me for all the self-centered things I've done. I've hurt so many people. Mom. Dad. Gram. Help me to embrace my roots, to pay attention to what my ancestors have taught me, and to be more considerate of other people in my life. Especially Brian. He's been so patient with me, I don't blame him if he wants to end our relationship. Please, help me. I don't want to make my own plans anymore. I no longer trust myself. I want You to tell me what to do and where to go. Please, God, take charge of my life. Now and always.*

Shaking, I rose from the table and went for a handful of tissues. I mopped the tears from my eyes and blew my nose. Learning that my biological mother had died giving birth to me had created an emptiness in my heart that I couldn't explain. I was an orphan, a child without a home.

Then, I thought about my folks, how they'd willingly adopted me and filled the emptiness with love and a future. The truth was, I *was* wanted. And loved.

Though Mom had written much more on those pages, mostly about Tom and his family, the rest of her notations were a blur. I must have read them to the end, but I couldn't remember anything she wrote beyond the information about Viviana.

I had questions. If Viviana was my mother, then who was my father? What had become of him? I had no other recourse but to turn to the two people who could give me the answers. I had to go and see Mom and Dad.

CHAPTER THIRTY-THREE

I shut the Bible, grabbed my purse, and stumbled out of the house. When I arrived at my folks' place, I found them in the kitchen eating dinner. Mom stared wide-eyed at me and set down her fork. Dad sat in his chair with his injured leg propped up on an ottoman, his brow crinkled with concern at the sight of me.

I found my voice. "Why?" I said, tearfully. "Why did I have to learn the truth this way, in a family Bible. And alone?"

Mom shook her head. "Oh, Francine, I knew I should have told you sooner, but I didn't know how. You were such a happy child. I waited far too long."

I fell into uncontrollable sobbing, dropped into a chair, and lowered my head, unable to look them in the eye.

Dad reached across the table and placed a hand on my arm. "Frannie, dear, please forgive us. You're right. We should have told you sooner, but we had such a solid family life. You had stability. We had Tom and—"

"Does he know?" I raised my head and searched their faces.

Mom shook her head, her face flushed, tears flowing down her cheeks.

"Uncle Giuseppe?" I threw out.

"He knows," Dad said. "But no one else."

"Then why tell me now? And this way?"

Mom leaned toward me. "When Gram learned we hadn't told you, she insisted we do it, so you'd know why she chose you to receive the house. She wanted you to get to know your ancestors before you learned about Viviana. She believed it might help you receive the truth about your birth."

I fell back against my chair, grabbed a napkin from the table, and blotted the moisture from my face.

"Please, Frannie," Mom pleaded. "Don't be angry with us. This doesn't change anything. You're still our daughter. We're the ones who raised you. We love you, Honey."

I shook my head. "I don't know. I need to think, to figure out what this means to me."

"Don't do anything drastic." Mom sounded like she was about to panic.

I managed a wry smile. "I won't," I murmured. I started to settle down and was breathing easier.

"I hope you won't leave town without settling this, Frannie." Dad's voice also held a hint of anxiety. "Stay and give us a chance to explain everything. We have to talk. And you know, it's not so bad. My beautiful sister gave birth to you, and then we took you to live with us. Think about it. She wanted you, and so did we, and we still do. More than life itself."

I looked back and forth at their two pathetic faces. "So, you're my aunt and uncle, not my parents?"

Distress clouded their eyes, and I was overcome with regret. I loved them. I didn't want to hurt them.

Nothing had changed. I still had my family. I still had a father I respected more than any other man, and a mother I'd always wanted to emulate. I still had a big brother who'd doted on me when we were kids and promised to always be there for me. So what was different?

My folks had been ideal parents, guiding me, teaching me, loving me. They'd never treated me like I was less than Tom, never gave the slightest hint that I wasn't as much their child as *he* was.

"So, who's my father?" I wanted to know. The puzzle still had a missing piece.

"I am—" Dad began.

Mom cut in. "Viviana never said. She only told us the boy had denied involvement and went off to college. We never knew his name. Never even knew she'd been seeing anyone." Mom shook her head with sadness. "Viviana took the truth with her when she died. Your mother was a very brave girl."

I rose from my chair and headed for the door. My folks sat quietly, like they didn't know what else to say or do. I reached for the knob, then I turned and attempted a smile.

"Give me time," I said. "I'm not going anywhere, not until I figure this out."

I went back to Gram's house and retrieved the album from the hutch, laid it on the dining room table and opened it to the photo of my biological mother. Viviana smiled back at me. She seemed to be saying, *Everything is going to be all right.*

"I wish I could have known you," I whispered.

I wanted to ask Dad to tell me everything he could remember about his sister. I wanted to know what was she like as a child, and as a young adult. What were her dreams? Her pursuits? Her accomplishments? Was she anything like me?

I sat there for a long time, staring at my mother's picture. I definitely had her genes. Perhaps I also had inherited her impulsiveness, maybe her intelligence, maybe her desire to do something more with her life than sit around Cittadina and vegetate. After all, she'd had a baby out of wedlock. Such happenings weren't unheard of in the early 1990s, but she still faced an uphill battle. I wondered, how was she received by the family in that condition? What was the reaction of the townspeople? After all, this was small-town America, settled by people from the old country, people who held to morality and expected their youth to do the same.

I flipped back to the photos showing Gram climbing mountains and riding zip lines and all the crazy things she did. I had come from wild stock, that's for sure. Whether I'd been born to Mom and Dad or to Viviana, Gram's genes flowed through my veins. They even surged, for I was a lot more like Gram than anyone else.

I closed the album and phoned Brian. He picked up on the third ring.

"Glad you called," he said. "I'm back in New York, and I have news I want to share."

"I have something to share too," I said, blinking back more tears.

"You go first," Brian prompted.

Then I lunged into a full explanation of what had happened that day. He listened quietly, and if not for an occasional, "Wow" or "Uh-hmm" from his lips, I feared he'd hung up the phone. When I finished, he let out a long sigh.

"Well, Fran. Your news was so much more intense than mine, I think I'll mull over what you shared and tell you my news when I come up there tomorrow."

"So, you're planning to come?"

"That's right. Just tell me, are you gonna be okay?"

"I think so."

"Is there anything I can do?"

"No, thank you for listening. I feel a little better now that I've talked to you."

"It's not such a hard thing," he said, his tone soft. "Some of us don't know if our folks even wanted us. My own father skipped out. But you have the assurance that Nick and Roberta wanted you and still do. And, if you ask me, they did a great job of raising you."

"Thanks, Brian."

We both breathed into the phone for a couple of minutes, like neither of us knew what to say. After all, how could anyone top the news I had spilled on him?

"I think what I have to tell you will get you feeling a whole lot better about things," Brian promised. "Let me wrap up things here and I'll hop on a plane tomorrow afternoon. I'll let you know my flight number and what time I'll be arriving."

"All right. I can't wait to see you, Brian. I have one more thing to share, but I'll keep it under wraps until we're together."

Our phone call was interrupted by a knock on the

kitchen door. I said goodbye, went to open it, and found Penny standing there.

She smiled sheepishly and lifted a box of doughnuts. "Peace offering?" she said.

Without saying a word, I went into the kitchen with Penny prancing along behind me. I removed the family Bible from the kitchen table and placed it inside the hutch with the other items from Gram's trunk. Then, being driven only on impulse, I brewed some coffee.

By the time I'd filled two cups and set them on the table along with two plates, Penny had already opened the box and eaten half of a bear claw.

She was behaving like nothing had happened between the two of us. I decided to play along. I selected a jelly doughnut and took a bite, savoring the burst of sweetness while brushing the powdered sugar from my blouse. I still didn't speak. This was Penny's show, and I wasn't going to steal her thunder. Besides, our last conversation had left me stunned. At this point, I wasn't sure how to react or what to say.

"I came here to apologize," she admitted, her eyes pleading. "You told me the truth, Fran. Jeff is a cheat and a liar."

I doctored my coffee with cream and sugar and waited.

"I should have listened to you," Penny went on, tearfully. "You wanted to help. I know that now. Even then I knew, but the thing was, I didn't want to hear the truth. I wanted to believe he'd changed."

"People in love don't listen." I knew I was making excuses for her, but she'd been my friend for such a long time. And I knew what a cad Jeff was, how he'd also tricked me and plenty of other girls.

"Listen," I said, setting my half-eaten doughnut on my plate. "Let's let it go and start over. We've been friends for too long to let somebody like Jeff Petrino come between us."

Penny's relieved smile told me all I needed to know. "You know what?" I went on. "Let's plan a vacation together, maybe

a white water rafting trip or someplace where they have a giant zip line. Won't that be fun?" I had to laugh at myself. It seemed Gram was having a big effect on me.

Penny broke out in giggles. "Yes, it would be fun, although I never expected someone like you to suggest such a thing."

"Well, I'm going through a change of life. Kind of like menopause, but better."

The rest of our conversation went pretty much like the talks we'd had as teenagers. Back then, we laughed and talked silly and planned exciting vacations that never materialized. It was time we did something for real. Gram had shown me a whole other world to enjoy.

Like Dad said, God could work good out of something bad. And I could see something good *had* come out of all that had happened. For one thing, I was changing. I'd sensed it from the first day I opened the door to Gram's empty house and stepped inside. Though I'd repressed the feeling that something was about to happen, I wasn't repressing it anymore. I was letting go, throwing caution to the wind, and making a new plan for my life, a plan that had no room for doubts and insecurities. For the first time in years, I felt free. Truly free.

CHAPTER THIRTY-FOUR

Brian's plane arrived at 5:30 PM, right on time. I was waiting in my car outside the baggage claim area at the Rochester airport. My heart did a little flip when he came through the double doors, pulling his suitcase, a deer hide carry-on bag slung over his shoulder.

I sprang from the driver's seat and met him by the trunk, threw my arms around his neck and nearly knocked him over. Somehow, between kissing and hugging me, he managed to set his bags on the pavement.

"It's good to see you, too," he said, grinning.

We stowed his bags in the trunk and sped away from the airport. During our drive, I asked about Brian's classes in L.A. His face lit up like a Christmas tree bulb as he spoke of the lectures, the study papers, the interaction with other students. He hadn't exhibited that much excitement since the day he hired on with the Judd Law Firm.

"It looks like you'll be moving up the ladder soon," I commented.

He simply smiled, like he had a secret to tell, but not yet. Instead, he asked about the house.

I filled him in on the finishing touches I'd made and assured him there would be no work for him to do this time.

"Wait till you see the place," I crowed. "I'm so happy with the way it turned out. The plants we put in are thriving, and the vegetable garden is holding up too."

By the time we arrived at the house, we both declared we were hungry enough to eat half a cow. Fortunately, I had prepared a dinner in advance. Pot roast, buttered noodles, and salad, plus banana cream pie for dessert. While Brian marched up the stairs with his bags and placed them in the bedroom he'd used before, I lit two candles and opened a bottle of wine. By the time he returned to the dining room, I had dinner on the table.

With flickering candles casting an ethereal glow on our surroundings and Beethoven's "Moonlight Sonata" setting the mood, I joined Brian at the table and bowed my head while he thanked the Lord.

As he ladled pot roast in his bowl, I spoke the words I'd been holding back for days.

"I made a commitment," I said, cautiously at first. "Not to myself or anyone else. But to God."

He stopped ladling and stared at me. "You made a commitment?" he said, incredulous.

I laughed. "Yes, finally, Francine Capellini has made a commitment."

He chuckled and finished ladling the pot roast.

"I prayed, Brian," I said, a serious tone filtering into my voice.

He lost his smile and gave me his full attention.

"I asked God to forgive me for being selfish and for not allowing Him to direct my life. I've been moving so fast, I haven't given God a chance to guide me. And I prayed for another chance—with Him, and with everyone—including you."

Brian reached for a roll. "Great for dipping," he said and plunged the bread into the gravy.

"Did you hear what I said, Brian?"

"I did, and I'm not the least bit surprised."

I gawked at him. "What do you mean?"

"I mean, I already noticed a change in you. A change in your conversations, even on the phone. You sound like a different person. Not the wired Francine Capellini I knew a month ago, but someone new and fresh, someone comfortable with her life. Someone who maybe had overcome a challenge and now was ready for the next step."

I gave him one of my unconvinced, skeptical reporter looks. "What do you mean, Brian?"

"What I mean is, in all those times I mentioned the possibility of marriage, I never thought I'd be able to do this and get the answer I wanted from you. Until now."

He reached in his pocket and withdrew a little black box, the kind that takes a woman's breath away. He placed it on the table between us.

"I'm asking you for what has to be the sixth or seventh time, Fran, but I feel confident that this time I'm gonna get a different answer than what I've gotten in the past."

I gazed, open-mouthed, at him. Then I extended my left hand and smiled. He returned my smile, opened the box, and slid a beautiful antique diamond ring on my finger. The circle of white gold had a row of tiny diamond chips on either side of a larger perfectly round stone in the center.

"It looks like one of Catherine's rose blossoms," I gushed.

He lifted my hand where the setting glistened in the light of the candles.

"I've seen this ring before," I said. "In the photograph of your mother on her wedding day."

He nodded. "This ring was my grandmother's before it belonged to my mother. It's very special, Fran, and I want you to have it."

Wordless, we both rose from the table and wrapped our arms around each other. Brian planted kisses all over my face and then found my lips.

"So, we're officially engaged?" he said, his eyes smiling with anticipation.

"I guess we are. But there's one problem." I backed away from him. "Logistics."

"Logistics?" he queried. "I don't see any problem. What exactly will we need to do?"

We returned to our chairs. I resumed eating my dinner and pondered how I would say what had been on my mind since that morning.

I swallowed and set down my fork. "To be honest, I've been struggling with a decision that might cause you to withdraw your proposal."

He also stopped eating and stared at me, concern filtering into his eyes.

"While a part of me wants to return to New York and resume my life as though nothing has happened, an even bigger part of me wants to move into Gram's house and live where my roots are."

I was about to remove the ring from my finger and hand it back to Brian, but he was chuckling now. I stared at him, confusion running through me.

"Not a problem," Brian said with confidence.

I looked at him in astonishment. "How can you say that, Brian? You know long-distance relationships don't work."

"We don't have to worry about that," he insisted. "You see, I could tell from our conversations over the past few weeks that your heart is in Cittadina. Always has been. You just didn't know it until now. But I could see it in your eyes the last time I came here. I could tell you loved this place, though you didn't want to admit it. I could hear it in your voice, every time we spoke on the phone and you shared what you did to renovate the house, and the way you spoke about the memorabilia your Gram left inside that old trunk. And how you shared things about your ancestors, people you never knew until now. How you talked about the letters and the gardens. It was obvious the house on Maple Street really did belong to you—and so did its history. Then, your latest news, that your grandmother's precious daughter gave birth to you—well, all of that tells me you belong here."

"But, my job—"

He chuckled. "You have a mobile career, Fran. You can work anywhere. Tell me, doesn't Cittadina have a decent newspaper?"

I thought about my dad and his grip on the *Gazette*. "It seems to. But you're forgetting one thing, Brian. What about *us*? If I move here, you're gonna be living and working almost 500 miles away. We'll see each other on a weekend now and then. What kind of marriage is that?"

"I'm telling you, we won't have a problem."

"Really? And how do you propose we solve it? You'll be in New York working your way up the ladder at Judd Law Firm, and I'll be picking vegetables in the backyard at Gram's house."

His face was glowing now, like he was about to burst. I searched his brown/gold eyes and broad smile, aware that he had something else to tell me.

"Fran, we won't be more than an hour apart. Ever. After finishing my class with flying colors and then taking that workshop, management asked me if I might be interested in starting an auxiliary office—and guess where?"

Dazed, I shook my head.

"Drum roll," he said, then announced, "In Rochester!"

"Really?" I was smiling with him now. "In Rochester?"

"That's right," he said, nodding. "I'll get a nice raise, and I can hire my own staff. I'll be in charge, Fran, and I'll be able to live in Cittadina and commute to work. Some of the time, I can even work from home."

I gawked at him, then found my voice. "Brian, is that the truth?"

His eyes sparkled and he laughed again. "Yes, darling. We can be married, and we can live right here in Cittadina. We can pick fresh vegetables from the garden. We can plant more flowers if you want. And we can make any other changes to the house you find necessary."

I allowed the scenario to flood into my brain. "I like it, Brian. We'll have the best of both worlds."

"Of course, I'll need to turn one of those bedrooms into a home office. But I'll gladly give it up when we start having children."

"Children," I murmured, and I could feel my face blushing.

"Tell me, Fran," he urged. "Who wouldn't want to grow up in a quaint little town like this, where a person can walk everywhere and know everyone? Who wouldn't want to live in this house? To be honest, I'm tired of the fast pace of the big city. I'm tired of climbing corporate ladders and rushing about trying to see how many restaurants and opening events I can take in within a year. I've reached the top of my personal ladder. Someday, I'll just slow down and enjoy the simple life. And, I want to do it here."

"What about all those adventures you keep asking me to go on?"

He raised his eyebrows. "Hey. We need to take a break from the everyday routine now and then, don't we? A cruise to Alaska, maybe a white water rafting trip down the Colorado River, or a camera safari in Africa. We can do whatever we want, go wherever we want, have our adventure, and then return for a period of rest and relaxation in one of the most calming places on earth, right here in Little Italy. Isn't that what your grandmother did?"

I was the one who laughed now. "Yes, Brian. If my Gram could do it, then so can I. We can go on those wild and wonderful excursions you mentioned. We can climb a mountain and ride a camel and catch a shark. We can do all those things Gram did and more. And then we can come home to our charming little cottage and write about our escapades in a journal. And we can leave it in the trunk in the attic for our grandchildren to find."

"The trunk's still there?" he said.

"I didn't have the heart to throw it away."

He reached for my hand. I freely gave it to him.

"There's one more thing I need to do," he said softly. "I need to get your father's blessing." He shrugged. "Call me old fashioned, but I have to do this. Maybe I should have done it first."

"Let's finish dinner, and then we'll go see my parents, and you can humble yourself before my dad. I also want to surprise them with the news that I'm gonna stay in Cittadina and live in Gram's house. I want to see their faces when I say it. And I want to let them know I'm no longer upset about the adoption, that I understand how much they loved me to have taken me into their home." I paused and considered the rest of my decision. "And, I want Dad to tell me everything he remembers about Viviana. I need to know her, Brian. She could have had an abortion, but she didn't. She gave me life. And my folks helped me to live that life to the fullest."

I stood and went to the hutch to retrieve the photo album. I flipped to the picture of Viviana and lay the page open before him.

"That's her?" he said. "That's your mother?"

I nodded. "My biological mother. The woman who mothered me is sitting in a Victorian house a few blocks away. She's waiting for me to come and tell her everything's all right."

Acknowledgements

Cittadina is a fictional town, but not so fictional to me, because I grew up in a little village, much like the one I created as a backdrop for this novel. Like Cittadina, which means "little town" in Italian, East Rochester, New York, was labeled "Little Italy," because of the great number of Italian immigrants who resided there.

Also like Cittadina, the 1 1/2-square-mile village I lived in consisted of main roads named after presidents and side streets named after trees. Growing up in a small town left an impression on my heart, and though, like Francine, I moved away and got a taste of big city life, those early influences never left me.

I appreciate the people who played a role in my growing up years. Teachers, like Miss Bird and Miss Redman, both of whom guided me into a writing career; Mrs. Quinn, who reached out to students on a personal level; and Mr. Miller, who taught me to love the older music.

I want to thank my beta readers—my daughter, Joanna Jones, whose eagle eye catches early mistakes; Delores Kight, whose editorial skills make my work so much better; and my friend, Laurie Rabold, an avid reader and voice of encouragement.

I want to thank Jenny Irwin, my cousin Frank Rizzo's daughter, for her hard work in researching our family genealogy and for sharing those findings that helped me create a similar history of Francine's ancestors.

Thanks go to Brigitte Shultz for her advice on real estate

matters, and to Belleview, Florida, Mayor Christine Dobkowski, who coached me regarding city council meetings.

Ultimately, the success of my work depends on the editing skills and words of support from my friend and publisher, Mike Parker of WordCrafts Press.

Finally, my expressions of gratitude would not be complete without a word of thanks to my Heavenly Father, the greatest writer who ever lived, for He left us the most important, life-changing document of all, the Holy Scriptures. To God be the glory!

A Pulitzer Prize nominated journalist, Marian Rizzo has won numerous awards for her writing, including the *New York Times* Chairman's Award and first place in the 2014 Amy Foundation Writing Awards. She worked for the *Ocala Star-Banner* newspaper for 30 years. She also has written articles for the *Ocala Gazette*, *Ocala Style Magazine*, and Billy Graham's *Decision Magazine*.

Several of Marian's novels have won awards at Florida Christian Writers Association conferences and Word Weavers International retreats. In 2018, her suspense novel, *Muldovah*, was a finalist in the Genesis competition at the American Christian Fiction Writers Conference. Two of her novels have earned Amazon "Best Seller" status. Through her membership with Word Weavers International, she's been able to hone her craft through interaction with other members.

Marian lives and works in Ocala, Florida. She has two children, three grandchildren, and a yellow lab/mix named Buddy.

9 781957 344089